HEROES
OF THE
EMPIRE

BOOK 4: THE CAPTIVE

HEROES OF THE EMPIRE

ISRAH AZIZI

Page Turner Press LLC

Published in the United States of America by PageTurnerPress LLC. Visit page-turner-press.com

Title: Heroes of the Empire/ Israh Azizi

Other titles: The Captive

Cover design by Damonza

Identifiers: Library of Congress Control Number: 2025917826

ISBN: 978-1-958688-10-6 (Hardback)

ISBN: 978-1-958688-08-3 (Paperback)

ISBN: 978-1-958688-09-0 (ebook)

Printed in the United States of America

10 9 8 7 6 5 4 3 2 1

First Edition

For my siblings. We are all fingers of the same hand, unique in our own way, and when we come together, we make an unbreakable fist.

PRONUNCIATION AND CHARACTER GUIDE

Andvora (and-vore-uh) — Vidrun villager
Aria (ah-ree-ya) — Elder, Velamir's sister
Aylis Barindaughter (EYE-less) — Saga's sister
Bear (bay-er) — Aylis, Svorgin, and Saga's father
Bodvar (ba-ud-var) — Britta's father
Britta (bree-tuh) — Saga's best friend
Clara (claw-ruh) — Vidrun villager
Coralie (cora-LEE) — queen of Verin
Daghvin (dokh-veen) — Britta's brother
Draven Valent (DRAY-ven VALL-ont) — late prince and
     king of Ayleth
Dunya (doon-yuh) — head of the Elders
Erda (air-duh) — Tariqin captain
Esme (ez-may) — Vidrun Village shavka
Fox — part of Queen Guin's guard
Frumgan (fur-rum-gin) — Jax's former Shadow Manos
     mentor
Guin (goo-wen) — queen of Devorin

Hesten Hartinza (HES-tin HEART-inza) — Honzio's late brother

Honzio Hartinza (HON-zee-oh HEART-inza) — emperor of Karalik Empire

Inlo (EN-low) — Captain Erda's second-in-command

Jaxon Tana (JAX-en tan-nuh) — Velamir's best friend

Jirco (Jeer-coh) — Chishman, village inspector

Kalpara (CALL-par-ruh) — Saga's rumlok

Latimus Blayton (LAT-ih-miss BLAY-ten) — Honzio's head advisor

Leno (Leh-noh) — Britta's partner

Lilly Tana (lil-lee tan-nuh) — Jax's cousin

Lore Blayton (LO-ore BLAY-ten) — Honzio's personal assistant, Latimus's brother

Madame Zelnat (zell-knot) — head housekeeper at Castle Yakh

Marcella (MAR-sell-uh) — former Shadow Manos

Melevore (mell-eh-vore) — king of Ayleth

Mole — part of Queen Guin's guard

Moralis Vane (MORE-al-less vein) — Honzio's cousin, Aylis's husband

Mordon Vaz (MORE-dawn) — Verin general, Coralie's husband

Morosta (MORE-ros-tuh) — Shadow Manos, Prolus's former right hand

Natassa Hartinza (NAT-ossa HEART-inza) — Honzio's late sister

Olava (OH-lava) — Vidrun villager, bread baker

Pistir (piece-stir) — Britta's late rumlok

Prolus (PRO-lus) — deceased Dark Lord

Pvlora (pov-lore-uh) — legendary Savorian warrior

Rasdor (RAZ-door) — legendary Savorian warrior

Rose — maid at Castle Yakh

Rost (roh-ist) — Elder

Saga Barindaughter (saw-guh) — Svorgin and Aylis's sister

Sheyvis (shay-vees) — Aylis's late rumlok

Silopar (SEE-low-par) — Savorian

Svorgin Barinson (sa-vore-gin) — Saga's brother

Thorsten Hartinza (thor-stin HEART-inza) — Honzio's late brother

Vandal (VAAN-del) — Velamir's horse

Velamir Raga (vel-uh-meer) — Alaric, Aria's late brother

Vykus (VI-kiss) — mercenary king, Jax's former kidnapper

Weria (wear-ree-ya) — queen of Ondalar

Yuva Elevedaughter (YOO-vuh EL-leave-daughter) — Saga's mother

Zenrelius (ZEN-rel-ee-us) — former Ondalarian general

IMPORTANT LOCATIONS AND TERMS

Ayleth (EYE-leth) — one of the four kingdoms

(the) Borderlands — once a defensive stronghold against the Tariqins

Chishma (chish-muh) — Prolus's elite soldiers and graduates of the Chishman Academy

Deedans (DEED-aans) — soldiers in the Awal, rejected from the Chishman Academy

Devorin (DEH-vorin) — one of the four kingdoms

(the) Docks — lawless city containing mercenaries and illegal trading ports

Galvasir (GAAL-va-sir) — high-ranking soldier in the Empire

Hearcross (HEER-cross) — capital of Karalik Empire

Karalik Empire (KAARA-lik) — land of the remaining four kingdoms

Lagrima Sea (la-ree-ma) — sea by Savoria

Mavaalin (MOV-aw-lin) — Savorian farewell meaning wind in your sails

Ondalar (on-DUH-laar) — one of the four kingdoms

(the) Qistool (kiss-tool) — once known as the kingdom
  of Beriyal, now a haunted remainder of the great
  kingdom
Red Bridge — a bridge in Savoria named because of the
  blood that changed the color of the wood
Rumlok (RUM-lock) — wolf/bearlike creature
Savagelands — also called Uluz, an arid environment
  housing tribal groups
Savoria (SAAV-or-ia) — large island conquered by Prolus
Shikista (shi-kis-ta) — castle in Ayleth
Tariqi (TO-RIH-qee) — realm consisting of nine kingdoms,
  eight of which used to belong to Karalik Empire
True Manos — Imperial healer
Verin (VER-in) — one of the four kingdoms
Castle Yakh (Yah-kh) — castle in Devorin

A DEPICTION OF
KARALIK EMPIRE
AND SURROUNDING
TERRITORIES.
AS DRAWN BY
IMPERIAL CARTOGRAPHER
MASTER JOWSHA
Savoria
Port
Lagrima Sea
For
Castle
Ondalar
Port of Ayleth
Ayleth
Karakan
Zarosari
Castle Shikista
Flonom
Wallington
The Pit
The Ja Sea
The Savageland
The Ja Desert

The Red Bridge
Mines
Topragar Fortress
Realm of Tariqi
Kalea Acadamy
Port of Savoria
Awal Military Base
The Qistool
Fortress Yadigar
Verin
Red Eagle Forest
Castle Verin
Namaar
Raqa Manor
Verintown
Castle Yakh
ondin Woods
Devorin
Hearcross
Savastown
Sok Town
Mines
Karalik Palace
ds
Whispering Woods
The Docks

VAZCOR THE MAP MAKER

SAVORIA
THE RED BRIDGE
VIDRUN VILLAGE
PORT OF SAVORIA
HOUSE OF BARIN
LAGRIMA SEA

PROLOGUE

SAGA'S SHRIEK TORE from her mouth, fogging the cold air. A hand clamped over her lips, followed by desperate whispers to be silent. Saga squeezed her eyes closed, but her brows drew together when she didn't feel the pain she'd been expecting.

"I haven't done a thing yet, dummy."

Saga opened her eyes to find Britta watching her askance. She held the needle so close to Saga's ear that Saga could swear the point grazed her skin. A low growl erupted, and a shape burst from the snow-covered trees to dart in front of Saga and snarl at Britta. Saga delved in her mind for the link connecting her to the rumlok and sent forth commands to be still, but the bond between them was still shaky, and the rumlok evaded the signals.

"Hush, Kalpara. Britta bears me no harm."

At her verbal command, the young rumlok pulled back but still stretched her lips, displaying her fangs at Britta. She was quite small, her head barely taller than Saga's knees, but she made up for it with viciousness.

Britta's brows shot up.

"She is so protective of ye. Pistir wouldn't care if I

"

was even breathing if not for the fresh meat," Britta said, a wry smile on her face as she mentioned her own rumlok.

"Because ye are making him a slug like yerself."

At the snide remark, both girls turned to glare at Daghvin, who sat upon a rock a short distance away, sharpening his newly forged axe. He looked up and shrugged. "What? It is no falsehood. Mam gives us tasks, and ye leave the work for me. Even now, my time is wasted. If the two of ye are caught, I will be in a whole lot of strife."

Britta batted her lashes at him. "But ye would do it again for yer one and only sweet sister."

Daghvin rolled his eyes and muttered under his breath, "Spoiled." He glanced over his weapon, pride glinting in his gaze as light burst over the metal and high-lighted the sharp edge.

"*I'm* spoiled?" Britta exclaimed. "*You* are the spoiled one. It is not fair that ye got yer axe. Ye still have a year before ye choose a craft."

"Well, I suppose that just means Da thought I was prepared." Daghvin gave his sister a victorious grin.

"That decision remains in the hands of the shavka," Saga piped up.

"Ye are the last to speak, Saga Barindaughter. If yer mam knew what ye were up to, she would flay all our hides."

Saga pouted. "But I am following the custom."

Britta nodded. "There is nothing wrong with getting an earring to remember yer loved one."

Daghvin sighed. "It is wrong when yer mam forbade

it. And Sheyvis wasn't even yer loved one. The rumlok belonged to yer sister."

Saga gave him another glare. "Sheyvis was as dear to me as he was to Aylis. He fathered Kalpara."

"Ye can defend yerself to me as much as ye want, but I'd ponder the excuses ye will give yer mam when ye get home."

The words tugged at her nerves, and worry pooled in Saga's gut. She put on a brave face. "That is none of yer concern, Daghvin."

He shrugged. "Finish up so I can get home. The folks will only believe our hunting tale for so long before someone comes looking."

Britta readied herself, leaning closer with the needle before her gaze locked with Saga's. Their eyes were both blue, Britta's pale as the sky and Saga's dark as a flowing river.

"Are ye ready?" Britta asked, a coat of sweat visible on her brow.

Saga bolstered herself and nodded. "I am."

She wanted to be like the older women who wore golden hoops in their lobes. She wanted to feel grown-up and accepted in the village. To be looked upon as though she had a place among them instead of being seen as just a child. The needle slid through her skin. Saga hissed at the sharp stab in her lobe. Warmth overtook her ear, and when she reached up, blood welled around the needle. Britta watched her with wide eyes.

"It wasn't as terrible as I thought it would be," Saga said, a smile growing on her face.

Britta retrieved the metal ring Daghvin had crafted

in their father's smith and shoved it through the hole the needle had created. Tears spurted in Saga's eyes. She coughed.

"That was worse."

Britta clicked the ring in place and then grinned. "Now it's my turn."

Daghvin leaned forward. "And who, precisely, is yer deceased loved one?"

Britta's lip quivered. "But I want one too."

"Too bad." Daghvin stood. "We ought to return."

He coaxed them up by waving his threatening axe. Together, they trudged through the snow toward their village. The closer they got, the more nervous Saga became. She imagined her mam's face when she caught sight of the jewelry dangling from her ear. Saga winced. She would be furious.

"Is that smoke?"

Saga looked up at Daghvin's comment. Plumes of gray billowed in the air in the distance. Far more than was normal for their village. Then they heard the shouts. The screams.

Britta's eyes widened. "What's happening?"

Daghvin shot forward, racing for the village. Foreboding crept up Saga's spine. She whistled, and Kalpara bounded up to her. The rumlok's thick white fur was coated with even whiter snow.

"Wait for me!" Britta called.

They neared the edge of the trees. Saga sank behind the low bushes and watched the scene before her. Her village was aflame. Women were gathered in the square, wielding glinting weapons as soldiers garbed in black and red approached with masks welded over their faces. Saga spotted her mother among the women. She stood, moving to go to them, when Britta grasped her arm, yanking her back down. Kalpara growled at the movement.

"What are ye doing? Have ye lost yer senses? Stay with me," Britta said, trembling.

Daghvin had already joined the women, and more youth left the shelter of their wood-constructed homes.

"Who are they?" Saga whispered.

Her eyes flicked to the harbor, where two large ships were docked. She spotted more in the distance dotting the sea as they approached. A flag wafted over each of them, a horned and smiling mask emblazoned upon the fabric.

"I do not know." Britta's hand squeezed Saga's.

"Where is Da?" Saga said, fighting the urge to join the fray and search for her loved ones. She spotted her brother and sister. Both appeared as unyielding as her mother, but her father was nowhere in sight.

Her heart lurched as she watched her family and the faces she had seen every day for the seven years of her short life launch into battle against the masked soldiers. They fought with a viciousness Saga had never seen before. Blood and screams filled the air. Despite her people's ferocious stance against the invaders, the battle was short-lived. Her family and neighbors were disarmed and shoved to their knees. Any who resisted were slayed.

Britta sobbed when her aunt's motionless form was deposited in a pile of other lifeless faces. Saga searched the features of those she could see, relief overwhelming her when she made out her mother, brother, and sister, injured but alive. There was still so much fight in them.

Nevertheless, worry burned through her. Where was her father?

Her question was answered when the men of the village were led to the square by more masked soldiers. A man stepped to the forefront. His hair was wavy and brushed over his shoulders. "Vidrun Village, along with countless others, is henceforth under the rule of Lord Prolus. Those who refuse to submit will meet their ends by our blades. If you wish your families to be spared, you will not rebel against us." His distinct Savorian features, along with his blue eyes and pale skin, betrayed his heritage, leaving Saga to wonder why he was aiding this insidious group.

He took all the men in the village and placed them in cages. Tears burned Saga's eyes when she saw her father among the prisoners. She shot to her feet, but Britta pushed her down yet again.

"We will leave your families and children untouched, but failure to comply with our orders will endanger them," the leader said. "Act wisely."

With the men inside, the carts containing the cages rumbled away. The soldiers left along with them. As soon as they drifted out of sight, Saga broke out of Britta's grip and raced to the square, where she fell in front of her mam.

"Mam, what is happening? Where are they taking Da?"

But her mother stared off with a listless look. She didn't see Saga, not the ring threaded through her ear or the tears drifting over her cheeks. Saga's brother, Svorgin, enveloped her in a hug. He smelled like Da, but his gangly arms could not bring the same warmth her father's had.

"He will return," Svorgin whispered. "Until then, hold on to his axe."

Saga took the weapon and didn't care that it was so heavy. She carried it with her as she journeyed to the bridge that connected to the Realm of Tariqi. Some of the invaders had crossed it to enter their village on land rather than sea. "The Siren Bridge," she and Britta had named it. The water rolling beneath had sparkled ethereally in the night, but there was nothing magical about the bridge anymore. The men had fought upon it in a futile attempt to prevent the invaders from entering. So much blood had spilled that it had dyed the wood crimson. From that moment, it was deemed the Red Bridge.

Days passed and then months, but her da never returned. She asked her mother every day, but her mother would just shake her head.

"Please, Mam, can we go look for him?"

"Yer da is gone, Saga," her mother finally told her. "He now serves the Dark Lord Prolus. He will never return. Ye'd best forget about him."

Those words had sent Saga stumbling from their home. With tears streaming from her eyes and an aching heart, Saga journeyed to the center of the village, where axes were piled together in a mountain of metal. And under the moon's glow, with the stars as witnesses, Saga placed her father's weapon, honed with dedication and strong hands, among the others and pledged to avenge the fallen.

1

SAGA

SAVORIA

VIDRUN VILLAGE

THE AXE GLEAMED as it swept through the air, then split the wood in two. Saga tossed it onto the pile she'd gathered and continued, setting another block onto the bottom of the fallen trunk. She split the wood without mercy. Sweat poured down her temples, and hairs slipped free from her tightly braided locks. She wiped at her perspiration, glancing at the sky above. The midday sun hovered over her, giving her skin a reprieve from the biting chill.

She gathered the wood and placed it into her bag before hefting it over her shoulders. The heavy pack didn't slow her pace as she trekked to her village. The movements recurred so often that they no longer bothered her muscled arms and back. She held her axe in a rigid palm. Smaller versions of the wicked-bladed weapon hung from her belt and swung with each step. The common sights and sounds sank in as she stepped into the village. Olava was baking bread over an open fire. A line of Saga's neighbors waited to purchase the delicious, hot bread for their midday meals. Olava caught sight of her and waved.

"Come on over, lass."

Saga approached her.

"Did ye collect wood for me this morn?"

Saga nodded and slung the bag to the ground with a thud.

"Olava, I've got to be going," a villager complained.

Olava's hand shot up. "It will be just a moment, folks. I am sure ye can wait a moment for the best bread in the village."

There was a rumble of *ayes*, and Olava *hmphed* in approval before turning to Saga.

"How much, lass?"

Saga retrieved the wood she needed, and Olava dropped coins into her hand.

"How fares yer mam?"

Saga shrugged. "Unchanged."

Olava's mouth turned downward, and she patted Saga's arm. "Do not lessen the hope in yer heart. It will all be better."

Saga nodded, though she didn't quite believe the words. She never found a reason to smile any longer. It was the same task from morning till night: finding a way to survive while under the rule of their oppressors, finding a way to survive just like the rest of the village. Saga noted the Tariqins standing at their posts.

Their postures were relaxed, as though they didn't have a care in the world. Their expressions gave away their boredom. They'd slackened in their viciousness compared to the first days. Saga's eyes narrowed.

"Are there less deedans?"

Olava followed her gaze and nodded. "So I am not the only one who's noticed. Something has changed."

The change had begun four months before. The villagers who'd been Shadow Manos convulsed, some dying and some falling into a dark, vacant trance. The head of the village, Shavka Esme, was one of those who lived but had been forever changed and took to bed rest. Everyone's morale had dimmed since then, considering it an ill omen. The seers could no longer guide them or dole out crafts to the young ones. The young, who were now without any hope for the future, were so few already. After the conquest, there were hardly any men remaining. The village was swarmed with women, more old and less of the young.

Saga slung her bag back upon her shoulders and moved to leave when Olava called out.

"Take this, lass." She handed her a wrapped bread.

The freshly baked smell drifted into the air, making Saga's stomach rumble. She swallowed and shook her head. "I cannot. I don't—" The words died in her throat. She was too prideful to admit that she couldn't afford to part with a single coin.

"Take it," Olava insisted, pressing it into her palm. "Share it with yer mam."

The woman's eyes sparkled with kindness. Saga blinked back the sting of sudden emotion.

"May our heroes look down upon ye. May ye be bestowed with Rasdor's courage and Pvlora's blessings," Saga said.

Olava gripped her arm. "And ye, Saga, and ye. Do not lose heart. The sparrows will return."

The aged phrase sobered Saga rather than having the effect Olava had intended. Shavka Esme would always repeat it, but even she had stopped. What hope was left when even their shavka no longer believed in it?

Saga bid Olava farewell and quickened her pace as she neared the smithy, hoping to pass it as quickly as possible. She could hear the clanging of a hammer shaping metal, smell the smoke drifting out, feel the burn of the fire without even entering the smithy. She had nearly passed it when she heard her name being called. She forced herself to turn. Britta bounded toward her with a bounce in her step. She smiled, bright as the sun, as though the world were made of flowers and the sky never stormed. As though nothing was wrong in their village.

"Saga? I haven't seen ye in days." Britta grasped her hands, holding tight to her. Worry flickered in her gaze. "Is everything all right?"

Saga blinked. Of course everything was not all right. Nothing had been all right since she'd been seven years old. How could it be? Her eyes flicked over Britta's right ear, where three golden hoops hung. She'd lost her aunt, mother, and cousin that day. But three was so few compared to the rest of the village. Women who used to have one or two hoops now had no space for more. But she didn't say the words racing through her mind.

"Yes. And ye? How do ye fare?"

Britta's grin widened. "Wonderful, especially because of tonight."

"Tonight?"

Her light dimmed, and she searched Saga's face. "Ye do not remember?"

Saga looked down at the ground. "Remember what?"

"Saga . . . ye promised me ye would come. For my binding."

Saga forced her mouth to smile. "I am sorry, Britta. It was so long ago when we spoke about it. I forgot."

Britta hesitated, hurt written all over her face. A twinge of guilt swept over Saga.

"But ye will come, won't ye?"

Saga paused, then shook her head. "I have to head home and take care of Mam."

"Ye will skip yer closest friend's binding ceremony? It's a life changing event."

"I must be with my mam, Britta. Ye know how she gets."

"At least come in and see the rings."

Before Saga could reply, Britta yanked her into the smithy. The bright light cut off when the door closed behind them. Saga made out the figure bent over the anvil. Long, greasy hair covered his features. His muscled arm brought down a hammer, slamming it onto a long piece of glowing orange metal. Sparks shot out, red as the flickering fire beside him.

"Leno." Britta's joy could be heard through her voice.

The man turned, and a wide grin broke over his sweaty face. He set his hammer down and tossed the weapon he'd been working on into the water bucket. The metal hissed in response. Britta launched into his embrace, heedless of the perspiration dripping from him. Saga looked away, crossing her arms over her chest. As she avoided staring at the couple, her gaze landed on the old man sitting on a bench at the back of the smithy. His eyes shone, and his mouth spread in a tender smile as he watched the young couple.

"Well, if it isn't Saga," Leno said. "Ye finally decided to visit."

Saga's eyes flashed to him. Britta was tucked into his side now. His arm wrapped around her shoulder and hers around his waist. Britta's head tilted as she gave Saga a pleading expression.

"Leno," Saga said curtly. "I wanted to check on Uncle Bodvar."

Leno sniffed, showing he was unconvinced. The old man stood from his bench, spreading his arms and revealing the stumps of all his fingers but four.

"Saga Barindaughter."

Saga flinched.

"It is good to see ye, lass." Bodvar hobbled past the couple and enveloped Saga into his arms.

Saga patted his back, and he pulled away, his features so similar to Britta's. She had taken her father's looks and her mother's joyfulness.

"Will ye remain for the ceremony?" Leno asked.

"I am afraid I c—"

Britta cut in. "Love, show Saga the rings."

Leno's brow rose, and then he kissed Britta's temple. "As ye wish."

He retrieved two sparkling silver rings from his apron pocket. He extended them to Saga, who took them after a moment's hesitation. She examined the rings, noting the detailed design.

"They are beautiful," she said when she felt the weight of eyes upon her.

"Leno has become a fine craftsman," Bodvar said proudly.

"If only Daghvin were here. Then we would be complete," Britta said, her eyes far off.

Saga stiffened. Complete? The village could never be complete. But Britta would never understand. She still had her father, even if he had been spared from the Tariqins after the battle because of the loss of his fingers. She still had Leno, who had been considered too thin and sickly to be taken. She still had a home that felt like one. But so many were too fractured to ever become whole again. And others were still held too tightly by hatred to ever move on.

Britta's eyes met Saga's, and her brows lowered. "Saga?"

Saga stormed out of the smithy, too afraid she would say something she would regret if she did not leave.

"What is her problem now?" Leno's voice accompanied her exit.

Saga strode down the path, attempting to push down the fury boiling in her veins. Boots pounded behind her. Britta grabbed her arm, forcing her to a stop. Saga wheeled around.

"I am sorry, Saga. I wasn't thinking when I spoke."

Saga sighed. "It doesn't matter."

"It does. I know it hurts ye to think about it. About them."

"There is no point."

"But can ye not consider it?" Britta persisted. "They may return. Daghvin and Aylis and Svor—"

"The dead cannot come back."

As soon as the words slipped past Saga's tongue, she regretted them. Britta's features crumbled. "But—"

"I will always love ye, Britta, but do not expect me to care for that traitor."

Britta flinched.

"Leno sold himself to the Tariqins the day he gave them weapons. The day he valued his safety over our honor and attempted to melt down the metal that made up the axes of our forefathers. The day he tried to erase history and became a puppet for the Tariqins."

"Ye cannot mean that. And he didn't do it. He didn't desecrate the monument."

"Because I stopped him," Saga growled.

She could still remember the day as if it were yesterday. Leno had bargained with the Chishma in charge of inspecting their village. He'd agreed to craft for them in return for remaining in the village. Although they were invisible, their shackles were still around his wrists, and his servitude to the Tariqins had driven him to the monument in the center of the town, where he'd tried to take the axes to use for material. Saga had lost her mind and nearly killed him.

Saga stepped closer. "He takes their coin and gives them weapons in return. Weapons that have spilled

Savorian blood for years. I cannot stand by and act like I accept that."

Tears bloomed in Britta's eyes. Saga turned, leaving her in the middle of the path to walk through the forest. She glanced around as she headed deeper, but there were no deedans in sight. It was safe.

She whistled, the noise echoing through the trees.

Hastar.

Come to me, Saga replied in her thoughts.

There was a vibration in the air and then the thud of paws. Snow-white fur emerged from the trees. Then glowing black eyes and sharp canines.

"Kalpara," Saga whispered, outstretching her hand.

She bounded to Saga, her tail flicking with excitement. The top of her head reached Saga's shoulders. She had grown far bigger than expected. Saga hadn't been able to give her as much food as she would have liked over the years. For Kalpara's safety, much of her life had been in hiding.

"How are ye, my lass?"

The rumlok rolled on the ground, a loud purr rumbling from her. Saga leaned over to rub her belly, which only increased the purring. Saga kissed the top of Kalpara's head.

"Let's go home."

Kalpara sprang before Saga, knowing the path, her sleek fur shining under the dimming light. Saga spotted the small home ahead. The stones had been carefully placed. Her father's and brother's hands had touched each one. Saga stopped by the door, her fingers brushing over the carvings her brother had made.

Ize ov Barin.

House of Barin.

Saga blinked and pushed onward, rapping on the door. She steeled herself, waiting for the familiar sounds. The patter of steps approached, and the door flew inward. Yuva Elevedaughter stood in the doorframe, her lips widening when she caught sight of her daughter. Her arms wrapped around Saga before pulling away just as quickly.

"Ye are freezing. Come in before ye catch a chill."

She bustled into the home and Saga entered after her. Her boots clambered across the stone and brought melting snow over it. She leaned against the wall, Kalpara standing beside her and taking some of her weight as she tugged her boots off before they dirtied the freshly cleaned floor further.

"Come, lass. I've prepared potato soup." There was a little laugh, and then her mother's head peeked into view. "Yer da's favorite."

Saga sighed and set her boots on the rack before trudging into the house and placing wood onto the floor. She tossed a log into the dying flames, and embers shot up, hissing.

"How was yer day?"

Her mother sounded just as bubbly and cheerful as Britta. Saga could hardly stand it. Saga threw another piece of wood into the fire, her back to her mother.

"It was fine."

She turned, seeing her mother rub Kalpara and give her a piece of the meat Saga had almost lost her life to obtain. Kalpara's tail wagged.

"She's grown so tall. I swear it was only yesterday she was at my knees."

Saga clicked her tongue in agreement and took a seat at the table. Like always, the absence of the people who should have been sitting in the three other chairs was inescapable. Her mother set more plates on the table, steaming hot. Far too much food for the two of them.

"Mam, I told ye we need to save this. It is hard enough to come by as it is."

"Oh, don't be silly," her mam said. "Svorgin can eat this entire table himself."

Saga winced and forced herself to inhale. She reached into her bag and pulled out the wrapped bread. "Olava sent this."

Her mother clapped. "It will go perfectly with the soup." She unwrapped it carefully and then took a seat. Saga reached for the bread, but her mother slapped her hand.

"We must wait."

"Eat, Mam. Ye need yer strength."

Yuva frowned but didn't stop Saga this time when she tore the bread and dunked it into the soup. The warmth filled her mouth.

"It's delicious. Thank ye, Mam."

Yuva watched her with a disapproving look before she stood and moved to the window. Tension filled the room as she crossed her arms and began pacing from the table to the window and back again.

"Mam," Saga started.

"Where is yer da, Saga? He should have returned by now."

Saga's fingers tightened around her plate.

"Svor as well." Yuva's brows furrowed. "And Aylis, where is that lass? She didn't help me with the mending."

"Mam—"

"Something may have happened to them." Yuva rubbed her arms up and down her sleeves. Her eyes sharpened, and she strode to the opposite wall, grabbing the axe mounted there.

Saga stood from the table and followed her mother to the door. "Mam, what are ye doing?"

Yuva whirled toward her. "What do ye mean? I will go searching for yer siblings and da. Something happened to them out there."

"Ye cannot go."

"Why not? How dare ye tell me what to do?"

Kalpara growled a warning at the rise in Yuva's tone. She drifted around Saga, coming before her in a protective stance.

"Down, Kalpara," Saga said, and she relented, retreating behind her.

Yuva reached for the door, but Saga grabbed her arm, pulling her back. Yuva's eyes flashed.

"What are ye doing? Unhand me."

"I cannot allow ye to go out there. It is too late. Let us finish eating and get some rest."

"I will not leave yer da out there."

They struggled against each other. Yuva yanked her axe-wielding arm free with surprising strength, but Saga didn't relent. When she realized her mother would not stop, she used her full power to wrench the weapon from her hand and thrust it aside. It clanged over the stone. Yuva stared at it with wide eyes.

"They are gone, Mam!" Saga's chest heaved. "They are all dead. Da. Svorgin. Aylis. It's just us here. No one else."

Yuva's face crumpled, and she shook her head, falling to the ground with unrestrained wails. Saga sank down beside her mother and pulled her head onto her lap, stroking Yuva's hair until her tears dried and she fell into her trancelike state. They'd all left, abandoning her and her mother. Saga swallowed bitter tears. She would give her last breath before she ever forgave them.

2

THE TIP OF the quill traced the parchment. The black ink appeared blue in the light pouring in from the window. Honzio paused, the quill stilling in his hand. He pondered for a moment, collecting his thoughts before writing again. Singing sparrows fluttered by the window. Spring had come, and Ayleth was awash with flowers and merry songs. Honzio pushed the finished parchment away and watched as the ink dissolved into the paper, disappearing from view. Then he tapped his fingers on the desk while awaiting his head advisor's reply. Latimus was always timely with his letters.

Honzio leaned back, marveling at the sunlight streaming into the circular purple-domed tower. How strange for such a bright place to have housed one of the vilest people he'd ever known. Honzio cast aside thoughts of the deceased King Draven. His villainy was long gone. Ayleth had a new king, just as Ondalar had a new queen. Honzio's steps in ensuring the Empire didn't fall back to ruin were coming to fruition. He leaned against his chair, his eyes drifting closed as sleep pressed down on him—until a knock on the chamber door startled him, yanking him upright again.

"Enter."

Lore stumbled inside, wielding a tray of food. The gangly, long-limbed lad caught himself and the tray and thrust his shoulders back, his eyes finding Honzio. "Your Supreme Majesty. Good morning. I hope you had a pleasant rest?"

"It is midafternoon," Honzio grumbled.

Lore smiled, the brightness in his eyes never dimming as he stepped closer. "King Melevore requested you have some of the food from his table when you didn't attend brunch."

"Perhaps because I already attended his breakfast."

King Melevore was a good man. Honzio had known him since childhood, which was partially the reason he had chosen him to be Ayleth's king. Draven had no relations to take the throne after him, and Honzio wasn't sure he would even want one of Draven's relatives on the throne if he had. Melevore was of noble descent and strong-minded, with a penchant for peace and a meal between each of his meals. He would lay down his life for the Empire before seeking to control it.

"Set the tray there."

Lore did as he was told and stepped back. "Any orders, Your Majesty?"

Honzio rubbed his forehead. He had grown up surrounded by servants ready to do his every bidding. That had only worsened when he'd become emperor. For a while, he had needed the assistance. There had been so much to do, and he couldn't accomplish the tasks alone. But being under the constant surveillance of his people, guards, and servants had taken its toll, leaving him no privacy or a chance to explore avenues of his own enjoyment. In short, he had no personal life. In an effort to ease the suffocating supervision, he'd limited the servants tending to him and changed the ruling of the Cadellion. Instead of six bodyguards, he'd lowered it to three. Another servant was the last thing he wanted, but when Latimus requested he find a position for his younger brother, Honzio couldn't refuse him. His head advisor had sacrificed much for the Empire, leaving Verin and Ondalar behind for good and moving into the Grand Palace with his expecting wife. He'd been cut off from his mother and the land he'd grown up on to become locked within the palace, with duties day and night. Honzio hadn't known of any other use for Lore— so personal assistant it was.

"Normally, I would ask you to fetch a cloth, but you didn't spill this time." Honzio motioned to the tray.

Lore beamed. "I am improving, aren't I?"

"I didn't say that."

Lore deflated before asking, "Will we have our lesson today?"

Honzio shook his head. "There is no time. We will simply have to practice on the way."

One thing he appreciated about Lore was his willingness to learn. Over the past months, Honzio had dedicated all of his spare time to learning the Savorian language. He'd instructed Lore to do so as well, since it would benefit him greatly once they reached the island.

"Are the Savorians prepared to set off?" Honzio asked.

Lore bobbed his head. "They are awaiting you, Your Majesty."

"And General Mordon?"

Lore nodded again. "He is readying as we speak."

Honzio searched the room to find something for the boy to do. His eyes landed on the nearly empty bottle of ink. "Didn't I tell you to fetch me more ink?"

Lore paused. "About that . . ."

The door flung open, and a rounded woman with wild purple curls bustled inside. "I do not know what you think I am made of, Majesty, but I am a human with red blood and blue veins. I am not a machine capable of producing ink for you at your whim."

Honzio blinked, a bit startled. He still hadn't gotten used to the former Shadow Manos's exuberance. Marcella stopped in front of him, planting her hands on her hips. Lore inched toward the door. *The coward.* Honzio waved him off, and he dashed out of the chamber.

"Marcella," Honzio began.

"Don't you 'Marcella' me." She huffed. "This ink doesn't sprout from trees. It takes weeks to create, even longer now that I do not possess my shadow's ability. In fact, you should be thankful I can even create it still. If I hadn't written down the recipe, your magical means of conversing would not be possible."

Honzio stood, reaching out with a placating hand. "I apologize, Marcella. I have been pushing you too hard. You know how much I need the ink. I am communicating with leaders around the four kingdoms. This is the fastest way we can fix the Empire. Isn't that what you wanted?"

She crossed her arms and raised a brow.

"I will have a second balcony installed to your home in Hearcross."

At those words, just as he'd expected, a smile spread across her face.

"Why, you dearie." She reached out to pinch his cheek before seeming to think better of it. "I'd best be going. I have patients to see."

Honzio nodded, and the door closed behind her. He sighed and sank back into his seat, turning to the parchment. Words drifted across the paper. Honzio leaned closer to read Latimus's response.

Your Majesty,

All is well in Hearcross. Do not worry. I will take care of things until you return from Savoria. We've increased the servants' wages and caught two slavers entering the capital from The Docks. The trackers located Zenrelius's cloak outside the Karakan's cave. The rumlok itself was dead. It had been skinned. Human bones rested beside it. Besides that, there is no trace of Zenrelius. I am sure Queen Coralie will be enraged to hear it. When he disappeared from his cell in Verin, we thought the mercenary Vykus may have helped him escape, but our spies have located his camp, and there is no sign of Zenrelius. By the time I sent a troop to capture the mercenaries, they had sought refuge in The Docks. It will take time to prepare a full assault group to flush them out. I think it is best we wait for your return. Though there is no proof of it, I believe Zenrelius is dead. And although I am sorry we couldn't execute him publicly as he deserved, he met his fate under the cruel claws of the Karakan.

Queen Weria continues to send aid to Verin. Moralis and Aylis have remained with her to assist her. She is trying to make up for the damage Zenrelius caused.

Forever your loyal servant,

Latimus Blayton

Honzio sighed, thankful the traitorous general had met his end. Latimus had been obsessed with finding him. It seemed to be a personal need to see him die. Queen Weria had been an Ondalarian shieldmaiden, and though she was illegitimate, Honzio had overruled the Book of Codes and allowed her to become queen. Honzio flicked the parchment, and Latimus's message dissolved, leaving a clean sheet behind. He folded the parchment and slid it into the cylinder tube he wore on a leather band around his neck. The tube clinked against the beads brushing his collarbone.

"I will return before you know it."

The deep, familiar voice rumbled its way through the window. Honzio stood, leaning over the desk to peer down at the gardens below, where two figures stood close together. The man was as tall as a giant, with toned muscles and thick black hair, and his queen stared up at him as though her world were falling to pieces. Honzio had considered ordering Mordon not to journey with them, but the man had volunteered himself. He wanted to see the Savorian men he'd been enslaved with in Prolus's camp return home.

"I know," Coralie said.

Mordon leaned closer to his wife, caressing her cheek. "What is troubling you?"

Uncertainty was written across her features. "I didn't want to tell you without being certain."

Mordon's posture grew tense. "What is it?"

Coralie wrung her fingers together.

Mordon clasped her hands with his, stilling her anxious motions. "Tell me, Coralie."

She searched his gaze before disentangling her hands from his and reached up, cupping his bearded jaw in her palms. "I wasn't feeling well. You know it. I spoke to another True Manos yesterday."

Mordon shook his head, stepping out of her grasp. "Do not tell me you are ill."

Coralie's eyes bloomed with tears.

Mordon continued shaking his head. "I cannot lose you."

"Mordon."

"We will find another healer. A better one. You will be cured."

"Mor—"

"Come with me."

Honzio watched as Mordon grasped his wife's hand and tried to pull her forward.

"Mordon, there is life in me."

Mordon turned. "What do you mean? Is it a temporary illness?"

Coralie nodded, wiping away stray tears.

"What is it?"

Coralie took Mordon's hand, placing it over her stomach and lowering his hand farther. "There is life in me, Mordon. Part of me and part of you."

Mordon's jaw went slack, and he stared at his wife numbly. He blinked. Once, twice. Then his eyes fell to their hands. "You—you are with child?"

Coralie nodded, laughing. Honzio drew in a relieved breath. Part of him had been as confused as Mordon.

Mordon's eyes lit with emotion. He released a victorious cheer and lifted Coralie into his arms, spinning her around. His exclamation turned the heads of several gardeners. The couple's laughs filled the air. Honzio withdrew from the window, giving them their privacy. He sank into his chair. Seeing their warmth and love made him realize how alone he was. He had an entire empire under his command, yet there was not a single soul he could call his.

3

AT THE KNOCK on her door, Aria creaked the wood open. Rost smiled his wide grin—the one he used when he went undercover as a merchant and placated people with his charm. Aria slammed the door in his face. Before she could twist the lock, he grabbed the knob. There was a moment of struggle as they both pressed against either side until Aria's energy seeped out and she backed away. Her door flew open, smacking the wall with a bang. Aria didn't even flinch. She slipped onto the chair at her desk and sank her face into her hands.

"You didn't give me a chance to speak!" Rost protested, far too jolly when the sun hadn't even risen.

"What do you want?" Aria grumbled into her palms.

"Emperor Honzio sent a request to us. Master Dunya wishes you to handle it."

"Let someone else do it."

Silence elapsed. Though she could see nothing but darkness with her eyes shielded by her palms, she could picture him so clearly. That contemplative look he had whenever he was planning something, the concern he wore whenever he looked at her. Aria was tired of it. Tired of the stares of all the Elders. For the first time since she had joined the cause, she wanted to run away. To escape the pitying glances and encouraging words. None of them could understand what she was feeling. She didn't want them to. All she wanted was to be left alone to try to heal.

"Will you stay here in this dark chamber filled with morose thoughts and pity yourself forever? How long do you plan to do nothing?" He was trying a different tactic. To antagonize her. And blast him, it was working.

Aria's calm demeanor slipped away, and she shot up, nearly grasping a karambit from the rack sitting upon her desk. She stilled her hand at the last second, deciding not to resort to violence. It was not the way of the cause. She stepped before him.

"My brother died, Rost," she hissed. "Give me a moment to breathe. Give me time to recover."

Sympathy swirled in his eyes. "It's been four months, Aria. You are only harming yourself by shutting yourself away. Accept the mission. It will help you move on and recover."

Aria turned away from him so he wouldn't see the

sudden tears that poured over her vision. She blinked them away and turned back to him. She knew he was only trying to help her. Rost was a kind soul who cared for her as if she were a niece, checking in on her even when others had stopped.

"What is the mission?"

A smile crept along the edge of Rost's mouth. "After hearing our suspicions about Queen Guin of Devorin, Emperor Honzio has decided to investigate the matter. He wants us to infiltrate her castle and find any evidence that she was assisting Prolus during the war. That she's a traitor."

Aria nodded, then sighed as she returned to her seat. She took a karambit from the rack and dug the tip of the curved knife into the wood of her desk. "I will think about it," she finally said.

Rost nodded, relief evident in his features. "Good. Give your decision before the end of the day, or Master Dunya will have no choice but to pass the mission to another Elder."

Aria didn't reply. She leaned back against the chair, resting her neck and staring aimlessly at the ceiling until her door clicked shut. Aria's faith was unshakable, but sometimes, she wondered if her family was cursed. She could still smell the smoke of the battle all those years ago. See the fear in her mother's face when she had raced to retrieve her brother. Aria hadn't seen either of them after that. And after believing her father had moved on with a new family, she had dismissed the idea of contacting him for good. But then Alaric had returned to her life—or, as he'd preferred to be called, "Velamir." It had been all but an hour that she'd gotten to see him. Such brief moments without a chance to sit and talk properly. And then she'd lost him.

Aria swallowed, opening her drawer and extracting the letter he'd sent her.

Dear Aria,

I wish I had good tidings, but I am afraid everything is madness. Prolus has summoned me to Ayleth alone. He is threatening me with Jax, my closest friend. I know it is a trap. Jax might not even be there, but if he is, I cannot afford to lose him. I cannot chance Prolus murdering him if I do not come. I wanted to tell you that seeing you again, after all these years, was very meaningful. I wish we had longer. I do not know what will happen in Ayleth, but I wanted you to at least get this letter from me. And I have one request. If I cannot rescue Jax from their clutches, please find him. Find him and take him out of whatever prison they have locked him in.

Aria glanced over the rest of the letter, where a description of Velamir's friend and his full name and the names of his family members were written. She brushed her fingers over the worn letter. The ink had faded, and the paper was so thin she feared it would tear. She returned it to the drawer. She'd searched for Jaxon Tana like a madwoman after learning of Velamir's demise, looking through registries and speaking with people in every inch of Devorin, leaving no stone unturned. She'd only been able to find measly bits of information. He'd grown up on a farm away from the town. He'd had an abusive upbringing. An older merchant had revealed that fact. She'd told Aria that Jaxon's uncle had sold him off to Vykus, the mercenary king, who, at the time, had abducted children for the Dark Lord Prolus. Jaxon's uncle had perished to an illness shortly after. He'd had a cousin who became indentured to Queen Guin of Devorin to pay off their family's debts. Aria had found nothing further. There was no trace of Jaxon Tana. She'd fallen prey to her grief then and shut herself away in her chamber in the Elders' shelter. She hadn't accepted any missions, hadn't stepped out of her room. Until now.

Aria forced herself up. If she infiltrated the castle, she could try to find Jax's cousin, Lilly. Perhaps she knew something, something that could assist Aria in her search. It was worth a try. Aria grabbed her blades, sliding them into the sheaths on either side of her hips, and set off to see Master Dunya.

4

Saga

Savoria

Vidrun Village

Saga SAT ON her mother's cot, watching over her. Her fingers brushed over the long braids in Yuva's thick plaits. Her mother had once done this for her, when she'd been just a little girl, before the Tariqins came. Saga had been fearful of the demons in the elder villagers' tales. Her mother would sit by her bedside and wait for her to sleep, and her father would stand at her mother's side, looking down on them both, his large, calloused hand gripping Yuva's shoulder. And Yuva would look up at him and smile after reaching to place her hand over his. Saga squeezed her eyes closed, drying the unshed tears. That had been a lifetime ago. She was no longer afraid. Now the wretched, the demons, her enemies would fear *her*.

Saga leaned over her mother and placed a

kiss upon her weathered brow. Yuva had become frail, a mere shadow of her former warrior self. Saga cleared the dishes from the table and placed her axes into her belt before grasping her large axe. She placed the dead bolt for the door in place and sprang out of their home through a window concealed on the side.

Come, Kalpara.

Her rumlok prowled through the darkness, white fur gleaming in the night air. Saga moved with the breeze, hopping over fallen logs and cutting through the trees with grace. Kalpara stalked behind her. Saga approached the town and slowed her pace. Torches lit the village. She heard the shrill whistles and claps and spotted the large fire in the center. Women danced about it, the beads in their hair shimmering in the light. She could make out the forms of Britta and Leno settled on their knees before the fire. She couldn't see from this distance, but she knew their hands were locked together as part of the ceremony.

Saga scowled and ducked away, heading into a different part of the village. It was dark and gloomy, devoid of life. Everyone had gone to Britta's binding ceremony. Saga approached a house and knocked. She heard no answer and pressed upon the door. It gave, creaking open. She stepped into the dim light, evading a table and grasping a chair as she made her way to the back of the home. A waning candle highlighted the solitary figure hacking coughs in a bed. Saga rushed to aid the older woman in her struggle to stand.

"Ye are not well. Ye must rest."

Shavka Esme wiped her mouth, and Saga was

alarmed by the trace of blood left behind on her tunic sleeve. "I must attend the ceremony." The shavka sagged down on the bed. "But perhaps I will take a moment to catch my breath."

Saga filled a tankard with water and handed it to her. "Ye are feeling better, then?"

Shavka Esme took the water thankfully. "Enough to leave bed, ye ask?" She shook her head. "I fear this illness is taking me, Saga. It was my shadow keeping me alive, and now that it's gone, the sickness is tearing my body to pieces."

Saga grimaced. She had long wondered what had happened to the shadows. Though they were a hazard to the person afflicted with them, slowly driving their bearer to insanity, they were also a gift. They gave unmatched wisdom and unnatural power, among other things. Those with shadows had long been respected in the villages and mourned as well, for a Shadow Manos did not live a long life. The shadows' corruption took over their mind before death ever came for them.

Saga examined Esme as she took grateful gulps of water. Though she was still young, not yet in her fiftieth year, she looked twice her age. The lines creasing her face, the sad, defeated look in her eyes, her weakened posture all spoke of the devastation she'd faced when she lost her shadow. Saga wondered how she'd lived. Most Shadow Manos lost their lives right after the loss. But Shavka Esme had been one of those who remained.

"I was stubborn," the shavka said, her voice scratchy.

Saga stiffened. It was as if Esme had heard her thoughts.

"I knew death was coming for me, but I did not want to give in. Not without a fight. Not without seeing my land free." Her voice broke, and she placed the tankard on an oak table beside her bed. "But it is too late, Saga Barindaughter."

Saga detested the defeat radiating from the shavka. She could not give in, not yet, not after everything they had hoped for. She glanced about the small home in search of something to restore Esme's spirits. Her heart lifted a bit when she noted the hanging birdcage. She moved toward it, brushing her fingers around the tiny bars. "Remember that day?"

Shavka Esme's mouth tilted in a soft smile. "How could I forget? Ye young foolish children hunting birds."

Saga's lips twitched. "We were terrified of ye then. All the children were."

She, Britta, and Daghvin had assembled their slingshots to catch a sparrow. Though they had feared the shavka, Esme's husband at the time, Esme herself terrified them far more. As soon as Daghvin and Britta had caught sight of her, they dashed away, but Saga had been so intent on catching her sparrow that she hadn't noticed. It was only after she'd struck the sparrow with a pebble from her slingshot and grasped the bird in a victorious fist that she realized her friends had abandoned her, leaving only Shavka Esme to glower down at her.

"Aye, I know. The children ran whenever they caught sight of me. But I had to impose rules for them as the shavka's wife." Her gaze brightened as they spoke of the past. "Yer pebble damaged the sparrow's wing."

"Aye," Saga said. "But ye didn't punish me as I'd

expected. Ye brought me here." She waved around the walls. "Ye taught me how to heal the bird."

Shavka Esme had instructed Saga on how to treat broken bones using the wing as an example. Saga would rush to her house every afternoon to check on the bird. It became a ritual, and Saga had learned something new with every visit. She grew close to the bird and was saddened deeply when she had come one day to find it gone.

It is restored, Esme had told her. *And returned to its friends.*

Saga had accepted this, although she'd been quite upset. She had never harmed a sparrow again. And once the Tariqins invaded, she never could, even if she had wanted to. The birds had all disappeared. Leaving Savoria without song. But Esme had never given up hope.

They will return, she'd said. *When the heroes of this island rise up against the evil, the songs shall come back.*

But it had been months since Saga had seen such a hopeful Esme. The shavka folded into herself, as if she, too, recalled those days.

Saga approached her and squeezed her arm. "The sparrows will return."

Shavka Esme placed her hand over Saga's and gave her a small smile, but the somberness still weighed heavy upon her. Saga needed her to believe it.

"They will," she insisted.

"They will," Shavka Esme whispered, and Saga's heart lightened somewhat.

She left the shavka's home sometime after, journeying to a back alley where she spotted a tall form leaning against the wall. He pushed up as she approached, a sneer crossing his face.

"Well, well, well, I thought you would not show."

"Ye thought wrong," Saga snapped and pulled the coin purse from her belt.

He extended his hand, palm upward.

Saga clicked her tongue and bounced the coin purse in her hand. "The medicine and information first."

He sniffed and shook his head. "So persistent."

Saga continued staring at him until he relented and gave her a vial of syrup.

"There won't be much more of this. You know what's happened to the Shadow Manos. Without their abilities, the chance of making more of these vials is almost impossible. We have few left, and I am risking my neck getting it as it is."

"Good," Saga snarled. "Let yer neck be at risk for once."

His brows lowered. "Such hatred. When will it end?" He tried to grasp the purse, but Saga kept it out of reach.

"The information."

He sighed. "You already know of Prolus's defeat. The Imperial emperor is rallying his armies. We are in desperate need of proper leadership before he brings them into Tariqi. Prolus's generals are scrambling to form some semblance of a defense against the emperor's men."

Saga smiled. "It took long enough. So, Tariqi's fall has begun."

"Careful, woman," he said, stepping closer. "That is my land you speak of. We are still powerful. Just reeling from the loss of our leader. But we will return twofold and make that emperor rue the day he was born." He placed his fingers around his sword hilt. "I could always turn you in to my superiors. Tell them of the rebel Savorian who is poking her nose into matters that shouldn't concern her."

"And would ye also tell them of the bribes ye were taking in return?" Saga bit out as she tossed him the pouch.

He shook his head. "I would say I played into your game to catch you. I would escape easily, but you . . ."

Saga remained silent. He jingled the coin purse.

"It seems less than before, especially after what I have given and told you. I deserve a greater prize."

"I have nothing to give," Saga said.

He pocketed the purse and leaned in, showering her with his foul breath. He reached out to touch her face. "You could give me a taste of this beautiful skin. I deserve it, don't you think?"

"Ye would do well to choose yer next step wisely," Saga informed him. "Lay a finger on me and ye will breathe yer last this night."

He chuckled and touched her cheek. "With what are you threatening me, girl?"

Saga grimaced and slapped his hand away.

He didn't relent. "I warn you. I will turn you in. Be a good girl." He ran his fingers over her chin, forcing her head up. "Let me see those pretty blue eyes."

Saga hoped he could feel the fire in her stare. He flinched, but his fingers remained upon her.

"So cold." His voice dropped to a whisper. "Why

so cold? Staring into your eyes makes me believe winter will never end."

"Let go of me." Saga enunciated each word.

"My fellow deedans say you people are unattractive. 'Ugly as a horse's behind,' if I recall correctly." He laughed.

The words *you people* drilled into her brain. Spoken with such malice, such blatant dislike. As if they were lesser. And they were, in the Tariqins' eyes. The Savorians would always be deemed worthless if they never rose up.

"But I disagree," he said, leaning closer, his fingers sliding into her hair. "I think you are quite pretty when you are submissive."

Saga yanked his arm from her hair and shoved his chest, sending him stumbling back. His smile faded, and a dangerous gleam entered his gaze. He approached again, looking determined this time.

"You will give me what I want, or I will turn you in." His vile hands trailed over her.

"Stay away!" she snarled.

She could kill him. End his life so easily. But to do so would have consequences.

"As you can see, it is just you and me. You are alone."

Something snapped in Saga. She would not tolerate this. She shoved him again and backed away, whistling. His eyes widened. "What are you . . . ?"

His voice trailed off when he caught sight of the enormous shape emerging from behind Saga. Kalpara's anticipation poured through the mind link when her glittering eyes focused on her prey.

"Who said I was alone?"

Kalpara lunged forward, her enormous jaws clamping around the Tariqin's throat and silencing his scream. Blood showered the ground and Kalpara's white fur. Saga watched as her rumlok ravaged the man's chest and extracted his heart—her favorite part of her meals. Kalpara glanced up at Saga. Her sharp canines glinted red as she revealed her teeth in what Saga recognized as her smile.

"Good girl." Saga patted her fur, heedless of the blood.

Then she leaned over the unrecognizable Tariqin and whispered, "My hatred will end once every one of ye vermin leaves this island."

5

HONZIO

KINGDOM OF AYLETH

HONZIO WALKED BETWEEN the graves. The midafternoon sun touched the exposed skin of his neck and the thick waves of his hair. He'd given up on trimming it months ago. The wind tousled the locks without the weight of his crown to hold them down. Honzio wasn't visiting the cemetery as an emperor but rather as a brother. In fact, if it weren't for the three Cadellion bodyguards tailing him and Lore at his shoulder, Honzio doubted anyone would have paid him a second glance. Civilians sat on the edges of their loved ones' graves, shedding tears for those they had lost. Honzio squinted when he heard a clatter ahead. Stable hands were attempting to settle an enraged horse. The horse pawed the ground and reared upward, heavy hooves narrowly missing a stableboy. Hands reached for the rope around the horse's neck.

"Now!" one man shouted.

The stable hands latched onto the rope and heaved the horse toward them. The horse resisted, thick mane billowing as it dug its hooves into the ground.

"That's Vandal," Lore murmured. "Velamir's horse."

Honzio marched forward and shouted in the commanding voice he'd perfected since becoming emperor. "Leave him!"

The stable hands glanced at him. Their leader gave him a narrow-eyed stare, clearly not recognizing him. "The horse has caused havoc in our stables. He entered Ayleth one week past and has destroyed every stall we put him in."

"I said release him."

They stiffened, and then the leader's eyes raced over Honzio's arm and the bodyguards behind him. He bowed his head to conceal the surprise in his eyes and placed a half heart to his chest. "Your Majesty."

The other stable hands dropped the rope and sank to their knees.

"You may go."

They hesitated before hurrying away. Lore approached the horse and reached out. The horse neighed and turned away.

"Latimus tried to tame him," Honzio said, recalling his advisor's words. "But it was useless. A lancer horse is forever bound to its rider. We set him free."

Lore glanced at him with wide eyes. "Vandal is looking for Velamir?"

Honzio nodded, placing his palm over the boy's shoulder. "And he shall search forever. But he will not find him."

A misty sheen covered Lore's eyes as Vandal approached the two gravestones in the center of the cemetery, and Honzio swallowed the lump in his throat when Vandal's muzzle brushed the dirt covering Velamir's grave. A pained whinny rumbled through his chest.

"What can we do?"

Honzio dropped his hand and strode forward. "There is nothing we can do."

Vandal looked up from the grave and shot off, hooves clomping against stone as he disappeared. Lore reached out.

"Should we stop him?"

Honzio shook his head. "There is no use locking him in a stall. He will not give up looking for his rider. He doesn't believe Velamir is gone. We can do nothing more than give him the freedom to search."

Lore nodded, his face settling into one of sorrow. Honzio stepped between the two graves before sinking onto the stone enclosing one. He motioned to the others, and Lore and the Cadellion backed away to give him privacy. Honzio sat a moment in silence before he reached out, brushing the words carved into the stone.

The Phoenix. Natassa Hartinza, Princess of the Empire.

Honzio bowed his head. "It has been 125 days, Natassa, since you left us," he began, his throat rough. "Since you returned to mother and Thorsten and Hesten. You undoubtedly want to know what has changed. Or perhaps not. Perhaps you are content exactly where you are. At peace with our loved ones."

Honzio pressed his head against her gravestone, ignoring the fact that eyes were upon him. "But just in case you want to know, I will tell you. The mines are closed as you wanted. I have imprisoned every slaver I could get my hands on. The Savorians are now safer on Imperial soil than their own land. Can you believe it? They can walk freely in the markets, no longer hiding within cloaks or other disguises." Honzio smiled. "And not only them, the Uluzar come and go as they please. We have maintained our treaty. I am sure Velamir would be pleased to know that."

Honzio's eyes shot to the opposite grave before he tilted his head against Natassa's gravestone. The cold rock pressed against his brow. "I opened a school in your name. A training school for young women to learn to defend themselves." He chuckled. "Just as Thorsten trained you once. I knew about that. I saw through your devious ways. But I turned a blind eye to it. Now no one will practice in secret."

He sighed. "I am departing to Savoria to liberate it, as I promised Svorgin. I hope he is still alive. I used to believe it as much as Bear does, but too long has passed. Even if my men have stopped searching, even if he is truly gone, I will keep the promise I made to him." He swallowed. "Until I return to speak with you again, take care of yourself, little sister."

He stood and walked past the Cadellion and Lore, who found themselves conveniently distracted by a butterfly hovering over them. They trudged after him as he approached Ayleth's dock. The ship was loaded with passengers, and a crowd of civilians waited to see it off. The crowd parted for him with mumbles of "Your Majesty." Honzio crossed the plank and hopped onto the deck. A gaggle of Savorians clustered together. Mordon stood in the midst of them, his arms wrapped over the shoulders of a broad Savorian. Honzio pinned his features at once and recalled his name. Silopar. Being a prince had its perks at times. Honzio's mind had been trained to remember every detail, every introduction, every possible ally, and master every potential deal since he'd been a boy. They broke out of their group as Honzio closed in and lowered their heads in respect.

"Your Majesty," Mordon greeted him.

"General," Honzio replied, "it is good to see you among us."

"I wanted to speak with you."

Honzio motioned for him to go ahead, and Mordon continued.

"I am not sure if you've heard the news. Queen Coralie and I are keeping it away from prying ears as best we can."

Honzio nodded. "I heard."

He didn't add that it had been his own prying ears that had overheard their conversation in the garden.

"I cannot leave the queen while she is in this state. Though I wish I could have journeyed with you."

Honzio waved away his apologies. "I understand, General. This is a time that you must be with your wife. You will be greatly missed, but we have spoken of the plan. This is a brief visit to gather the lay of the land

and our next move. There will be plenty more times we will journey into Savoria and chances for you to see the land yourself."

Mordon placed a half heart to his chest. "Thank you, Your Majesty."

Honzio spotted Lore inching closer and closer to Mordon and frowned. What was the boy up to? He stood just behind him and lifted his hand above his head. Honzio concealed a grin. He was measuring their heights.

"You've quite a way to go, lad," a heavily accented voice chimed in.

A tall Savorian with long, braided brown hair and gleaming brown eyes joined them on the deck and nodded at Honzio. Honzio observed the speaker. He was one of the Savorians from the party Mordon had brought with him from Verin.

"Daghvin, Your Majesty."

"Daghvin," Honzio repeated, pronouncing it as best as he could. "And I am Honzio."

Daghvin laughed, a crooked grin overtaking his features. "Oh, I know. I doubt anyone doesn't know of your name, Your Majesty."

"Since we will travel quite a distance and undercover, let's lose the titles, shall we?"

Daghvin nodded. "Honzio," he repeated. "I will keep it in mind."

Mordon glanced over his shoulder and peered at Lore, who took a fascinated interest in the cuff of his sleeve. "What are you doing?"

Lore blinked and looked up at Mordon. "Who? Me?"

Mordon gave him a slow nod. "Yes, you."

Lore beamed his specialty charming grin. "Just appreciating the wind. It takes the edge off the heat."

Honzio chuckled. The boy was right, though. The wind was on their side this day. It would propel them into the sea with minimal effort on their part. "We should take off."

The others nodded in agreement. Silopar issued orders to the other Savorians and Imperials accompanying them. Mordon stepped off the ship, joining Queen Coralie and King Melevore, who stood at the front of the onlookers. King Melevore, a brawny man with a thick mustache and close-trimmed beard, waved a hand toward Honzio.

"Your Majesty! May the winds be in your favor and the journey smooth."

"I thank you," Honzio replied.

"You make us proud. It is not often that an emperor leaves his throne, his home, and fights at the forefront. Fights not only for the good of his people but for the rest of the world as well. Long live Emperor Honzio!"

Honzio's chest thrummed at the praise. He wondered if he was truly deserving of it.

"Long live Emperor Honzio!" the crowd chanted.

"It is only with *your* help"—Honzio stressed the word, waving to all the observers—"only with the people's help that I have managed this. It is because of you all, the Imperials who longed for a change, and our just allies that we have progressed to the empire we have become. And we must stay united if we are to continue. For freedom!"

Fists shot into the air as all shouted in unison, "For freedom!"

The calls for his long life resounded through the crowd once more as the anchor was lifted. The wind swept them away and eventually stifled the cries. Honzio walked up the thick wooden stairs to the helm and stood beside Silopar, who manned the wheel. Honzio's hair blew back as the sails lowered and caught the breeze, shooting them forward with greater speed. He gripped the railing and looked ahead at the endless blue, preparing for whatever was coming his way.

6

"FAMILY NAME?" THE burly woman in charge of the servants questioned.

Aria gave her a timid smile and glanced at her feet. "Loritan. We are but a poor family forced to make ends meet. I have young children at home and no husband."

The housekeeper raised a thick brow over her beady eyes. "What happened to him?"

Aria summoned tears. They came just in time, dousing her eyes with a wet sheen. "He passed of an illness some months past. I am desperate. I have nothing but Her Majesty Queen Guin's mercy. I beg of you to forgive the taxes we owe. We can barely make ends meet."

The housekeeper waved a hand at the

servant standing at her shoulder. "How much in taxes does the Loritan family owe?"

The servant flipped through a hefty book until she found the name. "Five hundred gold, Madame Zelnat."

The housekeeper, Madame Zelnat, clicked her tongue and shook her head. "The unpaid tax your family owes has gone far over the limit. A debt of this amount warrants the chopping block."

Aria fell to her knees and clasped her hands together, presenting the perfect pleading image. "I beg of you, forgive us. I have no one but the children. I cannot pay such a sum."

Aria's gaze slipped to the crowd behind her. A long line awaited their turn to be granted an audience, many with the same plight. She caught sight of Rost in the line. He gave her a slow nod, and she tilted her chin in response, assuring him that everything was going according to plan. It had taken the Elders a matter of hours to find Lana Loritan, mother of two young children. They had come to an agreement so Aria could enter the castle. Lana would remain silent, and the Elders would handle her debt.

Madame Zelnat's gaze raked Aria from the tips of her scuffed boots, up past her brown skirt and tattered vest wrapped over a frayed long-sleeved shirt, then up to her face. Aria knew she must look a sight. Her nose and cheeks were red from the biting cold, and her eyes were bloodshot from the lack of sleep from planning the night before. Her hair was covered in a modest servant's white head wrap.

"You look decent enough," Madame Zelnat finally

said. "You can work off your debt. It will take a year of hard work."

Aria grasped the woman's skirt. "I thank you, madame."

Madame Zelnat's mouth twisted, disgust creasing her face. "Get up before I change my mind."

Aria pulled to her feet, allowing a triumphant grin to slide across her lips for a moment as she followed Madame Zelnat into the castle entrance. She glanced back to where Rost disappeared into the crowd. The inside of the castle was just as cold and formidable as it appeared from outside. The colorless gray walls and stone floor were almost transparent. Mirrors hung everywhere she looked, and her many reflections stared back at her. An uneasy shudder went through her. She felt exposed. The mirrors seemed to send a message. *You are being watched.*

"You will stay overnight," Madame Zelnat said, flinging open a door.

Aria stepped inside, scanning the long chamber. At least fifty beds were positioned along the walls of the room. Women glanced up at their entrance with bored looks, though some stiffened at the sight of Madame Zelnat and occupied themselves with a task.

"Rose, give the new girl the proper apparel."

The woman darted to a closet at the end of the chamber and returned with gray clothes. She extended the folded garments to Aria, who took them with a hesitant look.

"You will wear these from now on," Madame Zelnat

told her. "All of you maids dress the same. Do nothing special. No face powders or lip color."

Aria frowned. "Why is that?"

Madame Zelnat swept out of the room without answering. "Get changed."

Aria shifted into the clothes as quickly as she could while feeling the weight of eyes upon her.

"The queen doesn't appreciate it," Rose said while examining her.

"Pardon?"

"You asked why we couldn't get a bit fancy, make up our faces." Rose leaned closer. "Queen Guin doesn't like it."

The other women hissed for her to be quiet, some darting uneasy glances toward a mirror.

"Why?" Aria couldn't help but ask.

Rose lowered her voice to a whisper. "She wants the castle to be uniform and drab, including all of us. We are all part of her game. Chess pieces. Pawns easily destroyed."

An uncomfortable shiver raced over Aria.

"Come," Rose said, urging Aria to follow her. "Madame Zelnat will get angry if we tarry."

They stepped into the hall and found Madame Zelnat waiting. She gave an approving nod at the plain clothes and head wraps.

"Your only task is to clean the first and second floors, just like the other maids. Wipe down the stairs and banisters, mop the floor."

"I can do that," Aria said.

"Good." Madame Zelnat stepped closer, looking

down at Aria. "Only the first two floors. You are absolutely forbidden from going to the tower. No one can go past the second floor. Do you understand, girl?"

Curiosity flickered through Aria. So, the queen *was* hiding something.

"Understood."

Rushed boot steps approached. Madame Zelnat turned. The castle's defenders and the queen's loyal warriors advanced. They were dressed entirely in dark gray, with a blue patch in the center of their chests. If someone asked Aria how cold Devorin was, she would have motioned to the man at the front of the newcomers. His blue eyes were chips of ice. His jaw as hard as a mountain. Light lashes and brows did nothing to soften his face. His short hair exposed thin ears.

"Blade." Madame Zelnat lowered her head.

At the title, Aria's spine stiffened. The Queen's Blade, often mentioned in hushed conversations amongst the civilians, was a heartless man who did whatever Queen Guin ordered. He paid Madame Zelnat no mind. He almost appeared to be in another dimension entirely. He strode past them. The men and women following his lead were just as silent and vicious. They barely made a sound, yet their presence spoke volumes. A shudder racked through Aria. She glanced at Madame Zelnat.

"That is the Blade?"

Madame Zelnat's brows lowered. She seemed to consider not replying but then said, "The queen's right hand. Do not dare meddle with him, girl, if you know what's best for you."

Madame Zelnat gave her another look before

nodding and walking away. Aria exhaled. The first part of the plan was complete. She was now inside the castle. Her hand slid into the pocket of her gray skirt and fisted around the hilt of her karambit. The curved-moon blade had escaped Madame Zelnat's appraisal.

Rose motioned to a few maids, and Aria got to scrubbing the floors alongside them. She tried to converse with them as they cleaned and led the conversation to Jax's family. She asked about his cousin, Lilly, but the other maids said they had never heard of her—the ones that spoke to her, that is. Most of them simply shook their heads, a tamped-down sort of terror marking their faces. Aria scrubbed harder, her frustration getting the best of her.

"Getting the hang of it, new girl?" Rose appeared, sweat beading her brow and white apron stained.

Aria nodded, stilling in her fierce scrubbing to catch her breath.

"The others are wary of you." Rose settled down on the stair Aria had not yet polished. "I know I should be too. You are new, after all. But there is something about you that makes me want to trust you."

Aria wasn't sure how to respond to that. Was it a compliment or an insult?

"Yes." Rose nodded. "I have made up my mind. You seem like a decent sort. I do not want you to disappear, so I will warn you."

"Disappear?" Aria repeated, perturbed.

"That's what happened to others. The ones who asked too many questions."

Rose glanced about. But it was just Aria and her on the staircase. Well, them and the eerie mirrors.

"I heard you talking to the other maids. Asking about someone. I don't know who she is to you, family or acquaintance, but if she came here and you don't see her, she is most likely one of those who disappeared."

Rose spoke in such a hushed voice that Aria struggled to hear her.

"Do you know her? Lilly—"

"Stop!" Rose's voice rose, and she darted another fearful glance about. "Do not ask about her—or anyone for that matter. *She* is always watching. If you do something to displease her, it will be your end."

Aria could see the terror plain upon Rose's face. It unsettled her. How long had the queen been getting away with removing the people she disliked? Far too long, Aria thought, because no one dared to speak up.

"And the ones that disappear. Do you know what happens to them?"

Rose paused. "No one knows for sure. All we know is that most don't return, and those who do never come back the same."

Madame Zelnat's voice echoed from a chamber nearby, and Rose jumped up, scurrying away before the woman spotted her. Aria went back to work, Rose's words weighing on her the entire time. She cleaned for hours, step by step, until she reached the second floor. Her bones ached. Sweat plastered her gray dress to her skin. Pieces of hair had slipped from her head cover and brushed her cheekbones. She tucked them back with her hands and winced when she caught sight of the ripped skin on her palms. She leaned over, catching her breath.

None of the other maids were in sight. She glanced at the staircase leading to the next level. Madame Zelnat's warnings lingered in the back of her mind as she gathered her courage and crossed the steps, her hand trailing a touch above the railing. This was the reason she had entered the castle. She had to learn what the queen was up to, and she had to find some clue to point to Jax's whereabouts.

She crested the stairs. There was something different in the air. Something darker lingered here. A strangled sort of silence that drilled a sense of panic into her. Aria gathered herself, pressing a hand to her Elder medallion and the thin necklace beneath it. The two intertwined the meanings of courage and faith whenever she doubted or feared—like a beam of light whenever she faced darkness. With renewed purpose, Aria moved through the corridor like a ghost. She caught a flash of fabric in the hall ahead and ducked against a wall. Her pulse was erratic. Aria glanced into the corridor. There was no one there, but the candles mounted on the wall flickered oddly, as though something or someone had moved past them at a quick pace. Aria pressed her hand to her chest and breathed in. She turned back, then slapped her hands over her mouth to hold back the scream lodged in her throat. Standing before her was a woman dressed in the same gray clothes as her, but cutting through her lips in a gruesome image was a thick black cord.

7

S AGA MARCHED TO the village square, exhilaration pumping in her veins. She slowed as she neared. Leno and Britta were standing, facing each other. Charcoal marked their foreheads and cheekbones with customary symbols. Britta's father, Bodvar, handed her a knife, the firelight highlighting the sheen covering his eyes. The people Saga had known her whole life hummed the binding tune, drowning out the crackling fireplace and the night owls. Saga's heart clenched. Voices from the past spilled into her thoughts.

"My binding will only be with ye." Britta's *thick blond lashes framed her kind blue eyes.*

"Ye will do it with more than me one day," Saga replied.

Britta shook her head. "But ye will be my first. My blood sister forever."

Saga swallowed the thickness in her throat as Britta cut her palm. Crimson welled upon her pale skin, but she didn't even flinch. She beamed larger than ever before and passed the curved blade to Leno. He swiped it over his palm. The humming grew louder, and they pressed their hands together in a moment that seemed to last a century. Uncle Bodvar tied rope around their palms, binding them together. A tear lingered on the edge of Saga's lashes, but she refused to acknowledge it or the pain that cut through her shield of hatred. She forced herself to push aside the agony that seemed to drain her of life and focused on her anger and fury instead, on her thirst for vengeance, the feelings that kept her living. She marched forward as the Savorians pounded hands to their chest—empty palms that once would have carried axes, as was the custom for the binding dance. A ceremony performed for those who weren't kin but wished to become so. A ceremony that made life partners and blood brothers and sisters. A ceremony where different blood became one.

A shout pulled Saga's attention. Tariqins emerged from the dark, their red-and-black uniforms instilling a sense of panic into the crowd. The Tariqins' faces were carved from granite as they marched into the throng of her people. They stomped upon the fireplace, turning the fierce flames into mere embers, just like they had broken the spirit of many Savorians over these long years. Torches were tossed into the snow, and people were shoved to their knees. Saga joined the commotion, her ears buzzing from the frenzied cries erupting around her.

"Chishma Jirco," Leno said, untying himself from the rope that wrapped around both his and Britta's hands as he addressed the lead Tariqin. "What is the meaning of this interruption?"

Chishma Jirco, their village inspector, rarely graced them with his presence. She despised seeing his smug features and proud stance. This night, however, only anger dominated his expression and posture. His dark brows drew together beneath the fold of his hood. His cloak blended with the night, the apparel of all Chishmans. He moved like a wraith, drawing up right before Leno. Leno, to his credit, maintained a brave face, unflinching as he met the Chishma's gaze head-on.

"We have granted too much freedom to your village, Leno," Chishma Jirco said.

"And we have given Tariqi loyalty in return for remaining unharmed."

"Is that so?" The Chishma's eyes took on a dangerous gleam. "Why, then, is one of my men dead? Slaughtered in cold blood. His skin is still warm."

Saga stiffened. She had known there would be consequences for her actions. But she hadn't expected them so soon. Not after carefully disposing of the deedan's corpse into the sea.

"What are ye speaking of?" Leno asked.

"A Tariqin was slain, Leno!" The Chishma's voice rose. "And one of your people did it."

"We have done no such thing. We have proven our loyalty again and again."

"Your weapons are but a mere advantage. Many villages offer the same thing as you. Think wisely. We do not need you as much as you believe, Savorian. We could enslave all in your village and ship you off to other lands like your predecessors."

Rage raised the hairs on Saga's arm. Her fingers tightened around the axes on her hips.

"Or you can tell me who killed him, and I will only take the culprit. Your choice."

Leno's jaw clenched. His gaze flicked over the crowd, scanning, searching for someone to sacrifice. His eyes landed on Saga and stilled. *Spineless coward.*

"There is only one who could have done it. We have dealt with her rebellion in the past. She is the one ye want. Saga Barindaughter."

Britta gasped, betrayal pooling over her features at Leno's admission. "No, not Saga."

He pulled her behind him. The Chishma glanced over the onlookers.

"Catch her."

"There is no need." Saga stepped through the crowd and came to the forefront. "I will not run like a weakling."

She walked up to the Chishma, meeting his gaze. His eyes roamed over her, and he nodded. "You are the one who has been causing trouble since you were a little girl. A bad weed in the garden. We will pluck you from here, and this will be settled." His gaze fell to her weapons. "Ah, and I see you are illegally armed as well."

"Leno," Saga heard Britta sob. "Do something."

"Take her," the Chishma ordered the deedans with him.

They stepped forward, when a firm voice called out, "Stop!"

All eyes turned to the woman emerging from the cluster to stand beside Saga. She was frail but still carried a powerful presence. Her pale eyes were frightening, and her gray hair fell past her waist.

"Shavka Esme," Saga said in deference.

Murmurs of "Shavka" echoed among the crowd.

Esme narrowed her eyes on the Chishma. "Ye will not take a single soul from this village. I do not grant ye permission."

"Is that so?" Chishma Jirco's tone emerged, mocking. "But we were getting along so well with Leno here."

"Leno is not the head of this village, lad," Esme said. "I am."

"Well, let's change that up a bit, shall we?"

Chishma Jirco turned to look at the deedans. Then he swiveled, flicking a blade from his hand. It swept through the air with startling speed and buried into Esme's throat. Horrified screams erupted. Saga choked on a breath, her chest clenching. Esme coughed as her blood welled around the blade. Her eyes went wide, and she stumbled, hands rising to her neck. Saga reached out in time, catching her, and sank to her knees with Esme in her arms. She watched the struggle on Esme's face—the pain, the horror, the blood. Esme looked back at her, her lips moving, but only thick gurgles emerged. Saga touched her cheek, the screams around her fading as she stared at the woman who had given her so much wisdom and kindness. Esme's struggles subsided until she stilled in Saga's arms and her pale eyes were unseeing. Pure rage poured through Saga.

"*Kvor sergha ye lis*," she whispered. The same promise she had made over the forms of so many dead. *I will avenge you.*

"There, now that that is handled, Leno is the new shavka. I am sure we will get along nicely."

Saga's head rose, her gaze rooting on the Chishma who was clasping a horrified-looking Leno's shoulder.

"The girl is spared, as we took one life." Chishma Jirco's brows lowered as he looked at Saga. "Be sure not to cause any more problems, or her life will be for naught."

He turned away, walking toward the deedans, who began marching. Tears streaked over the Savorians' faces. Britta cried, and Leno wrapped his arms around her. Saga stood, her fingers reaching toward her belt.

Leno caught sight of the movement and shook his head. "Do not, Saga! Do not dare—"

But it was too late. The axe whipped out of her belt and buried into the Chishma's back.

And chaos erupted.

8

WAVES CRASHED AGAINST the ship. Honzio noted that they'd grown harsher over the past hours. The ship tilted, nearly sending him toppling from his chair and clattering the low table before him. He slammed his fist over the table, holding the map in place. A few Imperials grasped the walls to catch themselves. Their faces turned green, and they dashed up the stairs to the main deck. Honzio grimaced.

"Ye all right there?" Daghvin asked, slapping a thick hand onto Honzio's shoulder.

The Savorians had been friendly and helpful. They looked at home on the ship. Daghvin stepped in front of Honzio, appearing utterly at ease. The ship never unbalanced him, Honzio had noticed. In fact, they seemed to move in tandem.

"I'm fine," Honzio said.

Besides the queasiness in his belly the first day they'd set off, Honzio thought he was handling this sailor business fairly well.

"We will enter the island from the western side under cover of nightfall," Honzio said, returning to the point at hand. He'd called the men down to discuss the plan a handful at a time so as not to disrupt the controlling of the ship.

"My village is near there," Silopar said. The brawny Savorian who was covered in scars had a look in his eyes that spoke of several lifetimes endured during his imprisonment. "I believe Daghvin's is closer though."

"We must avoid the Tariqins and enter Daghvin's village. That will be our first stop. We will investigate the area and figure out how many resources we need to make the Tariqins fall back. As we slowly take control of the villages one by one, the Imperial kings and queens will bring forth their armies and distract the Tariqins. They cannot fight two fronts. We will go to Ayleth for backup and return with greater forces to Savoria. Slowly but surely, we will succeed if we follow this strategy."

Eyes followed Honzio's finger over the map and around the villages. Though Honzio's Savorian was accented and still a bit rough, they had no trouble understanding him. Honzio himself, on the other hand, was struggling to keep up because they spoke far faster than his tutor. It was a good learning benefit though, so Honzio insisted they speak to him only in their tongue. So far, he'd picked up a plethora of new words that consisted mostly of curses.

"I cannot wait to return to my village. What say ye, lads?" Daghvin called.

"Aye!" they shouted in unison.

"I miss my mam's cooking," one man said, beaming as a hungry light entered his gaze.

"I cannot wait to see the wee ones," another replied, smiling fondly at the memory of his children. "Though they may not be so small any longer."

Honzio flinched as they continued recounting all they had lost and those they couldn't wait to reunite with. He did not have the heart to tell them not to be so hopeful. They did not know what had happened in their absence. There may be none who awaited their return.

"And you, Daghvin, is there anyone waiting for you?" Lore piped up.

Honzio noted that, instead of hovering around him, his personal assistant had become the Savorian's shadow, lingering by him at every opportunity, soaking in his words and the tales he was apparently famous for among his folk. Honzio was relieved that he hadn't had to entertain the boy with tasks, but a certain part of him was envious of the draw Daghvin had.

"My family, my da and mam, and little sis of course," Daghvin answered, but there was a brittle smile on his face, as though he didn't quite believe he would see them all. "And there's one other."

He looked away, ducking his head. Teasing shouts erupted around him, and his countryfolk drifted closer and slapped him on the back and shoulders.

Lore leaned in. "Who?"

Daghvin glanced up. "It has been so long, but I

hope she remains the brave lass I remember her as. She feared nothing and dared to do everything. A friend of my sister's."

More chuckles rang about, but everyone leaned closer with interest.

Daghvin rubbed his neck. "I doubt she remembers me now. She despised me, as far as I can recall, and I ensured she thought I loathed her just as much. I was afraid of her brother."

"Too scared to get a whooping?" A Savorian shoved Daghvin with a bark of laughter.

"Svorgin was quite fearsome then. But I was more terrified of his sister, if I am being truthful. I feared her rejection. And we were too young then. She more so. So, I kept it to myself."

Honzio stiffened. Was that a common Savorian name, or did Daghvin speak of the man Honzio thought he did? "Svorgin? Aylis's brother?"

Daghvin nodded. "Aye. Aylis was just as fearsome as him. I worried they would tear me to pieces if they discovered my care for their little sister."

Honzio's brows shot up. For a moment, he'd thought Daghvin's childhood sweetheart had been Aylis herself and wondered how to break the news of her marriage. After months of searching for her brother and finally retreating into working on other things to help the Empire, Aylis had married Moralis.

"She had a look about her. Something in her eyes that said she was meant for greatness. She knew it too. She would have made a great warrior, but she told me once she wanted to be a healer. I believe it was after her rumlok was injured. I almost admitted my own wish to her that day."

"What was that, lad?" a Savorian asked, and all ears perked to hear him.

Daghvin shrugged, a tinge of red drifting over his face. "I couldn't tell her, but I whispered it to the stars that night. That, when we both came of age, I would ask her to join me in a binding ceremony."

Honzio frowned, wondering at the custom. He'd never heard of a binding ceremony before.

"I told the stars that Barindaughter's and my blood would become one."

Honzio watched the way he uttered the words. So full of passion. As though he still intended to make that oath true.

"The Barin family's lass, eh?" A Savorian scratched his beard. "That fiery wee one, I remember her. She stole my hatchet once."

Daghvin laughed. "Aye, my sister challenged her to do so."

Commotion sent boots thundering on the deck overhead. Honzio stood, and mutters of confusion erupted among the Savorians. "What is happening?"

Honzio followed Daghvin up the stairs, and they stepped onto the main deck, where Savorians and Imperials were tending to the rigging and racing back and forth as they adjusted the sails. Heaving waves swept overboard, a portion dousing Honzio's tunic.

"There's a storm!"

Honzio whipped toward the voice. Silopar had

replaced the man at the helm. "Get down below! The ride will be a shaky one!" he called to him.

Honzio glanced overhead. The sky was clear, and the sun bore down on them. He saw no sign of a storm, yet the ship continued to rise with the highest waves Honzio had ever seen.

"There's something else!" a deckhand called out. He'd climbed up the mast and was looking through a spyglass at the approaching elevated waves.

"What is it?" Daghvin yelled up to him.

The deckhand froze, his mouth parting and the spyglass nearly slipping from his hand. He looked down, his face covered in fright. *"Havmeer skrimsli!"*

Daghvin paled and unhooked his own spyglass from his belt, taking a look himself.

"What?" Honzio asked, his pulse ticking faster. "What is it?"

Daghvin's lips thinned, and a note of foreboding sank over Honzio as the Savorian passed him the spyglass. "It is no storm causing these currents. It is a sea monster."

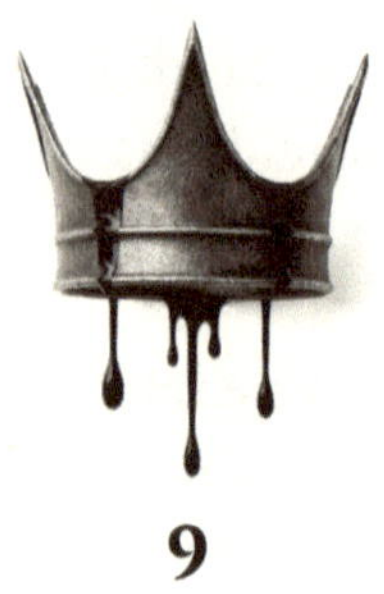

9

Aria

Kingdom of Devorin
Castle Yakh

Aria's scream emerged a voiceless cry into her palms. The woman's pale skin appeared pallid beneath the low light of the candles hanging in the hall. She was still and silent as she faced Aria. If she weren't standing upright, Aria would've believed her to be a corpse. The scent of rot permeating from her in waves only underscored that thought. Aria grimaced, holding her breath as she waited for the woman's next move. Would she bring her before Queen Guin, who would make her disappear like the others Rose had spoken of? Aria couldn't help the dejection that filled her. Her plan was over before it had even started.

The woman's arm lifted, and her stiff fingers grasped the air before Aria's face.

Aria's stomach clenched in fear. Her chest rose and fell quickly; her fingers trembled over her lips. She managed to lower a hand into the pocket of her skirt and gripped the hilt of her karambit. The Elders had a code. *Do not spill blood unless your blood is spilled first. Even so, do everything to prevent violence. Saving one life is equal to saving the world.* Aria didn't want to hurt this woman, but she couldn't have her cover blown. The woman's grasping fingers moved past Aria's head. Aria tensed, preparing herself. The woman pulled back with a candle from the wall. The flickering flame darted over her face, and Aria's heart lurched. Empty black holes remained in place of her eyes. The woman moved like a specter as she walked down the hall away from Aria. As soon as she faded from view, Aria sagged against the wall. *What in the four kingdoms is happening in this castle?*

"Get yourself together," Aria whispered and entered the next hall.

She swore to be more cautious as she continued investigating and kept her ears peeled for any strange noise. She spotted more servants, all with their lips sewn together. Though unlike the woman before, their eyes remained. Aria neared the end of a hall, where a large arched door stood. It differed from the other plain doors she had seen. She glanced back. There wasn't a soul in the long hall behind her. She turned the knob and ducked into the chamber. A quick examination proved she was alone. She released the death grip on her karambit and closed the door behind her. Piles and piles of books covered the floor and corners of the chamber. The shelves were mounted with more tomes. She grasped a candle and lit it with a hanging torch before furthering her survey. Though the room was large, the amount of clutter made it feel quite cramped. Aria ran her finger across a table, noting that it was laden with dust. No one cleaned here. Could this be where the queen stored her most private secrets? Aria swiveled around the table and held her candle over the heavy tome centered there. She hefted it open, and a cloud of dust burst forth. Aria waved a hand before her face as she was overcome by a surge of coughs. She placed the tiny flame close, and her eyes focused on the ink looping across the page.

Ameris Torsin

Shadow Manos

Type: Doer

Obeys well. He could not withstand the research tests.

I must improve the telepathic potion.

Status: Dead.

Aveida Ul

Shadow Manos

Type: Doer

Almost succeeded, but she couldn't last the entire procedure.

Status: Dead

This was the queen's journal. Aria's heart pumped

so loud she could hear it. They had always suspected she was up to no good, but all this? The blinded and mute servants? Testing that resulted in the murder of captured Shadow Manos? This was far more than Aria had expected. The names were arranged alphabetically. She glanced toward the door as she flipped through the worn pages in search of familiar names.

Lilly Tana

Non–Shadow Manos

The potion worked well for her. She is obeying without question. It seems the connection works better with non–Shadow Manos.

She broke free of my hold when she realized her cousin was with me. She tried to help him. I need to strengthen the potion.

Status: Dead.

Aria's blood chilled. Lilly. Lilly Tana. She *had* been here. She'd died here. And her cousin? Could Jax have been captured by Queen Guin as well? Aria searched through the tome in a frenzied haste, going backward to the *J* entries.

Jaxon Tana

Shadow Manos

Type: Doer

Prolus's men sent him as a gift, but he has no shadow. Either they lied or he lost his shadow somehow. I have begun experimenting with him.

*He is very strong and is now obeying
without question.*

Status:

The floor outside the door groaned. Aria's head shot up, and she moved like lightning, concealing herself in a secluded corner behind a tall shelf. The door opened with a long creak. A woman bathed in white cloth as pale as her thin skin stepped inside. Aria had seen her before from afar when she had addressed the people. Queen Guin. Aria swallowed, willing her pounding heart and skittering pulse to steady. Another form entered the room. The Blade. He stood there motionless, as if awaiting orders. Aria could only see his rigid back from her position. The queen hefted her skirts out of the way and sat before the table. She looked down and then frowned, her brows drawing together as her fingers doused the flaming candle and then traced the open tome. Aria nearly cursed. In her haste to hide, she had forgotten to erase her tracks.

The queen's scratchy voice filled the chamber. "Did you come in here?"

The Blade's head lifted. "I did not."

The queen abruptly rose. She walked around the table, a flurry of outrage accompanying her movements. She faced her Blade, her sharp features spitting venom. "Did you tamper with my things?"

He remained unmoving. "I did not."

The queen's hand shot out, her bony fingers grasping his jaw. Her nails dug into his skin and drew blood. The Blade didn't even flinch. "Who are you?"

"No one." The words were clipped. A mental battle seemed to wage between them as their expressions flickered, and the silence progressed.

"Who are you?" she shouted. "Say it aloud."

They were turned away from Aria. This was her chance. She could slip out while they weren't looking her way. She edged out from behind the shelf.

"Your weapon," the Blade uttered.

"Who?" The question was sharp and demanding, lethal.

Aria neared the door, opening it the smallest bit.

"Your weapon." This time, he answered with more conviction.

"Good. Very good." The queen released her brutal grasp on his jaw and caressed his face with the backs of her fingers like an apologetic lover would. Aria's stomach squeezed in disgust when the queen brushed aside the beads of blood she'd drawn.

Aria ducked into the hall before she was seen, then moved as quickly as she could, making her way back the way she had come. But then the scuffing of shoes neared, forcing her to cut down another hall and proceed onward up a curved staircase. She raced up the steps, her feet pounding in time with her heart. She crested the top and found herself in a round tower built with gray stones that gave the interior a foggy atmosphere. Light seeped in from a single arched window. Aria moved toward it, and her breath caught. She could see the entire town and beyond. This was the queen's tower. Known as the tallest building in the Empire. Aria's dazed stare was broken by the sound of a pained moan and clinking chains. She spun, withdrawing her karambit. A figure was silhouetted across from her. She approached with cautious steps. It was a man curled upon the cold stone floor, the chains around his wrists bound to the wall. Aria's heart jumped to her throat when she saw the horrible scars crisscrossing the span of his back.

10

"GET BEHIND ME!" Saga screeched at the women and their children standing closest to her.

The Tariqins surged toward her. Chishma Jirco remained unmoving, face-first on the ground. The deedans unhooked their kilisham whips from their belts and lashed them through the air, sending crackling sparks. Leno's pleading went unheard. Two of the Tariqins swung at her in unison. Saga slammed her heavy axe into the snow and jumped over the sizzling whips. She flung the small axes from her belt toward the Tariqins. They sliced through the air and embedded into their brows, splitting their foreheads into separate halves. They collapsed on either side of Saga as she landed on her feet and reached down, retrieving her main axe.

Deedans swarmed around her, dozens at once, too many for even Saga to handle alone. And alone, she was. The villagers watched from a distance as Leno herded them away. He was grasping a wailing Britta's arm, forcing her at bay. Saga blocked out the screams and focused on the deedans. She spun in a circle, using her momentum to thrust her large axe through the air. It flew with power, smashing into the approaching deedans and slowing them. Saga leaned over, grasping the handles of her small axes and wrenching them free. The slick sound of metal sliding from bloody flesh and bone filled the air. Saga continued battling. She let out a piercing whistle, and in a moment came the growl she could always rely on. Deedans stumbled back in fear when they caught sight of the white beast covered in bloodstains.

"Rumlok," they uttered, scrambling away. They thought they had taken every rumlok from the village. That they were safe since they had imprisoned them away in their camps.

Kalpara roared, a dominant sound that sent chills over Saga.

"*Nvore!*" she screamed, pointing an axe ahead. *Attack!*

Kalpara charged and tore through flesh. Saga ran alongside her rumlok, cutting and slicing and tasting blood on her tongue. Warm rivulets trickled down her face and coated her skin the more she stabbed, showering from the wounds of her enemies. These were the moments she lived for—when those who had oppressed her paid for every drop of blood they had stolen with their lives. But though the Tariqins were fearful, they were many. They gathered their strength and regrouped before leading another assault on Saga. She was outnumbered; not even with Kalpara could she hold back so many. The kilisham whips flicked and transformed into gleaming swords. Three flashed toward her head. An axe blocked them. Saga's mouth parted, and she glanced to her side. Her savior, Olava, thrust the kilishams back. Saga nodded gratefully. All around her, more Savorians came forth to aid her against their enemy. Leno released Britta, who rushed to join them with a battle cry. Though he was clearly conflicted, he also lifted his double-edged axe from his back and launched into the fray. Before long, the Tariqins were lying in lifeless piles around them. Saga dropped to her knees in the center of the mass. She heaved heavy breaths, her skin painted a watery crimson from the hot sweat coursing over her. The Savorians stood uncertain. Wee babes cried, and their mams attempted to shush them.

Leno marched toward Saga. He glared down at her. "Was it worth it? Ye have destroyed the peace I worked so hard to attain for our village." Saga looked up at him. His fingers strained around the handle of his axe. Blood trickled from his temple. "Ye have ruined us."

Saga slowly rose. "Peace? Is that what ye call the lives we've led?"

Silence hung around them as all eyes focused on them.

"We have been living off scraps of food. We have been living in fear of death every day. They took our families. They took everything."

Leno scoffed, leaning over her as he nearly spat his next words into her face. "Not all of us were damaged as greatly as ye. Some of us moved on. Some of us were happy with the lives we have now." He motioned toward Britta, who watched the conversation with a frown. "But ye have destroyed it. Ye've destroyed everything. When Chishma Jirco's superior doesn't hear from him, they will send a troop to check the village. And they will kill every single one of us."

Saga shoved his chest, sending him stumbling back. Then she closed the distance she'd created, seeking the upper hand with the move. "Will we wait about like lambs for the slaughter? We will fight back, Leno. We will take back the other villages. We will take back Savoria."

He laughed and wiped his hand over his face. "Ye are dreaming. Our army comprises old women and young girls who never learned to wield an axe because they were never permitted to use one. What army do ye speak of? Look around ye!"

Saga followed his hand motion, scanning the hopeless features watching them. He was right. They were too old, too weak, too helpless. And those among them who could fight were too few. Saga swallowed and turned back to Leno, who peered at her with disdain.

"Think what yer actions have cost us. Because of ye, Shavka Esme is dead."

The words were brutal and punishing, slamming into Saga's mind like a cold slap. She looked at Esme's body motionless in the snow. Guilt bloomed through her. Leno stormed past her, and slowly, the other villagers did as well. Saga sank back to her knees, her fingers gripping tight to the hilts of her axes. Kalpara nudged her shoulder, and her warm body curved around Saga's slumped form. Boots stepped into view, stopping in front of Saga. Saga looked up to see Britta staring down at her.

"When I saw ye, I thought ye had come for my binding ceremony." Tears spilled from her eyes. "I thought ye had come for me. But ye are still, as always, after the past. After a revenge that will only ruin ye."

Saga flinched.

Britta kneeled before her. "Ye will kill yourself and take all of us with ye on this path of vengeance."

With that, she left Saga to her torment. It wasn't until hours later that Saga returned home. She ignored her mam's shouts of concern when she saw her covered in blood. Her mam stripped Saga's ruined clothes and filled a wood tub with steaming water. Saga stared ahead, dazed, as Yuva scrubbed her skin until it was raw. But the heat of the blood remained, just like the guilt festering in her heart. Yuva tucked her into her bed as if she were a little lass again and then sat beside her. Saga handed her mother a needle and a gold hoop. Her mother acted without questions, and Saga was grateful. She pierced her ear and pushed in the hoop. Saga didn't flinch, didn't blink. And yet that small needle pained her more than the bruises she had endured in the battle.

"Who passed?" her mother finally said.

Saga thought about not responding but then said, "Shavka Esme."

Her mam frowned. "Who is that?"

Her mother was still living in a different time, when

they'd had another shavka. When they'd been a different village entirely.

"And these? Who are these for?" her mother asked, brushing her fingers over the four other hoops dangling from her ear.

Saga handed her mother a wooden comb. "Will ye brush my hair?"

Her mother nodded, and Saga leaned against her. The comb ran through the thick locks of her wet hair. Tears formed in Saga's eyes. Her mam hummed the song she'd sung to Saga since she was a little girl. And Saga's lids grew heavy until she yielded to her fatigue.

11

Sea monster. The words petrified him, and his fingers shook as he lifted the spyglass to his eye. The world around him stilled as he concentrated on the movement in the waves. At first, he saw nothing but the high drifts of water rising far more than ordinary. Then he glimpsed the scales slicing through the blue with speed. His blood chilled. It was nearing the ship. He lowered the spyglass, and the shouts returned, pounding against his eardrums. Savorians and Imperials rushed about the deck. Silopar screamed orders at the terrified group of sailors. The Cadellion closed in, the three of them forming a triangle of protection around Honzio.

"Return to the hold, Your Majesty," Daghvin told him, reverting to formalities, placing ranks between them to signify how important it was to keep the emperor safe.

Honzio wanted to protest, to stay with them, but he knew nothing about managing the ship, and he would only be in the way. He nodded and whistled to Lore. The boy darted to him, and Honzio shrugged past his bodyguards. He grasped Lore's shoulder, hoping his grim expression laid bare the seriousness of the situation. "We must return belowdecks."

"But I want to—"

The boy's words were cut off when a tentacle landed in front of them, long points jutting out of it; the end of one was only centimeters from Honzio's throat. A scream burst out of Lore. Honzio wrenched him back. The Cadellion snapped into action, forming a line before them and extending their double-bladed staffs. Despite their bravado, their slackened jaws revealed their shock and unease. Honzio watched in mute horror as the tentacle slithered back into the depths, tearing pieces of the ship away with it.

"*Havmeer skrimsli!*" the Savorians continued shouting.

"Move!" Honzio said, pushing Lore toward the stairs.

Lore looked with wide eyes toward Daghvin. "How can we kill it?"

Daghvin appeared resigned. "We cannot. We cannot kill the ruler of this sea. We can only hope to outrun her."

Honzio's heart thumped with terror. He hefted Lore toward the stairs as a wave plunged over them, soaking them with water. Lore slipped out of his grasp. The tang of salt filled Honzio's mouth, and strands of hair plastered to his face, blinding him. He spat and shoved the locks back. He tilted to the right, and confusion assaulted him when he couldn't keep his balance. The Cadellion were too far behind him, struggling to find their footing themselves. Honzio's boots slid along the deck as the ship tilted precariously to one side until he slammed against the wood rim. He exhaled a soft sigh of relief that he'd managed to catch himself.

"Your Majesty! Your Majesty!" Lore's terrified shouts filled him with alarm.

The boy was moving far too fast, tripping over his feet as he careened toward the edge of the ship. Honzio braced himself and reached out just as Lore toppled over. His mind left him, so stuck on the fact that he'd missed him. Then Honzio felt the solid weight clinging to him, and his numbness wore off. He adjusted his stance and leaned over the tilting edge. The beads circling his neck caught on the wood grain. Lore's fingers were locked around Honzio's wrist with savage desperation. The boy swayed in the wind, looking down in dread at the nearing sea.

"I've got you," Honzio called down. "Do not focus on the water."

Despite his confident tone, Honzio wasn't so sure he could haul the boy's weight with one arm. Still, he didn't reveal his doubt.

"I need you to focus, Lore. I need your assistance."

Lore finally looked up, and his features became resolved, even as his fingers slipped farther down Honzio's wrist. His strength was waning. Both of theirs were.

"You will heft yourself using the side of the ship," Honzio instructed him. His face was dripping wet; he could no longer tell the difference between the water and his sweat. "Do you understand?"

Lore's fingers slid down a little farther. The boy nodded, his mouth thin with determination.

"On three," Honzio said. His arm was burning and shaking and tingling from the weight, but he kept himself together. "One, two, three!"

Lore slammed his boots onto the hull and launched himself up. Honzio heaved him at the same time, and with their combined effort, Lore was sprung from the dark depths and landed on the deck. Honzio's necklace tore, and the beads scattered along the floor. He dropped to his knees, trying to gather them in a panicked haste as they rolled with the movement of the ship as it righted itself. Lore was sprawled across the deck, stuck in a fit of shaking and wheezing. The Cadellion approached Honzio. They hauled him up, forcing him to stop his search for the beads.

"Your Majesty, you must get to safety."

Honzio nodded, though his chest felt ravaged at the loss of the beads that had helped bring him to peace during dark moments.

"We must go!" Honzio shouted at Lore.

He moved to the stairs, but another tentacle appeared, smashing the wood and the way down. Honzio scrambled back. He turned and saw Lore pulling himself up, then went to join the boy, when another tentacle crashed between them.

"Lore!"

Honzio was boxed between the tentacles. His Cadellion was trapped along with him. They brandished their double-edged weapons. The tentacles shook, and disgust twisted Honzio's insides as pale lumps formed beneath the skin.

"What manner of creature—" a cadel sputtered.

The lumps burst, spraying a foul yellowish white liquid resembling pus onto them. Honzio gasped as the gunk hit his face and trickled into his mouth. He gagged. He would have rather eaten from the rubbish collected in the streets of Hearcross than endure the horrid vileness of this hellish flavor for a second longer. He wiped his face and blinked twice. Spindly legs emerged from the holes the exploded lumps had left behind. The creatures clacked their legs across the wood and opened their mouths to expose sharp, wicked teeth that gnawed at the air. More legs appeared, stabbing through lumps not yet ready to give way. They emerged coated in the pus-like fluid and joined their counterparts as they raced over the deck, rushing toward Honzio and the others. Honzio whipped out his sword.

"Defend yourselves."

At the sight of the creatures nearing, the Cadellion broke out of their horrified stupor. Honzio slashed his sword at the creature nearest to him. It screeched as the blade sank through its hard shell. But that didn't stop it. The creature's teeth slammed together as it used its spindly legs to propel itself up Honzio's sword, uncaring as the blade sank deeper into its flesh. The teeth were a hair's breadth from Honzio's hand. He flung his blade over the ship's side, and the creature squealed as it met the salty depths.

Honzio's relief was short-lived. There were many of the little monsters. So many more emerging from the trembling tentacle. Honzio unsheathed his dagger and glanced about him. The Cadellion were overrun. The creatures clung to them, taking hungry bites out of their legs and necks, anywhere they could find purchase. His men cried out in agony. Honzio sliced at the ones clinging to the man closest to him, but it was to no avail. The creature bit into his head, and the cadel's eyes went dark. Remainders of his brain slipped onto the deck when he collapsed. Honzio gulped his revulsion and retreated a pace. But he had become the new target. The creatures scurried toward him with excited little shrieks. He tripped and scrabbled back on his arm. The closest creature barked at the others, and they stilled. It approached Honzio, teeth clacking. Orange eyes peered at him from within the shell. Honzio swallowed. There was a burst and a wet sound, and then a long tail emerged from behind it. Honzio froze, terror fixing him in place. His eyes rooted on the pronged point of the tail inching closer to him.

"Duck!" someone called.

Honzio flattened himself to the deck just as something blazing hot swung over him and buried into the creature. It screamed and retreated. The fire overtook it and sent the other creatures clattering away.

Daghvin hauled Honzio up and handed him another torch. "Fire's about the only thing that's keeping them at bay."

"But we cannot keep it burning. Not with all this water."

Their voices were loud to be heard over the crashing waves and screams. Daghvin didn't deign to reply, instead using his torch to scatter the creatures further. They released earsplitting screeches as they scampered over the ship's railing and submerged into the water. The tentacles retreated next, leaving wet residue behind. As soon as they slipped back into the sea, the ship went still. The waves ceased. The ship's occupants seemed to sigh as one.

"We've been saved," someone exclaimed.

Honzio could still hear his own heart as a dull echo in his ears. The ship had been greatly damaged but was still intact. His eyes landed on Daghvin, who was watching the water with a frown. "What's wrong?"

"The water," Daghvin replied. "I do not believe the *skrimsli* has retreated."

Honzio followed his gaze. He was right. The water was still. Too still.

"Emperor Honzio!"

Lore approached with a smile. Before Honzio could examine the boy for injuries, the ship trembled, a vibration that came from its center. Honzio stumbled. Then a groaning noise emitted from the vessel. Lines cracked over the center of the deck before splitting in half. Honzio flew backward, slamming onto the stairs leading up to the helm. Lore and the Savorians smashed onto the opposite side, several of them out cold from the impact. Daghvin rose, and it was the first time Honzio had seen the man so afraid.

Tentacles snaked around the ship, and a creature rose from the depths. Honzio saw teeth first before registering that they belonged in a mouth two times larger than the ship itself. His pulse picked up, pure fright pumping through his veins rather than blood. His gaze slipped higher, past the mouth and to a pair of red eyes. Spikes ran over the humongous head. The sea monster opened its mouth wider and released a roar that nearly sent Honzio over the side of the ship. His hair blew back, and the skin of his face felt as though it were melting from the pressure. A rotting odor emerged that Honzio doubted he could ever be able to scrub his skin clean of. Daghvin's shouts were swallowed into silence as the monster's jaws closed around the ship. Honzio tripped over a body, and his head smacked against a pointed object, sending his thoughts scattering into oblivion.

12

ARIA DARTED TOWARD the stairs and then paused. She glanced back at the chained man. He was a prisoner, unlikely to inform Queen Guin of her intrusion. And besides, perhaps he knew her secrets. Perhaps that was why the queen was holding him captive. Aria decided to approach—as quietly as possible so he wouldn't be alarmed. Aria's breath caught at the sight of his back. Lash marks had broken his skin open. The area was inflamed and infected. The decaying scent grew stronger as she kneeled beside him. She flinched, pressing her fingers to her mouth and forcing herself to swallow the bile rising in her throat. What great secret did he know to be so brutally tortured? Then another thought rose.

He hadn't moved a single muscle during the entire time she'd been in the tower. Was he dead?

Aria leaned over him and gently grasped his arm. He turned, falling onto his back with a loud groan. Aria gasped, retracting her hand. The man's face was concealed by long, matted blondish brown hair. The tops of his shoulders also carried whip scars, though nowhere near as brutal as his back. Sympathy welled in her, bolstering her resolve to aid him. She crouched down and brushed his hair from his face. Under the grime and dirt, she glimpsed youthful features. She used the pads of her fingers to clear away a dark streak cutting across his cheekbone. He couldn't have been more than a few years older than her. He stirred, his mouth moving in incoherent mumbles. Then his thick blond lashes fluttered open, revealing dark blue eyes. Aria held his gaze, but her hand froze on his cheek. She felt like prey caught in the sight of a hunter. His gaze roved over her features, his lips moving as he continued mumbling an unfamiliar word.

"What?"

He frowned, his brows drawing together. *"Viila?"*

"I do not understand," Aria whispered. "What is your name?"

He coughed before forcing out more scrambled words. "The potion."

Aria followed his stare to the table behind her. She lowered his head gently to the ground before moving to the table and searching it. She found a vial containing a shimmering golden liquid and returned to the man's side.

"This one?"

He forced his eyes open and nodded. Doubt flickered to life. Should she be aiding him? She already knew enough information to incriminate the queen. She just had to escape the castle and return to the shelter. But no, she was a coward last and an Elder first. *Leave no one behind, especially not the helpless.* Reciting those words repeatedly in her mind, Aria pushed her doubtful thoughts aside. She propped him up against her, and his head sagged onto her shoulder. The man was deadweight, heavy as a horse. She placed her hand on his neck, assisting him in lifting his head, before uncorking the vial and bringing the rim to his lips. He devoured it in greedy gulps, the stiffness in his posture settling as he did. A healthy flush overtook his face. Once he'd finished every drop, Aria withdrew and returned the vial to the table. Chains clinked, and she whirled around.

The man was standing. Her jaw dropped when the whip marks faded before her eyes, settling into thin scars. He braced himself against the wall, seemingly not from a lack of strength but rather as if he were unused to standing upright. He turned toward her. His long hair slipped over his shoulder in a tangled mess. He blinked, as if startled to see her there. "You are real, aren't you?"

Aria nodded, compassion filling her. He'd thought he was hallucinating.

"How far are we into the year?" he asked.

"It is the fifth month."

He spat out a series of words she didn't recognize, but they sounded like curses from the venom laced around each one. He tried to move but then stumbled and grasped at the wall again. "Four months. I've been here for four months."

"What does the queen want from you? What do you know?"

"Nothing she can have. I have resisted her for this long and am not planning to give in now."

"I understand," Aria said. "You are no longer alone."

He stiffened, tilting his head. "Perhaps you are a part of her game. I wouldn't put it past her to send a beautiful woman to coerce me into giving away what she seeks."

Aria paused at his admittance of finding her beautiful and then said, "I promise you I am not one of her lackeys."

"Prove it," he said. "Get me out of here."

Aria had never been one to leave a person in the hands of an oppressor. But her doubts rebounded. If she freed him, she would be hindering her mission. He could barely walk. The chances of them getting caught were high. She could leave now and return with help. But by then, he could be dead.

"She keeps the key for the chains in the wall behind you." He nodded his chin. His words still emerged hoarse, but the vial had restored his strength. A thick accent coated his sentences, and now that she'd heard him speak properly, she noted that he was Savorian. She followed his instructions and dug her fingers into the stone wall, searching for the metal.

"She likes to keep it in my sight so I can believe freedom is within reach, yet as long as I keep silent, I cannot take it."

The queen of Devorin was far crueler than Aria had assumed. Her fingers brushed something cold. She extracted the metal key and rushed toward the Savorian.

She glanced toward the stairs as she passed. There was no one in sight. The weight of the Savorian's stare was heavy upon her as she unlocked his chains. They fell with a clang. He shook his hands out, examining the marks circling his wrists in permanent scars.

"Is that enough proof for you?" Aria questioned. "I am not your enemy."

His head lifted. "Let us leave from here, and I will consider your words as truth."

"Jax," she said. "Jaxon Tana, do you know what became of him?"

He observed her. "Who is he to you?"

"He was a friend of my brother's."

"I cannot give out information so readily, *viila*."

"I just freed you, and I don't even know your name," Aria shot back. "Surely, you can tell me what you know of Jaxon."

He swept past her, well enough in his stride that he even gained a swagger in his step. After months of imprisonment, that was quite an impressive feat. Aria rolled her eyes and followed him. They trekked down the stairs. Her heart beat faster as they neared the bottom.

"Anyone?"

The Savorian shook his head. They entered the corridor and dove into the next hall. He wasn't much taller than her, perhaps half a head, but he was bulky, which didn't help their stealthy trek down the hall. Each of his steps seemed to make the floor tremble.

"Can you be any louder?" Aria winced. "You will bring the castle down upon us."

"Apologies, *viila*. Not everyone can be as delicate as you are," he shot back in a semi-quiet whisper.

That was the first time in her life someone had called her delicate. Agile, yes. Graceful, perhaps. But delicate? Aria wasn't sure what to make of it.

"What does that mean?"

"What does what mean?" he replied, far too innocently.

"*Viila.*"

He glanced around the edge of the corridor once they reached the end. Aria looked back the way they had come. It was empty.

"Trust me, you don't want to know."

"So, it *is* an insult." Aria crossed her arms. Just as she had expected.

"Of the worst kind."

Aria's mouth dropped open. "What? Do you normally call people who save your life by insults?"

He grabbed her arm and yanked her through the hall. Aria struggled against his iron grasp.

"I like to give nicknames to everyone I meet."

"Let go of me, you big oaf."

He shot her a bewildered look and released her arm.

She gave him an overly sincere smile. "Perhaps I will call you that from now on."

"I didn't know you were planning on sticking around with me for long." He smirked. "But I do have that sort of charm. Once you get a glimpse, you cannot resist."

Aria gagged. "What charm? A street con artist could sway me before you ever could."

"Oof," he grumbled. "Vicious."

He grabbed her wrist and shoved her into a shadowed alcove.

"What are you—" Aria's furious whisper was cut off when his hand clamped over her mouth.

His blue eyes gleamed with a warning. Footsteps neared. Aria's heart thumped louder. The Savorian leaned closer, as though to make himself smaller. How he thought that would work was astonishing. Aria breathed out through her nose. He was pressed against her, nearly suffocating her. He was in terrible need of a wash. But there was a promising undertone of musk under all the other odors. She glanced to the side and made out a servant slipping past. The heavy hand upon her mouth lowered, and she exhaled. She pushed against his chest, but he didn't budge.

"Svorgin," he said.

"What?"

"My name, you said you didn't know it. It's Svorgin."

She searched his face and found the humor there had receded. Life had carved its mark on this man. She could see it in every line of his face and form. He carried a history, a map on his very back. Part of Aria was curious and wanted to know more about him, while another told her he was trouble. She forced her thoughts aside. She was here for a mission. For a purpose. She would not be waylaid by a mysterious Savorian.

His eyes lowered, and he reached out, grasping the chains circling her neck. He barely surveyed the small necklace, focusing on the one with the pendant. Aria stiffened and snatched it before he could examine it, shoving it back into her dress.

"You are part of the Elders," he surmised.

He was too perceptive for his own good.

He touched the remaining necklace, tracing the button hanging from the thin chain. "And this? A token from your lover?"

"I will slice your throat if you lay another finger upon me," Aria hissed, withdrawing her karambit and leveling it against his side.

Svorgin simply smiled, unfazed by the sharp point digging into him. "I thought the Elders were pacifists."

Aria nodded, stepping closer to whisper in his ear. "I know seventy different ways to injure a man without killing him."

Svorgin backed away, raising his hands in surrender, and Aria moved past him. He followed dutifully. They had crossed down to the second floor when a loud horn blared, sending the servants around scattering in panic.

"They've caught on," Aria said, urging Svorgin faster.

They crossed down to the first floor. They lowered their heads as they swiftened to the castle entrance.

"Stop there," ordered a voice crackling like a fissure through a block of ice.

Aria looked up. Standing before them, blocking the gates, was a group of warriors clad in dark gray, and at their forefront was the Queen's Blade.

13

Honzio

Lagrima Sea

A STINGING ACHE SNAKED through his mind. Honzio groaned, touching his head. His fingers skimmed over a swelling bump. He blinked, peering through his lashes at the clear blue sky above him. Clouds sifted by too fast, increasing his already imbalanced state. He pulled himself up with a groan and nearly collapsed when his vision blackened. He waited for the darkness to elapse. His stomach twisted, and he leaned over, retching into the water. Where was he? Honzio glanced at the thick, curved wood beneath him. It took a second for realization to sink in. It was a part of the ship.

"The sea monster destroyed it."

Honzio's head jerked up at the voice. Daghvin was sitting at the front of the makeshift raft, using a long piece of wood to direct them forward. Honzio opened his mouth to speak, but his voice emerged broken. He licked his dry, cracked lips and tried again.

"The others? Lore? Are they all right?"

Daghvin glanced away, and a horrible feeling sank into the pit of Honzio's stomach.

"I do not know," Daghvin admitted. "But I believe there are other survivors. We will find them once we reach the island."

"The island?"

Daghvin jerked his chin ahead. Honzio leaned forward, scanning the approaching land in the distance. Despite everything they had just been through, a tremor of excitement gripped him.

"Savoria," Daghvin said in a longing whisper.

Honzio settled back against the raft. His head was splitting with pain. Whatever he'd knocked against, it had rattled him. It ached to blink, to look, to think.

"Rest. We shall arrive shortly."

Honzio wanted to refuse, to attempt to help the Savorian, but he couldn't fight his own body's weakness. He closed his eyes and surrendered to his exhaustion.

Honzio jerked awake when the raft settled against the land. Daghvin helped him stand. The Savorian heaved Honzio over the raft, where he sprawled on the cold snow. After several moments of lying still, the cold seeped into his skin until it grew into a burning sensation. Finally, Honzio forced himself up and trudged through the white blankets. He didn't hear any sound behind him and paused, looking back. Daghvin remained at the edge of the raft, staring at the snow Honzio had just lain in. He seemed uncertain, his fists tight at his sides.

"What is it?"

Daghvin's mouth twitched. "It has been an age since I touched this soil. Since I last breathed home. I am almost afraid to step on Savorian land, lest I awaken and realize it is all a dream."

Honzio stepped closer. "I will be the first to tell you it is no dream. It is only in reality where you will be forced to face your worst demons, including the sea monster we just barely got away from."

Daghvin chuckled. "Ye are right."

He placed one boot into the snow and then the other. And just as Honzio had admired how the Savorian seemed one with the ship, he appeared just as rooted to the land, unlike Honzio, who walked like a drunken fool and tripped several times. He wasn't quite sure if it was because he was adjusting to the lack of moving water beneath him or his head injury.

As they trekked through the snow, they did not encounter a single soul.

"We have entered from the west just as we planned. My village is closest," Daghvin told him. "It is odd that there are no Tariqins here."

Honzio made out a watchtower ahead. Daghvin grabbed his axe and approached it with caution. The door creaked open. Honzio entered behind him.

"It is empty."

"Where are the Tariqins?"

Daghvin shook his head. "I do not know. But we can rest here for the night. Until we catch our bearings."

"And if they return?"

Daghvin glanced around. "It seems no one has been here in quite a while. We will remain only for the night."

Honzio nodded in agreement. They built a fire in a hearth along one wall so they wouldn't freeze to death. When morning came, Honzio and Daghvin continued trudging through the island. They took breaks often when the pain racking Honzio's skull grew too much to bear. They eventually stopped by a large cave.

Daghvin built a fire and then told Honzio, "I will go search for other survivors. Ye can rest here. We will move to another location in the morning."

"I will come with you," Honzio said, rising.

Daghvin shook his head. "Ye need to recover, and besides, ye will only slow me down."

Honzio flinched but managed to nod. Daghvin disappeared from view, and Honzio warmed himself by the fire. He touched his head and winced when a sharp, stinging agony stabbed his mind. He heard approaching footsteps and glanced up.

"Back so soon?" he called.

But instead of Daghvin, a cluster of Tariqin deedans emerged into view.

14

Saga

Savoria

Vidrun Village

T HE FUNERAL PROCESSION walked in a single line. Shavka Esme was held on a wooden board above them, her body wrapped in cloth laden with symbols stitched to ward off evil spirits. Many hands clung to the board, as if longing to touch the body confined within the cloth one last time. Guilt awakened in Saga once again. Or perhaps it had never slept. Consuming her very being when she looked at her neighbors. At Britta and even Leno. Saga ducked behind the shadows of the long, spidery branches as the group approached. They were humming a low, mournful melody that could break even the fiercest of hearts.

They placed the board on the ground and took up shovels. The song continued as the villagers worked together to pull up loads of dirt from beneath the snow. Saga's mouth moved in time with them, reciting the verses for the parting hymn.

We are bones and flesh and beating hearts,
skin and muscle, and so fragile.
We live on the land yet belong beneath it,
where we will sink and fade,
leaving our souls behind.

The board was lowered, and the shovels went to work once again, covering the grave. The Savorians leaned over one by one, placing three fingers into the dirt and then pressing them to their brows as they whispered. Saga waited until the last of the familiar faces faded, and then moved toward it. She stood, the lone soul above the grave. The wind whistled around her and bit into her skin. Saga sank to her knees and pressed her fingers into the earth. She closed her eyes.

"*Mero sav*, Shavka." *Forgive me.*

She knew Esme would have, had she still lived. She hadn't been one to hold grudges. But the rest of the Savorians . . . Saga's shoulders slumped. It would take time to earn their trust again. Time Saga didn't have. She stared at the grave for long moments and then touched her fingers to her brow before standing. If no one in the village trusted her, she had to continue doing everything herself. Saga had left Kalpara at home to guard her mother in case any of the villagers came to exact revenge for what had happened in the square. Saga trekked past the trees and carefully examined all the Tariqin campsites. They would send another troop soon, and she had to be ready to eliminate them before they could request more aid.

She spotted the main Tariqin watchtower and glanced about to ensure no one saw her crossing the clearing. She reached the door and sensed something was off. She pushed it, and it creaked open. Saga's eyes narrowed on the fish remains left on the table and the dying embers in the hearth. Someone was here but a few hours before. Saga spun out of the tower and searched the ground for footprints. She found them at once. Whoever this was wasn't taking precautionary measures. Saga reached the large cave she and Britta had often played in when they were young and hid behind a cluster of rocks. There was a solitary man sitting across from a fire. He leaned against the cave wall and wasn't wearing the deedan guard uniform of red and black, but was dressed in sailor garb. Saga's confusion was dashed away when she heard the approaching thunder of boots. A group of deedans emerged into view and closed in on the man.

"Who are you?" one deedan barked in Saga's tongue.

The man looked up at them, and Saga noted the trace of fear flashing over his features.

"Why aren't you in your village?"

When the question still wasn't answered, the deedan stormed closer. "Are you deaf?" He slipped into Tariqin. "Do you understand me?"

The man dragged to his feet, his wavy brown hair slipping forward and shadowing his features. He winced when he rose, and Saga realized he was injured.

"Let us talk this over," he said in accented Savorian.

The deedans murmured in surprise, glancing at each other. "From where do you hail?"

"I am not someone you want to trifle with."

Their surprise turned into barks of laughter. The deedans unhooked their kilishams and pointed them at the man.

"We will slit your throat if you do not answer."

The man hesitated as his eyes shot past them and into the forest of trees. He was looking for something or awaiting someone. Saga was debating whether she should assist him when she heard the chirps. Her heart stilled. She looked up, and a soft gasp escaped her parted lips. Sparrows. There were sparrows settling on the ledge above the man.

15

H E ENTERED THE dining hall. It had once been intended only for the queen's soldiers. But they had all perished when that woman had depleted them of their shadows. The Sorceress, the queen called her, always referring to her with a bite in her tone. He could still remember bits and pieces of the woman. Her wide golden eyes and the jagged hair that had billowed around her face. The flashes of her were quite beautiful, and her drive to deliver the shadows home admirable. But he had no right to admire her in any way. She was his queen's enemy and therefore his as well. An enemy who'd nearly killed his queen when she'd separated her from her powerful shadow. She was the reason the hundreds of chairs in the dining hall sat empty.

He moved toward the cluster of familiar faces making up his squadron. All ten under his command looked up at him. They were the sole survivors of the Battle of Ayleth. The queen's top warriors. Nods circled about the table as he sat.

"Blade," the man closest to him said.

"Fox," Blade replied.

The man gave him a sly smile worthy of his name and leaned in. "What did she want?"

Blade shrugged, uncomfortable discussing his encounters with the queen. Fox may have been clever enough to worm his way into second-in-command, but that didn't mean Blade had to tell him everything.

The others ate in comfortable silence, so used to each other's company. The only noise erupted from the triplets, who glanced at each other and broke into heinous laughter every few moments, as though sharing a telepathic conversation. And perhaps they were. Blade had only known the queen to use such methods, but it was not so unbelievable for others to have learned her tricks. Though Blade doubted the triplets would be brave enough. She'd named them the Hounds. Her Hounds that tracked her every target and obeyed her every order. They would never dare to be disloyal.

"She didn't answer you, did she?" Fox pressed. His shock of red hair was growing out of the trim the queen required of her warriors, pointing up in fiery spikes. Blade ran a hand over his own head, buzzed close. Though her gaze had slackened in the past months because of her power slip, her eyes never missed him.

Fox sighed. "Don't tell me you didn't ask."

Blade glared at him, and Fox lowered his voice as he glanced at the others eating from their bowls of oats. Mole was the only one watching them, her cunning gaze focused and bright. She would run to the queen if she scented a hint of betrayal.

"I shouldn't have told you anything," Blade muttered. "Forget it."

Fox tilted his head. "But you did. And it's too late now. I'm trying to help you. This is unnatural."

Blade hushed him. One could not speak aloud anywhere in this castle without the danger of it getting back to the queen. He had been foolish to confide in Fox, but when the man had seen him unbalanced and shaking one night, perspiring after awakening from a terrible dream, the words had simply slipped out.

I am seeing things. Things I believe happened in my life before.

Fox leaned closer to him. "If she will not return your memories or tell you about your past, then you must gain them back yourself."

Blade looked ahead, trying to ignore him and his rebellious words. But he couldn't.

"It is impossible," he snapped.

Fox shook his head. "What if I told you it isn't? What if I told you I discovered the secret to regaining your past?"

Blade scoffed, devouring his bowl as a distraction. He withdrew the vial from his belt and popped the cork off. Fox grabbed his wrist, stopping his hand on its way to his mouth.

"What if I told you that I stopped taking the vials?"

Blade froze. Treason. It was treason what he spoke of and also a death sentence. Blade got a furious head-ache whenever he went too long without the liquid. He couldn't stop taking what his body screamed for.

"I'm starting to remember things," Fox whispered. "My name, for example. My *real* name."

Blade tore his wrist from his grasp. "Do not speak to me of your nonsense, or I will report you to the queen."

Fox fell silent, but his gaze was beseeching. Blade ignored him and gulped the vial back. At once, the strain in his mind dissipated and his focus cleared. Yes, he had one goal. He knew that now. He stood, and the others followed his lead. A woman's whisper flooded his mind, as powerful as always now that her telepathic creation was taking renewed effect. There was a disruption in the castle. An intruder.

The others slipped into place behind him as he strode from the dining hall. And when he blocked the way of the intruder and the escapee with her, the queen's voice lingered. Always there, always whispering. He wasn't allowed to break past his servitude. He had one mission in life. She was his queen. He was her weapon.

She is my queen. I am her weapon. She is my queen. I am her weapon.

But between each controlled thought was an image he couldn't erase.

A pair of familiar green eyes.

16

Svorgin

Kingdom of Devorin

Castle Yakh

S VORGIN BACKED UP, looking toward the stairs behind him, where more guards blocked the way. He cursed, scanning the area for a way out. But it was no use. They were surrounded. His eyes flicked to the woman, noting the desperation on her face. She, too, realized how trapped they were. The Queen's Blade—his true name a mystery to Svorgin—stepped closer, his icy-blue eyes probing them.

"Her Majesty commands your presence."

"And what will she give me in return for it?" Svorgin couldn't help saying. Humor was his greatest defense in perilous moments.

He heard a disbelieving huff and glanced at the woman. Her unearthly features stunned him, just as they had when he had first seen her.

The Blade ignored him, his eyes flicking instead toward the woman. A crease formed between his brows.

"Who are you?"

"No one of consequence," she replied.

"I've seen you," the Blade said, confusion twisting his features. "I know you from somewhere."

Svorgin examined her as well. He'd been barely conscious when a touch as light as a feather had brushed over his cheek. Then he'd seen her. Skin appearing soft as a cloud and glowing with an otherworldly light. Green eyes the color of spring. He'd thought he'd died and been greeted by a fairy. But the fairy turned out to be a human of flesh and blood and in just as dangerous a situation as him.

A fist knocked into Svorgin's chin, jerking him out of his staring and sending him flying across the floor. He shook the daze from his eyes. The Blade towered over him, his knuckles red from the strike, but that didn't seem to bother him in the least. He leaned over and hefted Svorgin up like he wasn't twice his size. The *viila* darted forward toward the Blade but was grabbed by the other soldiers. Though she struggled, she never once reached for her curved blade. Either she was saving it to use later, or she didn't want to spill blood because of her righteous cause.

Svorgin stiffened when steel pressed against his lower back.

The Blade's low, lethal tone wrapped around him. "Will you comply, or shall I use force?"

Svorgin nodded, his jaw steeling. "I comply."

The Blade shoved him toward the stairs and ordered his companions, "Bring the girl."

Svorgin and the woman were half dragged, half propelled up to the tower. That ominous feeling sprouted in Svorgin's chest as they entered the circular chamber that had held him prisoner for months. When he hadn't lain half dead from injuries, he'd had plenty of time to think while he'd been chained there. He'd wondered if they'd searched for him. His da, Aylis, Honzio. If they were still searching for him or if they had resigned themselves to his death. Had they given up on looking?

Svorgin was deposited before the wall, and then the chains that had nearly become one with his body were relatched around his wrists. The guards grasped the *viila's* arms, keeping her still across from him. Svorgin and the woman shared a glance. He'd been so close to escaping because of her, and she had been caught because of him. The recognizable click of heels made his gut twist. Then she emerged into view—the queen who'd made his life torturous for the past months. Her long white skirts flowed over the grime-covered stone as she neared him. She reached down, gripping his chin and forcing his head up. He growled, attempting to wrench free from her clawlike nails, but she only held him tighter. Her pale eyes gleamed.

"I see our prisoner has regained his strength without my knowledge or permission."

She released him, and Svorgin tore his head away, wishing to create as much distance from her as he could. She wheeled around, slinking toward the *viila*. A surge of fiery emotion swelled over Svorgin. He wanted to break free from these chains and prevent another person—but especially the *viila*—from being harmed. She had risked her life to save him and now would pay for her choice.

"And who is this?" The queen ran a nail along the woman's cheek.

The woman turned her head away, her mouth twisting in a grimace.

"She is one of the new servants."

The queen tossed her Blade an inquisitive look. "Why was she in my tower?"

"She wasn't," Svorgin said. "I found her on my way down and used her to try to escape. I threatened her."

The queen waved her finger at him. "Do you take me for a fool? I know these walls better than anyone. Now I will ask again. What. Were. You. Doing. In. My. Tower?"

"I was lost," the *viila* said.

"Were you now?" The queen smiled condescendingly. "Call Madame Zelnat."

Blade motioned his head at two warriors in his troop, and they sped off in search of the housekeeper. A lengthy silence developed as they waited for their return. The queen seemed to enjoy the rising tension. Her nails clacked across her table as she walked back and forth. She stared at both Svorgin and the viila in equal amounts. An intimidation tactic.

When the warriors finally returned with the housekeeper, Madame Zelnat fell to her knees at once and begged for the queen's forgiveness.

"I swear I told her. I gave her strict instructions not to go beyond the second level." The housekeeper glared at the *viila*. "But she is clearly lacking in the mind. She is a foolish widow with three children. She must have lost her way and went up the tower. I will remove her from the premises."

Three children? Svorgin almost whistled as he glanced at the *viila*. She scowled, sensing his gaze on her.

"It is too late for that, Zelnat," Queen Guin said. "She has seen my tower and my prisoner. I will take care of her. You can leave and await your punishment for your indiscretion."

Madame Zelnat paled and then bowed before retreating down the tower as fast as she could.

"Now then, let us get to work." She gestured to the Blade, and he reached for the whip hanging among other torture instruments that Svorgin had become closely acquainted with. "Will you give me what I want, or shall we proceed?"

Svorgin raised a brow. "I've told you many times over. I do not know where the Golden Crown is."

"How long will you play coy?" Queen Guin waved her long fingers at the Blade.

Svorgin's back tensed, knowing what was coming. The whip sliced across his back with a fiery agony that burned his skin. Svorgin gritted his teeth. The slashes came down upon him again and again. His skin burst open, and warm blood trickled down his back. Sweat coated his neck. He could no longer contain himself. A roar poured from his mouth.

"Leave him!" a woman shrieked. The *viila*. "Leave him alone. What kind of monster are you?"

It was oddly comforting to have someone coming

to his defense in this demented tower. Queen Guin lifted her hand, and her Blade stilled and stepped back. Svorgin raised his head, his dazed eyes on the blood-covered whip, watching each drop of his blood hit the stone. His shoulders slumped, and his head dangled forward, entirely spent. The queen grasped a vial from among her shelves and approached him. Svorgin couldn't help but lean toward it for the aid it presented. The queen clicked her tongue, pulling it back.

"You already had one today. And without my permission. I do not think you deserve another."

Svorgin panted. His fists clenched. The queen pouted her lip and patted his cheek.

"Oh, my dear, do not be angry." Then her expression shifted to one of pure malice as she lowered her voice to a hiss. "Tell me where it is."

"I cannot."

She leaned closer to whisper in his ear. "Cannot? Or will not?"

Her hand wound behind his back to dig into the opened flesh. Svorgin cried out, his chains rattling. When she retracted her hand, her fingers were soaked in his blood. Svorgin stared at the vial in her grasp with longing. He'd grown so attached to it over the past torturous months, the special concoction that healed his wounds after the queen's punishment. But she'd never granted it to him easily. She waited until his wounds festered, until a fever took hold because of the infections, and finally, when he thought he would perish, she healed him. Just to do it all again.

"It is clear that tormenting you will not produce

results. But will you remain so steadfast if someone else is tortured in your place?"

Svorgin stiffened, but his body still trembled from the pain wreaking havoc through his back. He shook his head as the queen motioned for the guards to hold the *viila* in place. Panic flitted across her face before she steeled herself.

"You will not get away with this. Emperor Honzio will learn of your treachery and end your reign for good," she said.

The queen's laugh tinkled around them. A sharp noise that rang in Svorgin's mind.

"I have gotten away with whatever I wanted for nearly forty years. You believe I will be stopped now, girl?"

The *viila* jutted her chin upward. "Cruelty is always vanquished. Whether it takes a day or forty years."

Queen Guin's features settled into an expression of wrath, and she nodded at the Blade. He paused, uncertainty flashing over his face as he looked at the *viila*. The queen's brows lowered, and the Blade broke out of whatever was holding him back and strode toward the *viila*. Svorgin's heart pounded. He couldn't allow her to be hurt because of him.

Queen Guin fastened him with a look. "Will you speak?"

The *viila* called to him. "Do not give in. Do not tell her what she wants."

"Silence!" the Blade growled, fisting the woman's head cap and yanking her back.

Svorgin hesitated. The whip rose. His eyes darted

between the queen and the *viila*. Queen Guin looked on with pleasure as the whip lowered. It cracked against the *viila's* work dress. It would only be a matter of lashes until the whip tore through the cheap cloth and cut into her skin. Giving her marks like Svorgin's. She gasped, squeezing her eyes closed. A tear escaped as the whip came down on her again. But when she opened her eyes, despite the shimmer covering her irises, she remained steadfast and stared at the queen with defiance. Queen Guin growled, her pleasure fading.

"More," she snapped.

The Blade increased his speed, and the *viila* screamed when the whip dug into her flesh. Blood spread over the gray cloth.

"Stop!" Svorgin's voice emerged raw. "I will tell you."

The queen swiveled. "What did you say?"

"No." The *viila* shook her head. "No. I can take it."

Svorgin continued watching the queen as she slinked toward him. "I will tell you where it is. But you must promise to set us both free."

The queen smirked far too eagerly. "Done."

Svorgin met her eyes directly, a wicked plan formed in his mind. "It is in a fallen Imperial kingdom. In the realm of Tariqi."

The queen tilted her head, a crease appearing between her thin brows.

"The Golden Crown is in the Qistool."

17

THE THROBBING ACHE slithering through her whipped back faded as she absorbed Svorgin's admittance. The Golden Crown. The fabled legendary item that was said to grant eternal life, endless power, and wisdom beyond desire. If wielded, it would allow its bearer to rule the Empire, if not all lands. Master Dunya had said it was nothing but a myth conjured by those who wished to control. Could it truly exist?

The queen placed her hand upon the table to steady herself, but Aria watched Svorgin's face. He seemed pleased with himself and a fair bit amused at the queen's reaction.

If the crown existed and was in the Qistool as he claimed, how did Svorgin know it? The hands gripping Aria's arms tightened. She grimaced as the movement sent agony through her back. She wondered how Svorgin had endured it for so long. Sorrow sank over her at the thought of him languishing against the wall, forever chained and whipped to oblivion. How had he remained sane?

"You speak truth?" the queen said, but the words emerged as a question.

Svorgin nodded.

"Prove it."

"I went fishing with my friends long ago—or, rather, we would go to the lake in Savoria's center under *the guise* of fishing. Our families attempted to prevent us. It was forbidden to hunt the creatures that dwelled in the lake. But we preferred they thought us doing so than knowing what we truly wanted."

"The crown." The queen's eyes gleamed.

"We found it. I dove in deep, and my hand grazed across it." Svorgin paused, as though falling back in time. He lifted his chained hand, and his fingers drifted through the air as though it were water. The queen followed his motion, utterly mesmerized.

"It was something unreal. A magic that didn't belong in this world," Svorgin whispered. "And I only held it in my hand. Imagine the sheer power I would possess if I crowned it upon my head."

Queen Guin sank into a chair, clearly rapt by his words.

"But the Tariqins came. I couldn't let them have it. I took it from the lake and abandoned home. The Tariqins hunted me down, but once I entered the Qistool, none had the courage to pursue me."

"Y-You," the queen sputtered. "You entered the Qistool and emerged alive?"

"I am here, as you can see."

Aria frowned. Something about this tale rang rather odd.

"I left the crown in the fallen kingdom. It is all a scheme. There are no creatures roaming the halls of the Qistool. Not a single presence remained of the old kingdom. Only the ruins."

Aria shivered as though phantom hands grazed her skin. The Qistool she pictured was far different from what Svorgin described. It was a place shut off from the rest of the world that enclosed the dead. A haunted castle that no one dared breach for fear of their lives.

Queen Guin stood and extended the vial to Svorgin. He took it at once, hunger lighting in his eyes. He gripped the cork with his teeth, yanked it off, and downed the contents. Aria watched in amazement as his wounds closed and he stood taller, regaining his strength. She tilted forward, longing for the vial to ease the pain racking through her back. Queen Guin approached her, and her long fingers snaked around Aria's throat.

Aria inhaled a sharp breath, fighting back terror as the woman's bony fingers tightened.

"I told you what you wanted. Now set us free as you promised. Keep your word."

The queen retracted her hand, and Aria gulped in air. "I will. I will set you free to breathe outside these castle walls, but not entirely."

"What do you mean?"

"I mean, young man"—the queen spun, facing Svorgin—"that you are the only living being to have traveled to the Qistool and returned unharmed. You are the only being who knows exactly where the Golden Crown is."

Svorgin sputtered, then said, "But I told you already. I gave you its exact location."

"Then you will have no trouble retrieving it."

Svorgin paled.

"And the girl will go with you to keep you in check. One wrong move and my Blade will slice her throat."

Svorgin shook his head. "I told you what you wanted. You cannot ask for more."

Queen Guin laughed, the sound ringing about the round chamber as she drifted toward the stairs. "You will set off for the Qistool in the morning."

18

ONZIO STUMBLED BACK, creating distance between himself and the nearing deedans. He lifted a branch he'd been saving for the fire and held it out protectively. He stepped farther into the cave, forcing the deedans to form a single line to attack him. He blocked a kilisham, but at the second strike, the weapon cracked his branch in half. Desperation filled Honzio. He landed a blow in the man's stomach, sending him into the deedans behind him. They recovered quickly, grasping his arms and thrusting him from the cave. Honzio crashed into the snow, and a hiss slipped from his lips at the sharp impact. Pain laced through his right arm more so than anywhere else—a reminder that it would never fully heal. Honzio turned over onto his back and saw blurry faces peering down at him. Their heads shook in a chorus of laughter. Honzio touched his belt. There was nothing he could use as protection. He pulled himself up, but a boot slammed onto his chest, snatching the air from his lungs.

The Tariqin forced him back into the snow and angled his kilisham beneath Honzio's chin. "Any last words?"

Honzio gulped, his throat bobbing against the weapon. The blade pricked his skin, and hot blood dribbled down his neck.

"Aw, he wet himself." Another Tariqin chuckled.

Amused laughter erupted. The Tariqin above him raised his blade, gripping the hilt in both hands. *Look up, Honzio*, he thought. *Do not fear. Do not focus on the deadly gleam of the weapon but on the sky.* And so he did. It was beautiful. A blanket of blue embroidered with patches of white clouds. A haven he hoped his soul would rise to and be enveloped by. He would see his family up there. He inhaled. It was time. Then he heard the clang.

A slight axe whipped through the air, sending the deedan's kilisham into a clump of snow. Gasps rang among the Tariqins, and their heads spun in the direction the axe had flown from. Honzio peered into the distance. A woman stepped out from behind a cluster of snow-covered rocks. Her hair was not blond but darker. The locks reminded him of melted gold swaying in thick braids. Her expression was fierce.

"Leave him be," she called.

The Tariqins regained their composure, some managing to smile again.

"What are you doing here, woman? Aren't you a bit

far from your village?" a deedan shouted before turning to his companions. "She may be lost. Shall we give her a helping hand?"

Those were his last words before an axe was buried in his throat. He stumbled back and fell into the snow beside Honzio. Honzio's eyes popped wide open, and he stared for a long second at the red stain spreading about the deedan. All traces of humor from the Tariqins faded entirely. They now cast livid glares at the Savorian woman.

"Leave now while ye can. I will give ye a running start," the woman said, unflinching, deadly serious.

The deedans snarled, their grips tightening around their hilts.

"The winner is clear. You are one woman against eight of us."

Her lips curled, but it wasn't a smile. It was an expression that chilled Honzio. "That is why I suggested ye run."

They gave each other baffled stares before she said, "Time's up."

She walked forward, pulling an enormous axe free from her back. The deedans rushed her. They could've been mere flies for how easily the woman battled them. She ducked and parried and swung her axe with practiced ease. As if it were as easy as breathing. Honzio blinked. The bodies fell around her until she was the sole one standing. She was covered in blood. And yet Honzio found he had never been more mesmerized by a woman in his life. She approached him and held out a hand. He was hesitant. But then he reached up and placed his hand in hers. She heaved him up and put her axe in place behind her back before collecting her smaller ones.

"You have my gratitude," Honzio started. "For saving my life."

She shrugged and hooked her axes on her belt. "I was protecting my land."

Honzio pondered her words, and when she started walking away without further comment, he trailed after her.

"There may be more of them," he said. "If they find their companions' corpses, they will attack your village."

"I am counting on it," she replied without stopping her rapid pace.

Honzio burned with questions. Who was this woman? He focused on her back, the only part of her he could see. She was dressed in thick leather that encased her from her shoulders down to a pair of large boots. Fur lined her neck and adorned every part of her apparel. Her braids started from the sides and top of her head and wove back into a thick band that gathered them together all the way down to her waist.

"I was awaiting someone," Honzio started again. "If you do not mind delaying."

She stopped so abruptly that Honzio almost bumped into her. She whirled around, and Honzio's breath caught. Though she was a good amount shorter than him, her presence was large enough to encompass him. Her wide blue eyes were emotionless as she scanned him. Finally, she spoke.

"I did not ask ye to come with me. Ye can wait for yer

companion if ye wish." She unhooked one of her axes. "Ye do not carry a weapon and ye'll not get far without one."

Honzio took it, and a question bloomed in his mind. "Is that the first thing you noticed about me?"

One of her brows quirked up. "Should I have noticed something else?"

Honzio's jaw slackened, and he couldn't reply. She turned away and continued to march through the trees ahead. Honzio's mouth spread into a grin. She hadn't mentioned his arm; her eyes hadn't even lingered upon it. His curiosity propelled him after her. He didn't speak, too busy trying to keep up. She stopped occasionally, looking over marks in the ground or trunks of the trees. She glanced at the sky often. Finally, she stopped by a trap and released a squirming rabbit into her palms. She made quick work of ending it while muttering a prayer Honzio could not understand. Honzio flinched at the animal's demise.

"Ye must be well-off," she said, "if the sight of an animal being slain disturbs ye." She gutted and skinned it as she spoke.

Honzio swallowed. He'd killed. Taken lives. She did not know what he'd done to survive. Nevertheless, the loss of life upset him.

"Here, ye must hunt to live. Ye choose either to feed yer loved ones or to pity the animals in this forest. The choice is simple."

"And you care for them dearly, your loved ones?" He didn't know why he asked when she clearly did. He'd never been so curious to learn more about a person before.

She leveled him with a look. "The Tariqins took much from me. I only have my mam now."

Honzio wanted to say something kind or reassuring, but he knew she wouldn't appreciate it. She seemed like someone who preferred cold hard truth over platitudes. In a way, she reminded him of Aylis, the Savorian woman who'd been enslaved in Hearcross once. Life had hardened her in ways nothing else could.

The woman continued moving, then stopped by a large stream. She kneeled before it, dipping her hands into the water and washing the blood from her knuckles. Honzio followed suit and hissed at the iciness. He forced himself to continue washing and wiped his hand through his hair and over his face. The woman was doing the same.

"My mam will have a fright to see me covered in blood so soon."

"So soon?" Honzio questioned. How often was she covered in blood?

She stood. "In order to endure around these parts, ye must kill, *Lsrar*."

Honzio stiffened at the familiar term. Svorgin had once used it to refer to Prince Draven. Had she figured out his identity?

The woman's mouth moved the slightest bit, telling Honzio she was capable of smiling. "Ah, so ye know the meaning of that word. Ye seem pampered and spoiled like a prince."

Honzio's shoulders settled in relief. "I have seen much war in my land and most recently faced a sea monster. I assure you, I am not pampered."

"A sea monster, eh?" She lifted the pack containing the rabbit onto her shoulder. "I am surprised ye still draw breath."

"Is it so hard to believe I have some skill?"

"I would call it luck," she replied and moved off.

Honzio muttered under his breath and followed her. They stopped before a small home. The woman whistled, and a shape lifted from where it was settled by the door. Honzio's lips parted at the large rumlok with snow-white fur.

"Inside, Kalpara."

At the woman's order, the rumlok's head nudged against the door, and it swung open. The woman followed the beast inside. Honzio remained outside, blinking to ensure his eyes hadn't deceived him. He'd been under the impression that the rumloks had gone extinct in Savoria. To see one so healthy and large, it made him wonder once again . . . Who was this woman?

She ducked her head out. "Are ye coming, Lsrar?"

19

Saga

Savoria

"Mam!" Saga called as she entered her home.

Yuva emerged from the tiny kitchen hand-crafted by Saga's father long ago. She wiped her thick, calloused hands onto the front of her worn apron and scanned Saga.

"Where've ye been, lass? The sun's setting."

"I know. I was checking my traps."

Saga gave her mother the sack containing the rabbit, and her mother hummed in approval when she noted it was already prepped for cooking. She turned back toward the kitchen and stirred the pot. Saga's stomach growled as a delicious aroma drifted from it. As long as she could remember, no matter how much or how little they'd had, her mother crafted magic. She began slicing into the rabbit meat with an efficiency she could never forget despite her mind slowly stealing everything else from her.

"I heard the hymns. Someone passed to the next realm?" Yuva questioned.

Saga nodded, telling her mother for the fifth time since the morning, "The shavka."

"Shavka," a warm baritone mumbled, reminding Saga of the new arrival. "I've heard it before. It means *leader*, doesn't it?"

Saga turned, scanning the man once again. He seemed ill at ease, standing stiffly as he examined their surroundings. His eyes were brown—not a dark brown or light, but somewhere in between, like tree bark when the sun hit it in the morning. Those eyes flitted to her. His hand drifted to his right arm. A movement she'd noticed he did frequently—when the Tariqins attacked him, when she'd first spoken to him, and when he'd been indecisive about whether to follow her. She'd told herself to walk away after saving him. To leave him to meet whatever fate was in store for him. After all, she'd caused enough trouble for her village already. But there was something about him. Something that made her curious. She didn't know where he'd come from, what his name even was. But the sparrows arriving at his presence were sign enough for her to risk it. And when he'd followed her, she couldn't help but be pleased.

"Aye," she answered his question.

He glanced about. "Do most Savorians live in such homes?"

Saga viewed the interior through his eyes. Small and confined, it had never been expanded. It remained a cramped space, with a kitchen and a spot for the table in the main room and only one additional room that contained two cots. Saga stiffened.

"What of it? We do not have the palaces ye are used to, *Lsrar*."

He raised a placating hand. "I meant no offense. It is a lovely home."

She quirked her brow.

"Small and tidy," he continued, rambling. "Warm, cozy."

The wood creaked overhead at that very moment.

"Stop talking," Saga muttered.

He grimaced and nodded. "That is a good idea."

"*Kla.*" *Daughter*, her mother said, pausing in her cutting and watching the man with narrowed eyes. "Who is this lad?"

"He is not from here, Mam." Saga hesitated then, unsure what else to say.

Her mam's fingers tightened around the hilt of her knife, and she swiveled to face him, thunderclouds on her face. "Is he one of them? A Tariqin?"

Saga shook her head at once. The man paled.

"He is a traveler from . . ." She looked at him.

"The Empire," he blurted. "I am Honzio H-Holonor of the Empire. I worked under my father in Hearcross for many years."

"Honzio of the Empire?" Yuva repeated.

The man nodded. His eyes flitted to Saga. "And you are?"

"Going to eat," Saga said before yanking out a chair and settling down. Honzio's mouth opened and closed.

He inched closer, his gaze on Kalpara, who had been sitting beneath the table the entire time.

"Do not fret, *Lsrar*," Saga said. "She won't bite."

He chuckled.

"For now, at least."

His humor faded, and he took the chair at the farthest end. Her father's chair. Saga gripped her spoon tighter.

"Move at once," her mother growled, smacking her large ladle on the back of his neck.

Honzio flinched at the impact and placed his hand over his neck protectively. He received a smack to the fingers next.

"Leave him, Mam. There is no one else who will sit there."

Her mam pointed the ladle at her. "Have ye gone mad, lass? Yer da will be arriving soon."

Honzio pushed to his feet. "My apologies. This is your father's chair?"

He gave her a look that seemed to say, *I thought you'd lost everyone but your mam?*

Saga stood and propelled her mam toward the kitchen, mouthing at him over her shoulder, *Sit.*

He obeyed, but a line of confusion still cut through his brow. Saga assisted her mam, and before long, they were setting bowls of steaming soup onto the table. There was a bit of bread left over from Olava's gift. It was hard as a rock. A sliver of embarrassment wormed through Saga, surprising her. Since when did she care about giving guests hard bread? Then another thought rose in her mind. When had they last had guests?

But to his credit, the man didn't complain. In fact,

he praised the meal enough to make her mam blush and lose the suspicious look she'd worn since she'd seen him. He copied Saga's movements, dipping the bread into the soup to make it soft enough to chew. Saga noticed him watching her often. For the first time in years, she wondered how she looked. She knew she wasn't as pretty as her sister had been or Britta was. But still, she felt self-conscious. Was her hair in order or in the shaggy disarray it was every time she returned home in the evenings? His eyes were too focused, saw too much. Saga swallowed and bit back a curse. So what if a strange man from another world watched her? He would leave soon, and she would never see him again. She reached out for the bread, seeking a distraction. Her hand collided with his. He pulled his back at once.

"Apologies."

He used that word far too often. Saga snarled and grasped the bread. She tore a sizeable chunk off, then threw it at him. He caught it, surprise lashing his features. A few hard crumbs broke onto his tunic. The comical expression he wore nearly made her laugh. The sensation swelled in her chest, warming the area that had been cold for so long. She didn't even remember how to laugh, she realized. And she didn't deserve to, not until she freed her village. Saga took a spoonful of soup and focused on him, catching his gaze.

"Ye say ye are Imperial. Ye must know of what happened there. With my people. I've learned many were shipped off to yer lands."

He nodded. "Unfortunately, they were enslaved

there. The Empire has laws, but many didn't follow them and traded them illegally."

Saga's fingers tightened.

"But the new emperor has promised to fix everything," he said quickly, his eyes roving her face, searching for something in her features. "He's changed much already and plans to save Savoria."

Saga slammed her fist onto the table, making the bowls rattle. "What has he done all these years?" Her voice rose. "A pampered silly emperor who knows nothing of the horrors of life. His words mean nothing to me."

He flinched. "But he is sincere. Many of your countryfolk believe him."

"He can go to hell," Saga bit out. "Where has he been all these years? While we were slaughtered? While we were herded like sheep and forced under the rule of Prolus, the dictator?"

"Such brutal words for a man you've never met."

"And I do not regret them. I wish I could tell him directly to his face what I think about him," she said. "That he is a foolish coward that probably sits in bed and allows his advisors to run his empire while he stuffs himself with the finest meals. He rolls about in silk, never feeling the thickness of blood or its smell. He is an absolute useless beast that has done nothing."

Saga stopped for a breath. Honzio watched her, his face completely blank before he managed to softly say, "But if he came now, wouldn't that matter?"

Saga stood and gathered the dishes without answering. She marched to the bucket in the corner and scrubbed the bowls. She returned to his side and glared at him before grasping his half-eaten bowl and marching back. Voices rose behind her. Her mam and Honzio. Speaking and laughing like old friends. Her mam had even produced a cloth filled with healing herbs that she wrapped around his head to aid the bump he'd suffered at sea. Saga growled in frustration, nearly cutting her fingers from the vicious way she was scrubbing. When she finished, she marched to her cot, grasped a blanket, and then extended it to him.

"Ye can use this."

He took it in measured movements. "Where will I sleep?"

"On the emperor's bed," Saga muttered. "Outside, of course."

His eyes creased in response.

"Ye won't leave the poor lad in the cold, will ye?" her mam called to her.

Saga marched to the door and hefted it open, motioning for him to leave. He walked up to her.

"It is no problem, Mam," he called to Yuva. "I will make do."

Saga's mouth dropped open. In just a few minutes, he'd won her mother over so completely that she'd given consent for him to address her so intimately. Saga hadn't been set on leaving him out in the cold, but he unsettled her. She'd been so sure of herself ever since she could remember that anyone who unbalanced her had to be distanced as far as possible.

"Saga!" her mam called.

"Saga," Honzio said, drawing out the syllables of her name. "It's beautiful."

Saga forced herself to remain firm. She gave him a little push, and Kalpara darted out with him. She slammed the door behind them and moved toward her cot.

"Where is yer da? The old critter is determined to kill me at this young age."

"Ye realize ye two were the same age," Saga muttered as she unraveled her braids.

"Where is that bugger?"

"He told ye he would return in the morning, Mam. Have ye forgotten?"

Her mam's brows knit as she tried to remember. "Did he now?"

Saga nodded and kissed her mam's brow. "Get some sleep."

She, herself, took several hours to drift off, her thoughts rampant with an infuriating newcomer. And when she did sleep, her dreams were full of brown eyes and singing sparrows.

20

ARIA
KINGDOM OF DEVORIN
CASTLE YAKH

ARIA SHIFTED AGAINST the tower wall, placing her brow to it. The frigid stone soothed her mind for a moment. The rest of her was racked with shivers that had plagued her for hours. But it wasn't just the iciness of the tower that had kept her awake. The pain from the whipping lingered on her back, making her wince every time she moved. If only Queen Guin could have given *her* some of her healing tonic. Aria glanced at the sole window in the tower. It was so far from her that she could only see the sky from it. The horizon was covered in a low light that deceived her. She couldn't tell if it was the fading daylight or the early morning arriving. The snores continued, resounding from the broad man who'd sunk against her. They rumbled from his chest and out of his nose. His mouth was slightly parted, and warm air brushed her neck. Aria lifted her shoulder, shrugging him off. Svorgin sank into a crumpled shape on the floor, his shackles clinking. Aria attempted rubbing at her own shackled wrists to ease the discomfort.

Footsteps approached, cresting the top of the staircase. Aria slid her lids closed and deepened her breaths as the arrivals neared. The first set of strides were light and airy, barely heard, while the second *thunked* across the stone with intention. Aria felt stares peering at her. After a long moment, as though satisfied that she was lost to slumber, the first spoke up.

"We have discussed enough." The eerie tone, so soft and yet sharp as a knife, sent chills down Aria's spine. "You will not go through the border as originally planned."

The Blade responded to his queen. "We shall take the tunnels as you ordered."

"I would rather you have safe passage through the border, but we cannot know what to expect from the Tariqins. After Prolus's defeat, our alliance is shaken. They may ask what we are after. I do not want curious eyes on my prize."

Aria contained her surprise, maintaining her façade of deep sleep. The queen of Devorin had allied with Prolus. Emperor Honzio's suspicions of her were correct. She was a traitor. She had sold out her homeland, the Empire, for Tariqi. Aria had to escape the tower at once and send word to the emperor. He had to remove her as soon as possible before she wreaked further havoc across the land.

"The tunnels it is," the queen whispered.

Aria dared to open her eyes, keeping them half lidded, and stared at the blurry figures through her lashes. The queen shifted, moving around her table. The Blade remained across from her, watching his queen with his head slightly bowed in deference.

"It has been too long since they have been traversed," Queen Guin continued. "I have heard dark things now lurk in them. Be wary."

"I will do as you order, my queen."

The queen smiled that wicked grin, exposing her brittle teeth. "Good. But your true test will be when you reach the Qistool." She flipped through pages of a hefty book until her long finger settled on one. Her nail scraped across, following a line of words. "Darkness resides there, they say. Creatures that dwell in the kingdom. In the tales, they refer to them as nojori. It is a word used solely by the Tariqins."

A chill gripped Aria at the menacing sentence.

"There are many different opinions on the meaning of the word, but most scholars agree on *undying plague*." The queen looked up from the book. "I doubt the creatures have lasted this long. There may be nothing there, as the Savorian said, but be wary. Once the Savorian shows you the crown, take it and leave. You know what you must do. None shall touch the crown. None shall see it until it is placed upon my head."

Queen Guin lifted her hands and settled her fingers over her white hair. Her lids shuttered closed, as though she were imagining the legendary crown already upon her tresses.

"I will ensure none survive, my queen."

At his ominous words, the queen's eyes shifted open, and she gave him an approving smile. She walked around the table and laid a hand over his cheek. She traced the line of his jaw. There was an almost romantic note about it, just as Aria had noticed before. Disgust filled her at the sight. The Blade remained frozen.

"Out of all my servants, you have served me best, Blade."

Aria saw his throat bob. His brows lowered, and then his flickering eyes met the queen's. "I asked for something once. In return for my service."

The queen's hand dropped, her pointed nails scratching down his cheek. He flinched in response to her evident disapproval. Long red lines marked his pale skin.

"What you ask for will only harm you. The past is over. Done and gone. You are now the man you were always meant to be."

The Blade looked down. The queen frowned, doubt crossing her features.

"Who are you?" she hissed.

"Your weapon," he said after a moment's pause.

"Good. Very good."

With those final words, she ducked out of the tower. Aria closed her eyes as the Blade turned toward her and Svorgin. It was simple to convince him she was sleeping with the snoring oaf beside her. The Blade approached her. His stiff fingers curled around her arm.

"Awaken."

Aria feigned a yawn and slowly opened her eyes and then almost closed them again. Seeing him this close was unsettling. Those wide icy-blue eyes appeared empty, like never-ending pools of darkness. She feared staring into them. As though if she did, she may drown in the sorrow there.

"We will set off soon," he said.

There was a tinkling sound, and Aria's gaze flitted to his hand. A vial rested within his palm. It looked like the healing potion. The golden liquid begged her to drink of it and be free of pain. But the part of her that had been trained to be wary doubted this sudden act of charity.

"Why?"

"We will not have time to tend to your wounds if they get infected on the road."

He motioned for her to take it, and Aria reached out with hesitance, her fingers slipping around it. She bit the cork off with her teeth and continued watching him as she brought it to her mouth. His expression didn't change. Emotionless the entire time. She drank the contents. A rush of warmth shot down her throat and hit her insides with a heady rush. The warmth extended within her, sealing away the pain for good. She nearly sighed in relief. The Blade reached for the vial. As he grasped it, she noticed his littlest finger was a mere stump beside the rest.

"What happened?" she couldn't help but ask.

"What?" the Blade said.

"To your hand."

He didn't answer, turning to place the empty vial upon the table.

"At least tell me your name, then," Aria said, testing the waters. "Or does she forbid even that?"

He froze, then finally turned back to her. "I am known as the Blade."

There was something about him, a mystery that veiled him. One she wanted to solve. He sought the past from the queen. Had he forgotten it? Or did he wish to learn of his ancestors, his family? Was that why he followed her blindly?

"Your true name."

Curiosity flared in his features—just for a moment before he cleared it away.

"I have none."

Aria forced a laugh. "Of course you do. Everyone does."

"I am simply the Blade," he hissed, then leaned in close. "You would do well not to delve into matters that do not concern you."

Aria shrank back from his frigid tone. He moved away from her and kicked Svorgin awake. The Savorian groaned in reply.

"Give me a blasted moment."

"Get up. We leave in a few minutes."

Then the Blade moved toward the stairs. As soon as he drew out of sight, Aria turned to Svorgin, who was wiping the sleep from his eyes.

"You couldn't have thought of anywhere besides the Qistool? Tell her you were mistaken. That the crown is somewhere else."

"Good morning to you too, *viila*," Svorgin muttered, giving her a sleepy smile.

Aria glared at him. "This is not a game. As soon as

he finds the crown, the queen has ordered the Blade to kill us."

Svorgin's sleepy smile lingered. Aria grabbed his chain, forcing him closer to her. He lifted his hands in surrender.

"Do you hear me? They will *kill* us."

"That may be a bit hard to accomplish," Svorgin responded.

"Killing me perhaps," Aria said. "But they will handle you easily. And in the process of trying to save you, I will be sacrificed as well."

Svorgin's brow shot up. "I am unsure if I should be insulted or flattered by that statement."

"The former."

Svorgin chuckled and then turned utterly serious. His tone was calm and foreboding at once. "What I meant was that they cannot find the crown."

Svorgin paused dramatically, and Aria waited with bated breath.

"Because it does not exist."

21

"WHA—WHAT?" SHE STUTTERED. Her mouth parted and eyes widened.

Svorgin nodded. "It was a tale I fabricated at the age of twelve." He glanced to the staircase to ensure no one was listening before continuing. "In order to protect my family, I risked myself as my father had done before me. I knew the Tariqins were after the crown, so I told them I would give them its location if they let my family be."

The *viila* watched him, disbelief coating her features as she soaked in his words.

"I escaped them then, but that was merely where my story began. I was placed behind the bars of *five* different dungeons." Svorgin leaned closer to her, emphasizing the number.

"If you made it all up, why couldn't you have chosen somewhere other than the Qistool?" the *viila* finally said. "Are you mad? You know what lurks there."

Svorgin chuckled, brushing aside her concerns. "It is a mere tale. The cursed kingdom of old is but a story told to children."

She tilted her head. "You do not truly believe that. You fear what resides there."

Svorgin wiped whatever expression had given her that impression clean off his face. He couldn't give her the satisfaction of knowing that she had hit very close to the mark. He'd given the Qistool as the location because he wanted to see Queen Guin punished for her actions. For the torture of innocents before him and the months he'd endured, chained and beaten and whipped in her tower. He'd wanted her to meet her end in the cursed halls of the Qistool. But she didn't want the crown enough to risk her life. She had chosen to send him and the *viila* with her men instead. Svorgin cast aside thoughts of the rumors he'd heard since childhood. The tales whispered in the night, speaking of the horrors of what lay beyond the tall walls.

"I fear nothing," he said instead. It emerged jagged and sharp. "I have lived too long and through too much to harbor the feeling."

The *viila* leaned away at his fierceness, but curiosity lurked in her features. "All beings fear something. Losing something or never attaining their goals. They fear their master or God. They fear disappointing their loved ones. There are endless things to fear, making it impossible not to fear anything."

Her words were soft but firm, a wisdom in them that also lived in her mesmerizing eyes. Svorgin could listen to her speak for hours. He could lie back and be lulled to sleep by her melodic tone. He blinked, forcing away the thoughts. He lowered his voice and asked instead, "And what do *you* fear?"

Her dark brows, which appeared to have been carved to perfection by the Maker, rose at his question. She broke away from his eyes. He had thought she wouldn't speak, when she uttered, "I fear I will not keep my promise to my brother, who has passed on."

Svorgin's hand lifted as if of its own accord, resting in the air just by her shoulder. Some part of him screamed at him to comfort her. After all, he knew the feeling of loss. He'd known it ever since his father had been chained and taken away. Torn from them forever. At least until Svorgin had seen him again and that impossible dream had come to fruition. He'd seen his father and his sister, Aylis. But that dream had been sweet and far too short, and he'd been torn from them once again. Now he knew not where they were or if they were well. His fingers closed into a fist, and he dropped it beside him, his chain rattling.

The *viila* turned those large eyes on him. "It is your turn. Confess a fear in truth."

Svorgin chuckled. She was determined to wrench one from him despite his denial. He thought of his ultimate goal. The one that had kept him alive for so long. During the whippings and torture. The sole thing that kept him from succumbing whenever death came for him.

"I fear never seeing Savoria free." The admittance

came easily, as all his words seemed to around this woman. "I will give my last breath to see it alive like before and no evil burdening the land. I want to see my home free with my own eyes."

She smiled. "And you will. We will get out of here. Get away from this group before we get to the Qistool and journey to Hearcross. Last I heard, Emperor Honzio was rallying a group to travel to Savoria."

A lump welled in his throat. Svorgin forced it back and coughed to conceal his sudden emotion. Honzio had done it. He'd kept his promise. Even if he believed Svorgin to be dead, he'd still kept it. He was a true emperor and a man of his word.

"But we cannot do so if we are dead." The *viila's* voice brought his focus back to her. "Which, if you recall, will be your fault. Think of something."

"I saved your life, *viila*. If I hadn't convinced the queen to spare you, you wouldn't be ordering me about right now."

Her following laugh was filled with sarcasm. "If I hadn't unchained you in the first place, my life would have never been at risk."

Svorgin nodded. "You have a point there."

Silence elapsed as they both fell into deep thought.

"Three wee ones, eh?"

"What?" she asked.

"I knew it was a lie." Svorgin waved a finger at her. "That was your entry into the castle, wasn't it? Helpful maid with a passel of children."

"Why does that matter?"

He lifted his hands in surrender at her irritated tone. "All right, all right. I am thinking of a plan."

The *viila* gave him a doubtful glance.

"Let me remind you, *viila*, of the dungeons I have been trapped in." He gave her a wicked grin. "I broke out of all five."

Svorgin could not concoct a masterful plan in time. The Blade's companions—a group of ten trained men and women—stormed the tower and dragged them out of the castle through the back door. The queen was still attempting to hide her heinous plots from the civilians who already suspected her. Svorgin stumbled over rocks concealed by snow. He heard the *viila* gasp as a man shoved her. Svorgin snarled, but he couldn't do much else with the swords trained at his back. He was forced to mount a steed that was tied to the saddle of another horse before him. He accustomed himself in the saddle. He'd always loved animals, especially rumloks. His heart gave a pining thump at the thought of his rumlok, now long dead. But something he'd enjoyed even more than riding was sailing. Traveling by sea. Moving with the dangerous waters beneath. He lived and breathed the salty air and the blue deep. It had been too long. Far too long.

He caught sight of the *viila* on the mount across from him. She was seated before the Blade—a reminder that they would kill her if he had told a lie or refused to guide them to the crown. The Blade's arm slid over her middle to hold her in place. Discomfort slipped over

Svorgin, and something simmered in his veins, but he forced himself to focus. Before long, they were off, traveling through the snow-dusted forests. It was hours later that Svorgin spotted a shape racing toward them. It was moving fast, a blur of muscles and hair whipping back into the breeze. A horse. Its hooves skidded across the ground as it halted before them, shooting up clumps of dirt and snow. Sweat coated its laboring body and dripped from its mane. It had journeyed far. Svorgin eyed it. The horse was as unforgettable as his rider.

"Vandal," Svorgin breathed. "Velamir's horse."

At his admittance, a shape darted from the Blade's saddle and toward the horse. Worry surged through Svorgin at the sight of the *viila* escaping the Blade's hold. He glanced at the Blade, prepared for an angry response, but the Blade's gaze was far off. He was looking at the horse in a daze. Svorgin blinked, forging past his confusion to watch the *viila*. She whispered to Vandal, brushing her fingers over his coat. A tear escaped her eye. Did she know Velamir? Why was she so attuned to his horse? And why did Vandal allow her to touch him so readily? Lancer horses were bound to their riders and despised any other than their rider tending to them or riding them. A more concerning thought arose. If Vandal was here, where was Velamir?

"Blade," a woman in the company called.

The Blade snapped out of his daze. "Let the girl ride the horse."

Uncertain glances swept around the group, but no one dared to defy his order. The *viila* mounted Vandal bareback, her fingers curling around his thick mane.

She hesitated for a moment, and Svorgin urged her without words. *Go! Get out of here while you have a chance.* But she didn't. The thought of escape, if it went through her mind, passed quickly as she focused on him. Svorgin knew she was respecting her Elder morals. Leave none behind.

They started forward again, and it wasn't until evening greeted them in a pink line across the horizon that they halted. The Blade glanced about, searching for something. Part of the company assisted him, while the rest stood guard. Svorgin walked toward the *viila*, using the opportunity of the soldiers' deflected alertness to question her. That was no mere thing she'd done with the horse. He grasped her arm, and her wide gaze shot down to his hand, but he didn't release her. He touched her chin between his thumb and forefinger, forcing her head up so he could meet her eyes.

"Who are you, *viila*? Tell me your name."

22

THE BLADE
KARALIK EMPIRE

THE HORSE. *THAT* horse. He'd seen it before. As familiar to him as the dream he had every night. The dream that had once been distorted but now plagued him with memories of another life. The girl approached the horse, speaking to it softly. She turned, and he glimpsed her eyes. His heart thumped. Her face morphed into one he knew so well: a man with olive skin, bent nose, and confident grin. He knew him. He knew him better than himself. So why couldn't he remember why? The memories were there, taunting him, urging him. But he couldn't go down that dark path.

Couldn't return to his old life. The queen forbade it. The past was over. And even though he desired it, part of him knew that going back would kill him.

Pain slithered through his mind. All these thoughts were worsening his headaches.

As soon as they reached their destination, he dismounted and gave orders to find the entry for the tunnels. But though he gave the appearance of being in charge, his mind was elsewhere. He strode into the trees, leaving the others behind, and leaned against a trunk. He breathed in and out, hoping it would ease the turmoil within him. But when that didn't work, he reached for his belt and unhooked a vial. He'd just lifted it to his mouth when a hand smacked it out of his grasp. Blade pivoted, his brow furrowed as the precious contents sank into the ground, lost. He moved in a blink, fisting Fox's collar and shoving him against the tree trunk.

"What is wrong with you?"

Fox was unrepentant. "That is poisoning you. You must wake up. I did. We all can. We do not have to be servants for her any longer."

Blade's chest heaved with rage. "We aren't her servants. We are her warriors. The ones she values most."

"We are nothing more than her toys," Fox spat.

Blade growled a warning, his grip tightening. "Careful."

"I remember who I was," Fox said. "Back before she captured me. I was a merchant, and I lived in Hearcross. I was a widower making do to provide for my daughter." He paused. "My daughter. Can you believe it, Blade? I have a *daughter*. And she is out there, alone in this harsh world. Possibly thinking I am dead or perhaps—" Tears welled in his eyes. "Perhaps she is waiting for me to return as I promised her the day I was taken. She was only a small child, barely walking, but perhaps she remembers. 'I will come back for you,' I told her."

Blade's fingers went limp. He released Fox's collar. Longing for his own past swept through him so powerfully it surprised him.

"Do not drink her poison any longer."

Fox strode away. Blade watched him go and steeled himself. He couldn't allow Fox to influence him; he couldn't break his queen's command. His sole focus was following her orders. The only path for him was that of the future and his queen. And he would be her weapon. That was the only thing that should matter.

23

Honzio opened his eyes and could see nothing but white clouds. They were wrapped about him, creating the warmest haven. Sleep threatened to take him back under, but he waded through his exhaustion. He blinked, but the white tufts didn't fade. They were far heavier than he'd imagined clouds were. Not airy and light as he'd expected, but with enough weight that it stole the breath from his chest. It took several long seconds for Honzio to recall what had happened. Saga had tossed him out of the home the night before, and he'd sat alone on her doorstep with her murderous-looking rumlok eyeing him. He'd been so cold he thought he would die of frostbite if remorse didn't kill him first. Thoughts of his companions plagued him. Daghvin must have grown worried when he returned to the cave and found the corpses of the Tariqins. Honzio hoped he'd found the others and especially Lore. Honzio never should have brought the boy with him. It was far too dangerous a mission for one so young.

A door creaked open, and boots thudded across the wooden steps. A loud sigh filled the air, and then a rough female voice muttered, "Good, he's gone."

Something told Honzio that he was the *he* she was referring to. The boots stepped off the platform and crossed over the snow.

"Come, Kalpara," Saga called.

A growl emitted from above Honzio, emerging from the thick pile of clouds curled over him. Panic drummed into Honzio. That was no cloud.

"Are ye refusing?" Saga demanded. "We must get to work. No time to be lazy."

There was another long grumble of complaint.

"Kalpara!"

At the brisk shout, the white rumlok lifted off Honzio. He got a good look at the massive animal's dark eyes up close as it stared down at him before clambering toward an open-mouthed Saga.

"You!"

Honzio inhaled a much-needed breath. The cold seeped into him now that he'd lost the shelter of Kalpara's warm fur. He pulled himself to his feet.

"Good morning." He attempted civility as he combed through his disheveled hair.

"How did—" Saga appeared ready to burst with anger, her eyes flicking between Kalpara and Honzio.

"First my mam and now Kalpara. What tricks are ye using?"

Honzio shrugged. "I wonder that myself." Then he muttered under his breath, "People rarely warm to me so quickly."

Saga huffed and continued on her way without further word. Honzio glanced at the house and then followed her.

"No breakfast?"

Saga came to an abrupt halt and whirled around. "Like I told ye before, Lsrar. This is no palace. Return to yer home, Honzio of the Empire. Ye do not belong here." She appeared earnest for the first time. Beneath her anger was a deep sadness Honzio could not begin to fathom.

"What if I told you I came here for a purpose?"

"Do ye have a death wish?"

"It was no mere ship I traveled on. My companions and I were sent by the emperor. Our purpose is to help save Savoria. We will not leave without doing so."

She stared at him for a long moment, as though she expected him to reveal he was jesting. "That cannot be true. Why would he help us? If he heard what we thought of him, he would turn back without a moment's waste."

Honzio shook his head, holding her gaze. "He wouldn't. Even if you all despised him, he would not abandon Savoria. Because he made a promise."

Saga frowned.

Honzio swallowed, toning down the emotion that was no doubt evident in his face and voice. "The emperor never breaks an oath."

Saga seemed to consider this before she finally nodded. "I will help ye search for yer friends. But first, I must complete my daily work."

Saga led the way again. She eventually stopped in the center of a cluster of trees, where she got to work chopping wood. Honzio admired and was slightly in awe of how she moved. She didn't pause for a break or to wipe the sweat dotting her brow. Her arms moved without rest as she hefted her large axe, cutting through logs like they were nothing.

"Give me a task."

Saga paused, her chest heaving as she examined him. She nodded at a large sack she'd brought along. "Place the chopped wood in there."

Honzio did as he was told. He felt her eyes on him as he maneuvered the bag into his damaged hand and threw the wood in with the other. Finally, he spat out the question that had been burning within him.

"Will you ever ask?"

Her axe split a log in two. She leaned over it and glanced at him. "Ask about what?"

Honzio motioned. "My arm."

"Why would I? It isn't my business."

Honzio almost laughed. He wished people in the Empire thought the same way. "You aren't curious about what happened?"

Saga wiped the sweat off her palms. "I've known countless people who have endured grievous wounds. Many who never recovered. But the wounds were not something to be looked down upon." Saga crossed the distance between them.

With her standing so close, Honzio found himself short of breath. She examined his arm. "It is the most interesting part about ye. Every wound, every scar is but a history of moments that make ye who ye are."

Honzio was lost for words. To hear it spoken of so beautifully, it was like his whole world, the way he knew it, shattered and was put back together in a dazzling way. A new frame of mind. Her eyes shot up to him, so cold and yet full of flame. Honzio wasn't sure if he would drown in them or burn if he stared any longer. He broke eye contact and instead looked at the gold hoops adorning her right ear. She ran her fingers over them often.

"Do they mean something? The rings?"

She stiffened and then touched them. "It's a Savorian custom. To honor the passing of a loved one. I've lost everyone but my mam."

"Then what your mam said yesterday . . ."

Saga nodded. "After my da was imprisoned, after they'd gone, it was like she froze in time, forever living in the moment when we were still a full and happy family."

Honzio doubted she would be pleased if he offered any pitying words, so instead he said, "I lost them too. I am the sole living member of my family."

Saga reached out, patting his arm. And for a long moment, they stood in companionable silence. They understood each other. The pain of losing their family. The pain that didn't ever heal. Saga glanced toward the trees when voices neared. Her posture became stiff as the sounds drew closer and leaves rustled and branches cracked. Honzio saw her hand before he registered it winding around his. She tugged him forward, farther into the trees, where she yanked him down to hide and await the approaching newcomers.

154

24

SAGA PEEKED OVER the underbrush. Honzio's eyes bored into her cheek, questions burning in them. His lips parted to speak, but Saga reached out, placing her fingers over his mouth. He froze, and Saga gave him a subtle shake of her head. He nodded in understanding, and she dropped her hand. The footsteps drew closer, pulling Saga's attention. Britta emerged into view from between the trees. She appeared determined, her brows lowered and mouth set in a grim line. She was marching without intending to stop. Leno appeared behind her. He grabbed her arm, yanking her toward him.

"Britta, what will ye gain by going to her? I've told ye countless times Saga will not benefit us, and we cannot help her. She has chosen her path."

"I told ye I needed distance, Leno. After

what ye did." Britta's lids closed, and her mouth turned in distaste.

"I did what had to be done. For our people. For us to continue living."

Britta's eyes flew open, and she shoved at Leno's chest. "Ye were going to give her to them. Ye were going to allow the Tariqins to kill Saga. If Shavka Esme hadn't come . . ."

Leno nodded. "And what happened to her? Shavka Esme *died* because of Saga."

Saga swallowed, her fingers curling around weeds.

"Because that is the fate of all who are close to Saga. Ye know it. She's cursed. More than any of us. The Seers said it all those years ago. Wherever Saga goes, death follows."

Saga trembled with rage. She wished to give Leno a solid punch.

"Her family's death wasn't enough. She will kill all those closest to her by her actions."

Britta looked up at him with tear-filled eyes. Leno stepped closer to her, grasping her hand to his chest. Saga watched them without blinking. She was so focused that she startled when fingers brushed her skin. Honzio peered at her with concern as his warm grasp gently coaxed her hand to release the death grip she had upon the thorny weeds. Lines formed in his brow when he examined the fresh tears in her skin and the blood welling forth. Saga couldn't feel the pain. It was nothing compared to the agony of watching her dearest friend nod at Leno.

"Do not let her doom us all, Britta. If she wishes to

kill herself, she can go ahead. But I will not—*cannot*—allow her to destroy the rest of us."

"At least leave her be," Britta said so low Saga almost didn't hear her.

"Ye know I cannot," Leno said. "The Tariqins will arrive angry, and they will seek revenge. We will give them what they want."

Britta shook her head, her lips trembling, and she burst into a sob. "Not Saga. Please."

Leno pulled her in, resting his chin over her hair. His solid, muscular arms folded her against him. "I am sorry, my love, but we have no other options." Though his words were regretful, his face was utterly serious and devoid of sadness as he stared off into the distance where Saga's home was located.

Saga's rage heightened. Her breaths were rough and angry. She barely kept her composure as she imagined different scenarios of lunging over the underbrush and attacking Leno. She tried to calm herself, considering she had no right to detest him this much. Not when he was right. She *was* the reason the Tariqins would return to exact revenge. She'd started this. She'd turned them all down this road they could never return from. Leno believed they would be appeased by her sacrifice, but the Tariqins would never leave until they stopped submitting to them.

Leno tugged Britta away, and Britta cast one last mournful gaze toward Saga's home before they disappeared into the trees. Saga stood and marched to her wood bag. She moved to lift it when Honzio called to her.

"You do not believe what they said about you, do you?"

Saga stiffened.

"About you being cursed."

She swiveled to face him. He moved hesitantly, as though he were a tamer approaching a wild beast.

"I do not heed their words any longer."

The lie burned her tongue. Honzio held her gaze, and she forced herself not to break it, lest she reveal her weakness.

"Stay with my mam until I return." Saga swung the bag over her shoulders. "They already want my neck as it is."

If they saw her harboring a foreigner, they may kill her themselves. She started forward.

"Wait," Honzio said.

He walked around her and reached down. His fingers closed around her wrist, and she stiffened again, unsure of his intentions. He lifted her hand, inspecting it under a critical eye. A loose curl slipped from the locks crowning his head and hung over his brow. Saga had the sudden urge to touch it to see if it was as soft as it appeared. Despite his clear experience with life, he had a boyish quality about him. A hurt wound that gaped wide. She dispelled the thoughts. This Imperial was nothing but trouble. Why then had she believed him when he'd said he'd come to help save her island?

"You are bleeding," he said.

He leaned closer, filling her senses with the salty scent that still clung to his skin from the sea. Saga's breath caught. Confusion warred with curiosity. She allowed no one to be so close. His fingers slid over her belt and tugged a small axe free. Just when she was wondering if he planned to use it against her, he stepped back. Saga took a quick breath of forest air and regained her bearings. Honzio used the axe to slice through the extra fabric of his tunic.

"It is not the cleanest, but it will have to do."

Saga watched as he grasped her hand again and carefully wrapped the cloth around her palm. Such gentle motions. A part of her cracked, and the young, trusting girl within her flared to life as she watched his brows knit in concentration. It was as if every shield she'd crafted around herself was falling with his every touch. He manipulated the cloth with one hand and then used his other to help tie it together. He grimaced. It clearly pained him to use both. But when he finished, he shot her a smile. Saga's own lips threatened to tilt up. She shot it down at once. How could she smile when there was so much cruelty and death in Savoria? She'd made a promise to herself that she would laugh only when her land was free. And this Imperial had nearly ruined that oath.

"Stay with my mam," she spat through gritted teeth.

He stepped back a pace at the venom in her voice.

"I will help ye search for yer companions when I return," she added to soften her previous response.

She didn't wait for his reply, marching toward the village square instead. As soon as she entered, she felt the tension lingering in the air. She approached her neighbors, the ones she sold the wood to, but every one of them turned their heads, some pretending not to see her entirely. Saga should have expected such a reaction, but the rejection still stung. She had no choice but to keep trying. How else would she earn coin for her and her mam's survival? Saga inhaled and squared her shoulders, thinking of an inspiring proverb passed down from generations before her. *The Lagrima Sea was filled with tears, but despite the heartbreak, it never failed to carry ships safely to land.* She was a Savorian. She had lost everything—her family, her home, her people, and even her own heart—but she was a Savorian. And the mountains would crumble before she surrendered.

Olava was standing at her usual stall, a fresh batch of bread, newly baked. She glanced up as Saga approached.

"Lass? What're ye doing in town?"

"I have to keep working, Olava. I've no choice."

Olava nodded, though her lips were downturned with sorrow. "Aye, I just thought after everything, ye would wait a bit before returning."

"I cannot leave the people without their daily wood," Saga said partly in jest.

Olava did not return the humor. In fact, she seemed despondent. "I am afraid I cannot buy from ye, lass."

"Ye too, Olava?" Saga whispered.

She expected it of everyone else but not Olava.

"I wish I could." Olava swallowed. "Leno has forbidden it. No one can buy from ye."

"Who is Leno?" The words emerged threatening. "He is not our shavka."

"There is no one else fit to lead, lass. After what has happened, most of the village is open to him taking charge."

Saga shook her head. "He will doom us all. He is ready to surrender to the Tariqins. To allow them to torture us as they will. He would willingly sacrifice any of us to save his own skin."

"I agree with ye, lass, but the people are with him. They are holding a meeting right now in the shavka's home. He is discussing ousting ye directly."

Saga had dropped her wood before the last words fell from Olava's mouth, already halfway across the square. She could walk to the shavka's house in her sleep from the number of times she'd journeyed there. Andvora, the girl who used to compete in combat matches with her when they were younger, stiffened outside the large wooden home at her approach. She stood at the door in a guarding position. Her hand slid to her axe. Saga didn't lessen her pace until Andvora cut in front of her.

"Ye cannot enter."

"Do not make me do things I do not want to," Saga said, settling her eyes upon the younger lass in warning.

Andvora drew out her axe. "Ye have done enough, Saga. We do not want ye here any longer. Yer presence brings us death and pain."

"Get out of my way," Saga ground out.

Andvora hesitated for a moment before her determination took over and she swung her axe. It cut through the air with a speed that Saga reciprocated, her own axe whipping out from her belt. The two weapons clanged, and then Saga manipulated her axe to hook over Andvora's, using the edge to yank the weapon from the lass's hand. Andvora stared at her axe as it went flying. Saga patted her arm.

"Put equal weight in yer arms when ye swing. It will not be so easy to disarm ye then."

Andvora sputtered as Saga swept past her into the shavka's home. She halted in the slight entryway, where raised voices drifted toward her from the cramped space in the main room. Leno's disparaging tone cut through them as he spewed the same rubbish about her that he'd told Britta earlier.

"Saga is cursed. We all know it. We will aid ourselves by removing her from the village before she does us more harm."

Ayes rang about. A pang hit her at the full agreement. These were her neighbors, the people she'd considered family, and yet they wished to feed her to the wolves.

"That is the only way we will survive this storm. The Tariqins will leave us be once we give her to them. We can continue on as before."

"For how long?"

Saga's voice carried as she stepped into the room. The conversation stilled. Her neighbors wheeled about on their chairs. Leno's mouth parted, and his preaching finger froze in the air. He stood, looking down upon the others as though he'd been granted leadership already. Britta was right beside him. But she was only his shadow. Saga's hurt at her friend's choice turned to pity. Did she not see that Leno valued nothing above himself?

"How long will they leave ye in peace? Until winter ends? Until the Imperials press against them and they need to replenish their forces? Until they decide our sons and fathers and brothers aren't enough and they come to take the rest of us?"

Saga stared directly at Leno before her gaze slid to Britta. They both watched with open mouths. "Ye may sacrifice me now and someone else the next time. But it will never end. Do ye not see that?"

Nods circulated and disgruntled mutters broke out amongst the crowd. Leno snapped his jaw shut before addressing her.

"And what do ye propose, Saga Barindaughter? What is the way to our salvation?"

Saga paused, feeling fully the weight of the stares upon her. She could feel it for the first time, even if they couldn't. Even if all they felt was terror at the inevitable return of the Tariqins, Saga sensed something she had buried deep within her long ago. Something that had fluttered back to existence at Honzio's arrival. *Hope.*

"I will tell ye this—"

Boots thundered into the home behind her, and a man staggered into the room. Saga broke off her sentence, dread filling the pit of her stomach as his features came into view. Murmurs of surprise and suspicion rang about.

"It's your mam, Saga." Honzio braced his arm against the wall as he heaved in breaths. "She is very ill."

25

ARIA
KARALIK EMPIRE

W HO ARE YOU, *viila? Tell me your name.*

The words lingered between them. Aria's face and arm flamed at the Savorian's touch. His fingers still gripped her chin and wrapped around her wrist, nearly heaving her against him.

"Release me," Aria muttered.

Svorgin stared at her with eyes the color of a midnight sky that contained the fury of a storm. "Why did the Elders send you?"

"Lower your voice," Aria hissed, glancing over her shoulder at the Blade's troop.

They were all focused on the ground, searching. The Blade had disappeared for several minutes, but he'd just returned from the trees, along with a redhaired man. The Blade's eyes caught on them, and Svorgin released her. His brows lowered before his attention returned to the ground. "There was an entrance here. It may have been covered by dirt over the years. Dig."

The troop got to work extracting their tools and cleaving the earth free from the area the Blade directed them to. Before long, the spot was cleared. The Blade crouched on his knees and reached down to heave a hidden door open. It groaned in protest, as if irritated at being awakened from a century of sleep.

"From this point on, we won't need our horses," the Blade announced.

The rest of his troop slapped their horses' rumps, sending the mounts heading back to the castle. Aria moved toward Vandal. The horse nickered low and moved his head so he could stare down at her with his large eye. She smiled and ran her fingers over his coat. Seeing him had sent a sort of peace through her. Vandal had stuck by her brother's side when she'd seen them all those months ago, a loyal horse through and through. And when her brother had passed, he must have gone in search of him. Alone, just like she was. But at least they'd found each other, even if it was only for a few hours.

Aria wrapped her arms around Vandal's muscular neck, holding him close as she whispered her farewells. She pulled away, and Vandal's large eye blinked, and Aria swore she could see sadness there. Then Vandal reared up and, with a harsh whinny, took off into the trees. Aria touched her chest, feeling the pounding of her aching heart beneath her palm. She glanced at the Blade, who had frozen in his crouch above the hidden door. His eyes locked on Vandal until he faded out of sight.

"What are you doing?" Svorgin called.

The Blade didn't deign to reply, his gaze cold as he glanced at them before he hopped down through the door. Aria gasped and moved forward on instinct. The troop went as well—one by one since the size of the entrance would not permit more. They shoved Svorgin down and then Aria. A wave of unease gripped her as she descended into the dark hole, while another part of her was excited to discover the depths below. Large hands gripped her waist and placed her on solid ground. Aria nearly thanked the person until she noted it was Svorgin. Nevertheless, even if it had been a captor, they didn't deserve her gratitude any more than he did.

"Chain them, lest they attempt to escape."

The Blade's voice was followed by his intense presence. Torchlight brought his cold features into view. His troop did as ordered and produced chains, clamping one around Aria's wrist and the other end around Svorgin's. The Savorian cursed and gripped the metal encasing. His skin beneath was rough and broken from his previous chains. Aria groaned inwardly. This would make escape even harder.

Three identical men led the way, torches in hand as they examined the narrow walls on either side of them. "The Hounds," she'd heard the Blade refer to them as. They were the guides, it seemed, calling for breaks every so often as they determined which way to go, judging by the softness of the ground and walls, the scent, and often checking the map the Blade carried with him. He walked directly behind them, barking commands and sharing his opinions on their suggestions. Behind the

Blade was his second-in-command. Aria deduced him to be his second because of the way he stuck by him. His flitting gaze was rooted to the Blade, a trace of unease marking his brow. His red hair stuck up and appeared aflame from the torchlight casting shadows upon the tunnel walls.

"Move!" The sharp voice was followed by a shove.

Aria stumbled forward, bumping into Svorgin. She scowled back and was met with a fierce glare from a small woman. The Mole was her name. Her stare was piercing and didn't miss a detail. She prodded Aria again, forcing her forward. The group's pace quickened as the Hounds got a better feel for the tunnels. Five more men walked behind the Mole. Their uniforms blended in with the darkness, the sole patch of blue in the center of each of their chests appearing like a twinkling star. The Hounds stopped when confronted by a fork in the path and consulted with the Blade's map.

"What were these tunnels used for?" Svorgin whispered.

Her Elder training hadn't been for nothing. She'd gleaned as much knowledge as she could.

"Prolus's spies dug them long ago. A way into the Empire after Emperor Malus had the Drivy constructed. They couldn't get through the Borderland wall, so they went under it. It took many long years to finish, but once they did, they had tunnels that led into Verin and many other places. That was how his Chishmans traveled into the Empire undetected. There are tunnels that go all the way to the Qistool, I've heard."

Svorgin shook his head in disgust. "Nothing ever stopped the Dark Lord when he wanted something."

"But once the Borderlands were conquered and the Drivy destroyed, there wasn't much use for the tunnels. Especially once the Imperials discovered a few entryways and made guarding posts there to catch Chishmans."

"Why didn't the Tariqins seal the tunnels if they'd been discovered?" Svorgin asked.

Aria shrugged. "I believe they did seal a few when they realized the Imperials had found them, but most, they kept purposely open."

"Why?"

A screech emerged from the distance, too far to be dangerous but disturbing enough to raise the hair on her arms. They all froze. Aria swallowed and realized she had stepped closer to Svorgin. She gathered herself and cleared her throat.

"They filled certain tunnels with creatures created by their Shadow Manos to ensure the Imperials could not delve through them."

Svorgin shot her a horrified look. "By *creatures*, you mean?"

"I never saw them, but it was another mutilated creation of the Shadow Manos. A mixture of a bat and a bird. Instant death if touched by its claws or beak."

"Oludrake."

Aria flinched at the new voice. The Blade had hung back from the lead and appeared before them.

"It was one of the queen's designs."

Aria gave him a look. "So she has been aiding Prolus for that long."

He ignored this. "The oludrakes are nothing compared to what lives in the Qistool." He glanced at Svorgin. "But if it is as empty as you say, we have nothing to worry about."

Svorgin nodded, forcing his mouth to curve into an easy grin. "Of course. Which is why you may as well release us. You can find it well enough on your own."

The Blade shook his head. "Oh no. We need your direct guidance."

Aria couldn't tell if that was a play at humor or if the Blade was being utterly serious.

The Hounds called for him, and the Blade returned to their side as they debated which path in the fork to follow. Aria's bones were aching, and her stomach rumbled. They had eaten once in the past hours of traveling. By the growling in her belly, it felt like weeks had elapsed since she'd filled it. She slumped down on a large rock. The Blade's troop used the opportunity to drink water, none of which they spared for Svorgin or Aria. Aria stared at the flickering torches, wishing for the warmth of the fire. She rubbed her arms to dispel some of the aching in her limbs. Svorgin sank to his knees before her. He had little choice in the matter. If he had remained standing, he would've been forced to bend his back because of the chain securing them together.

"You are cold," he said.

"I've been worse." Part of her was still annoyed at him for his brusque ways. But she knew they had no choice but to rely on each other. If they were to escape, they would do so together. She needed him just as much as he needed her.

His hands slid over hers. Aria stiffened as he enveloped her fingers and palms. He lifted her hands to his mouth and blew warmth into them. He appeared so wholly concentrated on bringing life back to her fingers. For the first time, Aria didn't feel the urge to fight. She remained still, utterly befuddled, and then realized she was softening to this large oaf.

"Aria." The word slipped from her mouth.

He stopped his ministrations and glanced up at her. "What?"

"My name is Aria."

His eyes creased. "It suits you."

She found herself confessing other truths. Of her brother, Velamir, whom she found Svorgin had also been acquainted with. He nodded, taking in all her words with a somber expression when she told him of her brother's passing.

"I want to honor his last request and find his friend Jaxon. And if I can, I wish to avenge him."

Svorgin's fingers tightened around hers. "He was a good sort. I am sad to know he is gone. You will keep your promise to him."

He seemed so certain when he said the words.

"How can you be sure?"

He smiled. "You do not look like a quitter, *viila*."

Aria found herself smiling in return. "I gave you my name so you would stop calling me that."

"Oh no." He smirked. "It will be stuck with you forever."

Forever. How long was forever when they were

living in a one-day world? Aria pushed aside the damp thoughts. "You still haven't told me what it means."

"You are welcome to guess."

"It is an insult. You have made that apparent already."

He gave an overdramatic nod in reply.

"Imbecile?"

He shook his head. "Not exactly."

"Fool? Idiot? Is it an animal? Chicken? Hog?"

"Wrong to all of those."

"That's rubbish!" Aria exclaimed.

"Getting closer."

She released a frustrated breath. "You are an oaf."

"You've made that clear."

She yanked her hands out of his and regretted it at once when the cold came back into her fingers. But then a strange fluttering on the tunnel ceiling caught her eye.

"But why is oaf a bad thing? Typically, large and muscular men are referred to by it," Svorgin continued droning on. "I clearly fit the criteria—although I am possibly among if not *the* smartest man you have ever laid eyes on."

"Be silent," Aria hissed.

Svorgin gave her an affronted look. "No need to get offended. It is true. I may be an oaf, but I am the best-looking and possess the most brains you've ever see—"

Aria clawed at his arm. "Svorgin."

He finally stilled and looked up, following her gaze to where at least two dozen pairs of unblinking red eyes peered down at them.

26

Svorgin
Karalik Empire
Tunnels

THE CEILING WAS alive. The creatures shifted, and their wings fluttered, but their eyes never slipped from their prey. Svorgin bit back the surge of panic and grasped Aria's hand, hefting her up from the rock she'd been sitting on. For the first time, she didn't complain about his manhandling. Her focus was rooted on the creatures, just as his was.

"What are you doing?" Fox, a member of the Blade's troop, asked.

"Those bat things. What were they called?"

"The oludrake?" Fox questioned. "No need to get your knickers in a twist. They aren't in this tunnel, or we would've been dead by now."

Aria shook her head. "They like to hunt. To play with their quarry."

The words sent more concern through Svorgin.

Another of Blade's men huffed a laugh. "It's just a story. They probably don't even exist."

There was a screech, and the man launched onto the ground. Svorgin stumbled back, yanking Aria against him. She clutched at his tunic to find her balance, and they both watched in horror at the enormous creature mounted on the man's face. Black wings spanned a great distance, the right almost touching Svorgin's leg. A long beak slammed down into the shrieking man's face, burying into the tissue and cutting off his shouts for good. The beak emerged coated in blood, and the oludrake chewed the flesh with satisfied slurps. Svorgin forgot how to breathe during the horrific moment.

The Mole reached for her sword, but the Blade lifted a hand, and she stilled.

"That will not stop them. We must run."

An endless moment of silence reigned until one man stepped back, and the sound echoed. The oludrake's head swiveled, and sharp red eyes fastened upon the man. Svorgin's blood chilled.

"Run!"

At the Blade's shout, the company erupted into movement. Svorgin pressed forward, pulling Aria with him. They moved alongside the Blade, approaching the fork ahead.

"Which path?" Svorgin shouted.

He glanced back. The swarm of oludrakes was descending. The creatures screeched and latched onto several of the troop at the back. Screams tore through the air.

"Which path?" Svorgin shouted again, desperate.

"The third." The Blade seemed uncertain, and Svorgin shot him a bewildered glance. "The third," he repeated with more conviction.

Svorgin didn't hesitate, lunging toward it, but a sudden weight yanked him down. He stumbled, and the pressure brought him to his knees. Aria was sprawled on the floor. She heaved herself up and started running again.

"You big oaf." She groaned. "At least give me a warning before you go barreling off."

Although he enjoyed sparring words with her, there was no time at present. The oludrakes were swarming closer, their wings flapping as they glided down from the ceiling just above their heads. Aria was a fast runner, but the fall had hurt her, dampening her speed. They would be the next morsels if they didn't pick up the pace. Svorgin reached for her.

"What are you doing?"

She shrieked as he hefted her up onto his shoulder and continued barreling down the tunnel. The Blade's troop had disappeared along with their torches, leaving the pathway in total darkness. Still, Svorgin moved onward, praying he wouldn't slam into a wall—or worse, encounter an oludrake from the opposite direction. Beating wings and screeching beaks were just behind him, pressing on his neck.

"In here, Savorian!"

At the shout, Svorgin veered right. He plowed through another tunnel, and when he emerged, he saw the Blade and company gathered, their faces highlighted by the glows of their torches.

"Duck!" the Blade ordered.

Svorgin threw himself toward the ground while shifting Aria to fall on top of him instead of landing on the hard floor. The Blade flicked a vial open and tossed it into the tunnel behind them. That was quickly followed by a torch. The entryway burst into flames and black smoke. Petrifying screeches emerged from the tunnel, and in the smoke, oludrakes fell to the ground in dying lumps.

"Keep moving!" the Blade yelled.

They rushed into another tunnel and didn't stop until they were no longer being pursued. Svorgin carried Aria the entire way. The Blade called everyone to halt. Svorgin sighed in relief and deposited Aria to the floor.

"Thank you," she said, staring up at him.

Svorgin shook his head. "Don't thank me. I just didn't fancy parting with my arm."

She scowled and looked away. Svorgin called to the Blade.

"Why didn't you use that potion earlier?"

"Because I have strict orders. The vial was supposed to be saved for the Qistool."

At the mention of the fallen kingdom, a queasiness returned and gripped Svorgin's belly. Aria sank against the tunnel wall.

"How long have we been traveling? It feels like years have passed."

"We have almost reached the second day," the Blade answered.

No wonder Svorgin felt so exhausted. He could curl up on the hard, rocky ground and drift off if given the chance. His stomach rumbled. "The least you can do is give us some food. Or do you wish us to starve before we reach our destination?"

The Blade nodded his chin toward Fox, who'd been carrying the supplies. "We have enough rations now that we are down five men."

A bag was tossed at Svorgin, and he handed it to Aria. There was only one flask of water within. Svorgin uncapped it and gave it to Aria. She muttered what he assumed was a thanks before she began drinking. Svorgin watched her, swallowing the dryness in his own mouth. She downed half the water in moments, parts of precious liquid trickling down her chin. Svorgin's mouth parted. His own thirst demanded he take the flask before she could finish it, but his mam had taught him better than that. He tore his gaze away, staring at the wall across from him as he tried to distract himself.

Something cold grazed his hand. Svorgin turned as Aria placed the flask in his palm.

"Your turn," she said.

She had left half for him.

"Do not thank me," she said, no doubt seeing his surprise. "I have no wish to drag about your dead body, and I don't exactly fancy parting with my arm either."

A laugh built in Svorgin's chest, burning up his throat until he let it loose. The chuckle burst into the tunnel— a joyful sound he doubted these dark, cavernous walls had ever heard before. The noise drew several irritated looks their way. Svorgin lifted the flask toward Aria in a dramatic motion before he brought it to his lips. The liquid was cold and refreshing, awakening all his senses.

He nearly finished the entire thing but managed to stop himself. He tucked the flask into the pack.

Svorgin examined Aria, following the patterns of dirt lining her face, the ends of her lashes brushing her skin, her long pointed chin jutting out as if to challenge the wall across from her. Even with her exhaustion and the dirt, she still carried that ethereal quality about her.

"I am not particularly fond of people staring," she muttered.

"Feel free to return the favor at any time. I, myself, quite enjoy being looked upon."

Aria sighed. Loudly. "I cannot believe how arrogant you are. After everything you've been through. How can you jest so easily?"

Svorgin leaned closer to her. "Because without laughter and cheer, what is the purpose of life? Shall I be doomed to live in darkness and misery because of what I've faced?" He shook his head. Aria turned toward him, those clever green eyes fastening on his. "I may have been a prisoner most of my life, but they cannot chain my very being."

She blinked, her eyes welling. Svorgin was utterly earnest as he held her gaze.

"I will not allow myself to remain captive. Even if it's only a smile or a laugh. They cannot take that from me."

Aria lifted her cuffed wrist and placed her hand over his. "You are right. I didn't understand."

They sat like that for hours as they waited for the Blade's orders. Svorgin babbled about his childhood and his family. Aria listened, and before long, she leaned against him. Svorgin froze, wondering at the meaning of the movement. He looked down, and through the light of the torches, he realized she was sleeping. He inwardly cursed himself. *Why else would she rest her head upon your shoulder, you lout? What are you to her? She is a member of the Elders. A group dedicated to saving victims. And what are you? You are a victim in need of saving.*

Svorgin glanced down at the top of her head. The material from the head cap had suffered a few scrapes, and parts of her black hair peeked out from it. He reached for the strands. They were softer than he imagined the finest silk would be. He fought the urge to caress them and instead tucked them back into her cap, safely out of his reach. She murmured something and pressed closer to him.

"Let's get going!" the Blade called out.

Svorgin gently shook her, and her eyes fluttered open. She stared at him in confusion for a long moment, sleep still holding her under.

"Good morning, sunshine." Svorgin smirked.

Aria scrambled away, only to fall back against him because of the chain linking them together.

"Insufferable," she hissed, then added, "Is it truly morning?"

Svorgin shrugged. "I do not know. We haven't seen the sun in at least a day, remember?"

Aria's shoulders slumped at the reminder.

"You are more tolerable when you sleep," Svorgin said. "Even pretty."

Aria's brows lowered, and her eyes flashed dangerously.

"But your snoring is on another level."

Her jaw dropped open. "I do not snore."

"You do," he insisted.

"I *do not* snore."

He laughed and stood, forcing her to rise with him. "You do."

They heard a scuffle and then a *thump*. The Blade had sunk down into a crouch, with his five remaining companions gathered around him in concern. He grasped his head.

"It is agony," he whispered.

"It will be so for the first few months," Fox told him, trying to help him rise.

"What did you do?" Mole demanded. "Why is he in pain?"

The Hounds glanced at each other, all seeming to realize something as they spoke at once. "The vial. He's not taking the queen's potion."

"You must!" Mole declared. "You are betraying her by not doing so."

The Blade opened his mouth, but then his face tightened, and he collapsed again.

"His vial broke," Fox told Mole. "Do not speak further—unless you wish to give him some of your potion?"

Mole went silent at once, though she still looked on with disapproval. Aria rose, moving closer to them, and because of the chain, Svorgin had no choice but to follow. The Blade looked up when they neared. His eyes fell upon Aria. Svorgin spotted the confusion contorting his face.

"Vel?"

Aria stilled. "What did you say?"

The Blade shook the daze from his eyes and rose. "Nothing. My brain was fogged for a moment."

"No." Aria marched up to him. "You said Vel. Did you know him? Did you know my brother?"

"I don't have the slightest clue what you are talking about." The Blade shook his head, though Svorgin could tell he was concealing something.

"Do not lie to me." Aria stepped even closer. "Who are you to my brother? How do you know him?"

27

H E LOOKED DOWN at the girl with furious eyes who demanded to know how he knew her brother. He swallowed, unable to answer because he did not know himself. Ever since he had first laid eyes upon this woman, his flashbacks of a previous life had worsened. He continued seeing a man with green eyes and an easy smile. The man meant something to him. He knew that much. And just now, after experiencing severe mental torment, the name had come into his mind with such clarity. *Vel.* That is what he'd called him.

"Who was he to you?" the girl probed again.

The words sent a wave of panic over him. He couldn't listen to her, couldn't continue to think about it. It hurt too much. Delving into that past was through a layer of blood and agony he knew he could never break free of. He was safe this way, he tried to convince himself. He was safe not knowing.

"I do not know what you are speaking of," he growled, then shoved the girl into the arms of the Savorian, who was glaring daggers into him. "Let's continue moving."

28

Honzio
Savoria
Vidrun Village

S AGA BRUSHED PAST him. Honzio remained in the house for a moment, regaining his breath after his run to the village. The occupants sitting in the home stared at him before confused mutters erupted.

"Who is he?"

"A foreigner? What is a foreigner doing here?"

"Saga is up to trouble once again."

"That lass will be the death of us."

Honzio stumbled out of the house, leaving the whispers and lingering stares behind. He spotted Saga in the distance. She moved at a rapid pace before breaking into a run. Honzio quickened his own pace to catch up to her. By the time he reached the house, she was already within, where Honzio saw her desperate for the first time. She was gripping her mother's hand between hers.

"I need ye, Mam. Stay strong."

Honzio used to be the one who lingered back in situations, waiting for orders from his father. But since he'd taken over the Empire, he'd broken that habit. He'd taught himself to act. "What can I do?"

Saga sniffled, her eyes red as she glanced at him. She nodded at a shelf. "Her medicine is there."

Honzio reached for the shelf and pulled a flask free. He gave it to Saga, along with a wooden spoon. She carefully lifted her mother's head and directed her to drink the medicine. Her mam was deathly pale, and her thinness didn't help the appearance of her frailness. If Honzio didn't know better, he would've thought he was looking at a corpse. Saga massaged her mother's hands and arms, working to revive her. She muttered prayers, Savorian words Honzio didn't understand. Honzio gave her whatever she needed. Cloth, water, blankets. Then he stirred the pot her mam had been working on before she collapsed upon the floor. He brought in wood to renew the fire, ignoring the sparks that shot out.

"How did it happen?" Saga whispered.

Honzio stilled in dishing out the stew. "We'd been talking when she suddenly collapsed."

Saga nodded. She smoothed the cloth over her mam's head and turned toward him. "The sickness is increasing. I have tried giving her less of the medicine to keep it longer, but it doesn't work. I must continue giving her larger doses."

"You need medicine," Honzio said. "That's what the chopping is for, isn't it?"

Saga looked down, a pained grimace on her face as

she admitted, "I use most of the money I make on the medicine and whatever's left on food. But it doesn't help. Nothing helps."

Her shoulders bowed, and her chin tucked into her chest. She slumped down on the side of her mother's cot, tugging the blanket up higher over her and smoothing it down.

"I will help you," Honzio said.

Saga shook her head, sadness reining in her features. "Some things, ye cannot fix. Some things are too broken, too gone."

A tear slipped from her eyes, surprising Honzio. He'd been growing accustomed to the frigid Savorian woman; it was strange to see her allow emotion free.

"It is me keeping her here. She wants to join my brother and sister. My da. But I am selfish. I cannot let her go."

Honzio recognized the feeling all too well. He placed the bowl down and moved toward her. He had never been one for physical contact, but at that moment, everything in him screamed to comfort her. Before he could think better of it, he pulled her into his arm. She went stiff with surprise. Honzio regretted his brazen action and was just about to release her when she softened against him. She lowered her head, resting it in the crook where his shoulder and neck met. Her breath brushed his skin.

"You are not selfish," he said in a low tone. "You are simply a girl who does not wish to bid her mother farewell."

Her arm slipped up at that and hooked around his waist. And then there was a bang at the door. Saga yanked away from him and turned toward her mother, reaching up to wipe away the runaway tear. The door opened just as Honzio managed to get himself together and stop thinking about how perfect she'd felt within his arm. The large Savorian man Honzio had seen speaking with the woman in the woods strolled inside. Leno. The woman, Britta, came in after him, along with a few other armed Savorian women. Saga reached for her axe, which she had left mounted on the wall. Leno clicked his tongue and pointed his long spear at her.

"Do not even think of it."

"How dare ye come barging into my home," Saga hissed.

"How is yer mam?"

"What do ye care?"

Leno's brows lowered. "It is over, Saga. Ye have done one too many things to bring down our village. To meet the end ye must desperately want. But none of us share yer feelings."

Honzio glanced at the other Savorians that had come in and found the same contempt on their faces as Leno's.

"And now ye have brought a foreign man into the village."

"He has come for a reason—"

"I do not care the slightest. I want him gone. I want both of ye gone. We all do."

Saga peered at the woman beside Leno, but Britta lowered her gaze as though she couldn't bear to look at Saga.

"We will have to restrain ye until the next Tariqin force arrives. Then we will hand ye and the man over."

Honzio reached for the thin kitchen knife. Leno cast him a sharp look, and Honzio froze. A growl erupted from outside the house.

"Call off yer rumlok, Saga," Leno said. "Or I will bring her down. I have ten Savorians aiming arrows at her outside."

Saga shook her head. "How can ye be so cruel? How can ye threaten to kill an animal that is going extinct because of our enemies?"

"I will do what I must," Leno said, unrepentant. "Surrender and no one will be harmed."

Honzio could see the fight in Saga's features. She wanted to battle Leno more than anything but couldn't risk harm befalling her mother and her rumlok.

"Fine," Saga said. "But do not hurt them. And let the man go."

Honzio stiffened. Why was she bargaining for his safety? He'd come here to help her people, not create more difficulty. Leno nodded his chin, and the Savorian women removed Saga's belt. He wrapped rope around her wrists and then tugged her toward the door. She cast a look at her mother. Britta stepped toward Saga's mam.

"Don't worry," Britta said. "I will take care of her."

Leno approached Honzio, sizing him up. A flash of curiosity lit his features. "Who are ye?"

"Why do you want to know? To increase my worth when you hand me over?"

That cracked a smile across the Savorian's face. Saga struggled against the women's hold at Honzio's words.

"Ye promised to let him go!"

"I never agreed to yer terms, if ye recall," Leno said.

"And why would I allow this man to go free when he must have something of value to have traveled so far to our little island?"

"Well, I certainly didn't come for you," Honzio muttered.

Leno's smile vanished, and he gestured for one of the Savorians to bring him more rope. Honzio used the moment to dart for the door.

"Oh no ye don't," Leno called out.

The Savorian grabbed his tunic and hefted him back. Honzio stumbled against the kitchen table, knocking the stew onto the floor. Saga screeched and broke out of the Savorian women's hold even with her hands tied. Leno slammed a fist into Honzio's face. Honzio staggered at the impact. His lip burst, and he tasted the iron tang of blood. Then Leno slammed his head onto the table. Darkness coated Honzio's vision, and when he recovered it, he found his hands were bound. They were taken to the village square and tied to a pole in the center. Their feet were bound as well as an extra measure of precaution.

Leno gave a nod of satisfaction and issued a schedule of Savorians to keep watch over them before he left. Honzio was dazed and lightheaded. The cold was getting to him. Out in the biting chill, with darkness falling, he wondered if he would actually get frostbite this time. Saga was on the opposite side of the pole, but she hadn't lost her fight yet. Not one ounce of it. She grunted and growled, struggling with her ropes and letting out a few curses at any Savorian who looked their way when passing by. Honzio leaned back, placing his head against the pole and hoping that, if nothing else, at least sleep would claim him. His thoughts drifted to Lore and Daghvin once again. Saga would have helped him search for them if the day hadn't gone so wrong.

"These are too blasted tight," Saga grumbled. "I cannot loosen them."

"Well, you Savorians are sailors. I am not surprised they tied an expert knot."

"Are ye really complimenting the knots that are binding us right now?"

Honzio chuckled but turned serious after a moment. "About earlier . . . You don't believe what they say about you, do you?"

Saga stilled her struggling, and he knew she was listening.

"I used to do everything I could to earn my father's approval. One of the things—well, the only thing—he would praise me for was jousting."

"Jousting?" Saga repeated.

Honzio had said the word in his tongue since he didn't know it in theirs.

"It is a game where two riders charge at one another with lances and try to knock each other off their horse."

"Sounds foolish," she muttered. "I am surprised ye haven't broken yer back."

"No, I was lucky. Many faced injuries far worse than mine."

She was silent, then said, "Yer arm."

Honzio nodded. "It never healed properly. And neither did I. I would float about as my father's shadow. Until rumors started spreading. People called me cursed."

Honzio paused. Saga didn't say a word.

"It nagged me for a while. For years, in truth. Their perception of me became my reality. I was captive to their whispers. I was a useless cursed man with a lame arm. And then one day, I stopped listening. Because it wasn't true. None of it."

Honzio glanced toward her, making out the line of her jaw and the muscle flexing in her cheek.

"I don't know what they told you or why it began, but you are not cursed, Saga. In fact, you are the very opposite. You are blessed. You are a fighter. And that's what Savoria needs."

Saga was quiet for so long that Honzio feared he'd insulted her. But then she glanced at him, her face utterly serious.

"Thank ye." There was no bitterness in the two words. Only gratefulness, as though he'd pulled her out of a well of self-doubt only she could see.

She sniffed and cleared her throat. Her nose and cheeks were pink from the rough wind and cold. She glanced at the Savorian women on watch. Honzio followed her gaze and saw they were laughing together and not paying the slightest bit of attention to their prisoners.

"I have a gold pin in my hair. It is sharp enough to cut our bindings."

Honzio nodded, and when she stared at him expectantly, he tilted his head. "And how can we get it?"

"Clearly, I cannot," Saga said, sarcasm filling her tone as she nodded down to her bound hands. "Shift closer to me."

Honzio kept his eyes on the Savorians on watch as he pivoted around the pole. His arm burned at the movement because of the awkward way it was bound. He continued moving until his shoulder bumped against Saga's.

"Quickly," she said and tilted her head toward him.

It was easy to see the pin. It sparkled in the center of her braid, keeping the shorter pieces of her hair in place. Honzio leaned toward it and clamped his teeth around it. His nose buried into her hair, and the smell of sweet flowers engulfed him. He froze for a moment that seemed to shift into eternity, basking in the scent.

"Honzio," Saga hissed. "What are ye doing?"

Her voice snapped him into action, and he pulled the pin free before he did something ridiculous. Like burying his nose into the mass of her golden hair again.

Saga lifted her bound hands farther up, and Honzio dropped the pin into them. She worked fast and, despite cutting herself several times, didn't lessen her pace. Before long, she'd severed the rope and was doing the same for him. Time passed, and the Savorians barely looked at them. Honzio rolled his wrists once his bindings were off. Saga stood and reached down to pull him up. Together, they slinked off toward the forest.

"I need to check on my mam, and then we can go looking for yer friends. Perhaps my people will start listening once they see all of ye."

Honzio nodded, praying his men had survived. They had barely made it to the tree line when cries of alarm started up.

"Leno! They've escaped!"

Honzio and Saga exchanged a look and then dashed into the woods.

29

Saga

Savoria

Vidrun Village

S AGA TORE PAST the trees, her chest heaving with vicious breaths that colored the air white. Branches cracked alongside her as Honzio struggled to keep pace. He didn't know the forest like she did. Didn't know how to bend to its will and allow it to shield him. She skidded to the left and grabbed hold of his shirt, yanking him into the shadow of a large tree. He stumbled against the oak just as her back hit the trunk. A low branch cut into her cheek beneath her eye. She winced, the burn spreading through her skin, and the hot trickle of blood wormed its way down her face.

Boots tore past as Leno and his accomplices searched for them. Saga leaned closer to Honzio. He took a step back, his boot crushing a twig. The snap echoed. Saga's head swung toward their pursuers. Most had disappeared into the foliage ahead. All but Leno, who stood frozen, his ears attuned to the surrounding noise. He pivoted and focused on their tree. His eyes would adjust in a matter of moments, and then he would see them.

"Come on," Saga breathed out and shoved Honzio into motion.

They sprinted into the tangle of trees. A shout echoed behind them as Leno called for reinforcements. Saga's eyes grazed the familiar trail, and her heart pattered when she realized where they were heading, but she didn't allow her swelling fear to stop her. She continued until the sound of rushing water reached her. She stumbled to a halt just before the edge of the waterfall. Honzio was staring behind him and nearly toppled down into the blue depths. Saga grasped his tunic, and he flailed his arms, a terrified shout escaping him as he dangled for a singular moment before she hauled him back onto solid ground. He cast her a worried glance.

"Where do we go now?"

Saga didn't answer and instead turned to the rustling leaves as Leno burst into view, the faces of her once neighbors and friends flanking him. The women wielded their weapons in intense grips, the flint in their eyes just as unrepentant. They would use force, draw blood if they had to. Leno lifted his arms, opening them on either side as though to welcome her.

"Ye do not have to do this, Saga." His voice was cheery, with an odd brightness to it that sent chills down her spine. "Ye have caused enough trouble."

"I will not be a sacrifice for yer game," Saga spat out.

Leno shook his head, his arms dropping. "Ye wouldn't be a sacrifice, Saga. Ye would be a savior. We would remember ye as such. All yer past crimes will no longer matter if we hand ye over to the Tariqins. Because of ye, yer people will live unharmed."

"Do not believe him," she told the women standing alongside him. But they didn't heed her. Instead, they inched closer and closer with Leno as he approached. Saga glanced at the waterfall. The rushing water deafened her. It sped down in a luscious sparkling blue cascade and looked far more welcoming than Leno's twisted words and open arms.

"We can work this out, Saga."

Saga stepped farther back. Her boots sent rocks showering over the edge into the spray of water. Leno frowned, paling as she edged closer. Honzio glanced at her in disbelief. Saga reached for him, clasping his hand in hers.

"Do ye trust me?"

Honzio stared at her, wide-eyed. "Not particularly."

"Saga . . . what are ye doing? Do not be foolish," Leno said.

"Good," she whispered and then lurched down into the spray, taking Honzio with her.

30

ARIA STARED AT Blade's back as he strode away. Though he hadn't answered her, her question had unsettled him. Perhaps he knew what happened to Velamir's friend Jax.

Svorgin looked at her. "You all right?"

She nodded, brushing her dress off after Blade's brutal shove. "We need to get away from the group."

"You think I haven't thought of that?" Svorgin said, keeping his voice low. "But how can we? We've gone too far, and the way back is through those oludrakes."

Aria grimaced. "We have no choice. If you recall, they plan to murder us."

"Let's move!" the Blade boomed from ahead, and the Hounds shoved them forward.

Aria stumbled and barely righted herself. She shot the triplets a scowl and continued forward. They moved nonstop. Aria plotted the entire while. The comforting feel of her karambit lingered in her sleeve. Thankfully, it had gone unnoticed. She racked her mind, considering different escape methods. They couldn't go back, as Svorgin had said. And she couldn't attack their captors until Blade guided them out of the tunnels—though the darkness of the tunnels may have given her a slight advantage if she ambushed them. Then there was the matter of the chain linking her to Svorgin. Any attack they tried would fail because of how differently they each fought. They would likely end up injuring each other rather than their captors.

The Blade stopped at the end of the tunnel and heaved a door open above him. A sliver of light appeared. He hefted himself up and out of sight. A rush of anticipation gripped her. She couldn't wait to feel the sun on her skin and to be away from the dampness coating the tunnels and creating a rotten scent. They were lifted up, and much to Aria's disappointment, the sky was gloomy and soulless.

"There is no sun," she said sadly.

"There never is," the Blade muttered. "Tariqi's skies have long been darkened due to the creations of the Shadow Manos."

"How do you know this? Have you been here before?"

A panicked expression overtook the Blade, as though he himself wondered how he knew. He cleared his features. "It is common knowledge."

Svorgin nodded. "It is far better than it was when I was here years ago. The Shadow Manos's innovations polluted the air. But without their craft, Prolus would not have been able to take so many kingdoms."

"Eight," Aria said. "Eight kingdoms."

"Exactly."

The Blade waved his hand, and the group proceeded. Aria slowed her pace, feigning exhaustion. Svorgin walked beside her, and the Hounds moved past them, apparently tired of urging them faster. Blade and his companions checked on them every so often, but their eyes were more focused on the map and their destination.

"Do you know where Tariqi's harbor is?" Aria whispered.

Svorgin nodded. "Yes, I was brought to the Empire by ship."

"Good. Once they stop for rest, let's escape."

He scratched his neck with his free hand. "I do not know the exact coordinates. It happened so long ago. I can only guess at the location."

That wouldn't do. They had to be able to reach the harbor as fast as possible without any confusion on the path, or else the Blade would find them.

"The map," she said, lowering her voice further when Mole glanced over her shoulder at them. "We need to steal the Blade's map. But how?"

The Blade tilted his map up, examining it with apparent frustration. They were surrounded by endless dry land and foggy mist. She jerked her chin toward the Blade as she returned to her conversation with Svorgin.

"See how possessive he is of it?"

Blade's fingers seemed to caress the map as he tucked it into his tunic and turned to speak with Fox. Svorgin nodded at Aria and then moved toward them. Aria trailed along, barely keeping up with his long strides.

"You will not get what you seek," Svorgin called.

Blade and Fox halted their conversation and turned to face them. Mole crossed her arms, and the Hounds watched with the same sly smile on all their faces.

Blade's brows lowered. "What do you mean?"

"The crown isn't in the Qistool. I just said it was because I wanted your queen to suffer when she couldn't find it."

The Blade strode to Svorgin and grabbed his collar, yanking him close and probing his face with those ice-cold eyes. "Watch your mouth when you speak about Her Majesty. What game are you playing?"

Aria watched the interaction, the tension building with every passing moment.

"The crown is not within those walls. But if you release us, I will tell you its true location."

Blade hissed. "Another lie? Why don't I just kill you now?"

"Because Her Majesty would not approve." Svorgin grinned. He reached out, tapping the Blade's chest for emphasis. "You are her mutt. You cannot even make one decision without her consent."

The Blade's fist plowed into Svorgin, sending him to the ground. The chain rattled between them, digging into her wrist and yanking her down beside Svorgin. Blade shoved Svorgin down, looming over him as he landed another blow to his face. Blood poured from Svorgin's nose. They rolled across the ground, wrestling for the upper hand. Aria was stuck in the fray, her hand an instant from being torn off her wrist. The metal cut into her from the pressure and drew crimson forth.

"Blade!" Mole shouted. "Can't you see? He's goading you."

Blade froze, then scowled and pushed off Svorgin.

"I know you despise her. That is why you are lying to me now. You will do anything to stop her from getting the crown. But it is in the Qistool as you first said. We have come this far. I will not turn back."

"You are making a mistake."

Blade raised his hand, pointing a long finger at Svorgin. "If you continue to protest, it will be *you* making a mistake. Choose your words wisely if you wish to survive." Blade glanced at his companions. "We will rest here for a few hours."

Fox produced bedrolls from his pack, and Mole started a fire. The Hounds stared at Svorgin and Aria without wavering as they settled on the ground.

"You're hurt," Aria said, wincing at the blood still pouring from his nostrils.

He smiled. "Worried about me, *viila*?"

She scoffed but tore off part of her dress and dabbed at his face. She felt his gaze upon her, warm and searching. Though he did annoy her at times, Aria was grateful he was with her. It was far less terrifying than being alone. For alone she'd been many times. When she was a young girl, closed off in a secret passage for hours. Even when she'd found the Elders. Though they'd welcomed her and cared for her and loved her, she'd still missed her own family lost to her forever. But she'd been especially lonely when she went on missions, occupied with all her worries and doubts.

"I am glad you are here," she said before she could think better of it.

Svorgin's eyes creased. "I never thought I would say this, but so am I."

She plugged his nose and tilted his head up. The bleeding had lessened. "What were you thinking by goading Blade into a fight? Now he is more watchful."

"Just a wee bit of a distraction." Svorgin winked.

Aria tilted her head. "Wha—"

Her mouth parted when he opened a portion of his tunic, revealing the edge of Blade's map tucked safely within. Aria smiled and shook her head.

"Come on. I am awaiting your praises," Svorgin said, his voice emerging strange because she was still pressing the torn fabric to his nose. "You can call me all the names I know are running through your mind right now. Talented, intelligent, gifted, has an unnatural capacity for genius ideas." He waved his hand to signify a continuing list of attributes.

Aria rolled her eyes. "A foolish oaf without a care for his life."

"And don't forget handsome. A handsome, foolish oaf."

She chuckled and shook her head again. A shadow fell upon them, and they looked up to see Fox holding out two bedrolls.

"We had extra," he said.

Aria took them, nodding at Fox as she tried to overcome her surprise. The man scratched the back of his head and trudged away. The time slipped by. Aria and Svorgin lay upon the bedrolls, waiting. One by one, the Hounds dozed off, their snores equally rambunctious. Mole sat watch, her gaze narrow and fixed upon them. Aria fluttered her lashes closed, hoping the woman bought the act. Fox succumbed to his exhaustion next. Blade didn't seem to sleep, his eyes wide and icy as he stared at the small fire. Eventually, he rolled onto his side, blocking his face from view. Aria groaned inwardly. Now they wouldn't be able to tell when he was sleeping. Mole's head hung forward and then snapped up again. She shook herself and pinched her own arm. But despite her efforts, she couldn't stop herself from at last surrendering to sleep.

Aria nudged Svorgin, and he nodded. This was their chance. They had the map and an opportunity they couldn't pass up. They slinked away and tore down a hill, putting distance between them and the camp. There was open land as far as she could see; if they didn't move fast, they would be obvious targets. They raced through the fog. The cold wind bit into her skin, and the chain rattled between her and Svorgin. An arrow sliced the air above her head. Aria ducked and continued sprinting. Svorgin quickened his speed. He glanced back.

"They've caught on."

Shouts echoed as their pursuers chased. Another arrow grazed her ear. Aria cried out and tumbled onto the ground. Svorgin's heavy weight collapsed on top of her, and all the air in her lungs huffed out of her.

"Aria? Are you hurt?"

She shoved his chest. "I wasn't until you fell on me."

He lifted himself and looked down at her. He touched her ear and winced. "That doesn't look so good."

His hand came away covered in red, and her belly turned queasy at the crimson dripping from his fingers. The pain in her ear crept into focus.

"You fools." Blade's bitter voice sank into her senses.

"We are surrounded, aren't we?" she asked Svorgin.

He gave her a small nod, tearing his midnight eyes from hers to glance around them. The Blade's troop had formed a circle around them.

"Where did you plan to go? There is nothing here for miles."

Aria stood, holding her ear to stem the bleeding. "I thought you have never been here before. How do you know that?"

Blade grabbed Svorgin and ripped his map from his tunic. He waved the parchment at her face. "Perhaps because I have been examining one of these and not wandering about following the tip of my nose. Next time, be a bit cleverer."

Aria winced, more concerned about the blood pooling in her palm than his ranting.

"You almost killed her!" Svorgin growled, hands fisting at his sides.

"If you had behaved and not gone running in search of death, that wouldn't have happened." Blade's mouth twisted, and he reached into his bag. "Come here."

Aria hesitated, but she was not about to refuse another healing potion. But instead of the gold sparkling vial she'd been expecting, the Blade withdrew a needle and thread.

Aria's breath trembled at the sight. The Blade stepped closer. She eyed the needle until it moved out of view. Then she felt it, the sharp point digging into her flesh. Her eyes squeezed shut, and she clamped her lips together to hold in her scream. She gritted her teeth and grabbed on to something solid. For an eternity, the needle wove in and out, sealing the rip in her ear. Until finally, the Blade broke the thread with his teeth and tied it closed.

Aria opened her eyes. A tear slid free. She wiped it away with a bloody hand and then realized she had been grasping on to Svorgin the entire time. His arm had turned pale and bloodless from her hold, and she could see prints where her fingers had dug into his skin. She gave him an apologetic wince and then turned to the Blade.

"Queen Guin trained you to be a healer as well?"

The Blade tucked his supplies away. "I believe I must have always had the skill. But every warrior should know how to tend a wound. Especially if there isn't a True Manos about to help them."

"You *believe* . . ." The words nagged her until she realized: "You don't remember anything about your past, do you?"

The Blade shifted uncomfortably.

"That is what you wanted from the queen."

His eyes snapped to hers, angry. "You were listening."

Aria stepped toward him. "What did she do to you?"

But like before, he brushed her off. "Keep four eyes on these two. We make for the Qistool. Let us reach it before dark."

Aria glanced at the sky overhead. How could he

even tell whether it was day or night? The thunderous clouds gathered, ominous and heavy. She could see no sun, no moon, no trace of stars to determine the time of day. Aria and Svorgin were placed in the middle of the group; they weren't taking any more chances. Before long, tall walls came into view. Walls she had only heard about in hushed whispers. They were higher than any she had ever seen. The entire group stilled at the sight of the Qistool.

"Hurry," Blade ordered.

They moved faster toward the looming walls. The Qistool was sealed all around, not a gate in sight. A hideous carving marked the stone, the phrase repeatedly etched by a blade's tip. Aria couldn't read the words.

"What does it say?"

It was the Blade that answered. "It is in the old Tariqin text. It says, 'Death resides within.'"

Aria shivered, and not because of the sudden gust of wind that swept over them. They waited a moment, all eyes rooted on the foreboding sight, before the Blade barked out, "We climb."

31

FOX PRODUCED ROPED hooks from his pack. There was a metal hoop at the top of each hook. Blade got into position, bow and arrow ready. Fox tossed the rope into the air, and Blade's arrow released, the point flicking through the hoop and dragging it over the wall, where the hooks clamped around the stone high above. They continued the same way, until eight ropes dangled down the wall. Blade was a good shot, Svorgin thought, a very good shot. He had only seen one person who had been as good an archer. Aria's brother, Velamir.

Mole motioned to him and Aria. She wrapped the ends of the ropes around their waists. Fox grabbed Svorgin's leg, hefting it up so he could access his boot, where he attached a triangular metal blade.

"What are you doing?" Svorgin said.

"Helps with the climb," Fox provided before adding the metal to the bottom of Aria's shoes.

The Hounds went first, starting the grueling clamber upward. They went one at a time, per Blade's orders. Each one gripped their individual rope with eyes focused on the top of the wall. Once they'd made it a good distance, Blade nodded at Svorgin.

"You two are next. You will go up together."

Svorgin noted Blade was wisely putting them between his troop so they would be boxed in the center, unable to escape.

"Together?" Aria sputtered. "How can we climb that way? At least unchain us."

Blade shook his head. "I have risked enough with you two. It will be as I say."

Mole adjusted their ropes, circling them around both their middles. Svorgin found himself pressed even closer to Aria. Their faces were inches apart. Aria winced when Mole tied the rope into a harsh knot.

"You won't have time to try anything foolish because you will be too occupied keeping yourselves alive," Blade said. "Up you go."

Svorgin didn't have much choice but to do as ordered unless he wanted to receive one of those vicious arrows to the heart. He grasped the rope and heaved upward. He stabbed the metal points into the cracks between the stone wall, using them to aid him in the climb and to keep himself from falling.

"You might want to hold on to me," he told Aria.

"Like I have any other choice," she grumbled.

He hauled them farther up. Aria gasped as she looked down at the increasing distance from the ground. Her free arm snaked around him, and she placed her face into his tunic. Svorgin watched the climbers above him, emulating their movements, and concentrated on keeping himself steady. But he'd only crossed a fourth of the wall when his arms began to tremble. Lifting Aria's weight along with his own was no simple task. His muscles ached, and sweat trickled down his brow. He worried he would lose his mind if he thought about the strain in his arms any longer.

"Distract me," he said.

"What?" Aria mumbled against his tunic.

"Say something."

Her head lifted, and her eyes grazed his face. Her brows lowered when she saw the struggle in his features. "There are so many tales about the beginning of the war between Tariqi and the Empire. There is the version the Imperial children have memorized. A tale they spout of how they cared for the Tariqins and gave them whatever they wished, but Tariqi's cruel Dark Lord betrayed them and took over their lands."

Aria's calming voice took Svorgin's attention away from the shaking in his arms. He slammed his boots into the stone, the metal blades keeping him in place so he could rest for a moment.

"Then there is the version the Tariqins say. That the emperor was a dictator they broke free of. That their leader, Lord Prolus, desired to free the other kingdoms from the dark rule of Imperial sovereignty. And thus began the war for the salvation of humanity."

Svorgin looked down at her, seeing her eyes lost in thought. "And the other version?"

Aria's green eyes flicked to his. "The last version, discovered by the Elders, who took up the pained task of learning the truth of the matter, is that there was once a small kingdom called Tariqi that was surrounded by the powerful Empire. The Imperials hated the idea of Tariqi, since it was such an insignificant kingdom bordering their land. The emperor at the time wished to claim it. He sent his ambassadors to Tariqi, urging them to join the Empire. But the slight population of Tariqi refused. And when pressured by the Imperials' insistence, Lord Prolus fought back. He attacked the neighboring kingdom first, starting with the towns and then overtaking the capital. It became easier with time. He convinced the rulers of the kingdoms that if they joined him, they could be free of the emperor's malicious rule. That they could set their own laws and become a peaceful realm. Many accepted."

"Until one."

The voice startled Svorgin. He looked down, spotting Blade just below them. The man lifted himself up the rope until he was beside them. It was then that Svorgin realized the others had grown silent while Aria spoke, all ears intent on listening to the tale of the past.

"The kingdom of Beriyal."

At the name, Svorgin could swear the hairs on his neck rose. It sounded like something forbidden. Even the mention of the kingdom seemed like it would bring the dead back. As if history would awaken.

"They were loyal to the emperor. One of the largest kingdoms. They did not submit to Prolus. He knew he would have to take a riskier chance to claim it. He would not put his own neck at stake, so he placed his trust in his right hand, a Shadow Manos named Morosta. Morosta was prized amongst the Tariqins. Many even wished him to be Prolus's successor. But when the topic came up to Prolus, the lord said a Shadow Manos could not rule after him. That the Shadow Manos were meant to serve, not rule. Morosta overheard this and was deeply upset. He'd admired Prolus, after all. Seen him as an uncle or father figure."

The Blade frowned.

"And then what happened?" Svorgin said. He began pulling himself up the rope once again.

Aria seemed just as invested, and Svorgin wondered if she even knew of this part of the tale. The Blade continued up, passing them.

"Morosta worked with his Shadow Manos peers to fulfill the task Prolus had given him, all the while stewing in anger. He crafted a poison like never before and took it to Beriyal. Some say that, before he heard Prolus's dismissive words, he was about to present him with a gift he been searching to find for ages. Morosta poisoned the food and water supply in Beriyal. Once he left the kingdom, he told Prolus if they didn't submit, they must die. The Imperials residing in Beriyal were wrought with illness that none of their True Manos could heal."

Svorgin continued climbing. "What kind of illness?"

"None were sure what it was exactly, but it rotted away the mind and took over the body from within. The people turned into rabid creatures. They were called nojori. Prolus had no choice but to order a wall built around the kingdom to stop the spread of the disease. Morosta was sentenced to death, but before his execution, he disappeared. None know what happened to him. Although . . ."

"Although what?" Aria pressed.

"There are newer rumors that say he began it all. We now know that Prolus was simply a name with many faces. Some say Morosta killed Prolus and wore a mask and became him. He knew they would never allow him to rule as a Shadow Manos, so instead, he became Lord Prolus himself."

The story sent chills down Svorgin's spine. "And the kingdom?"

"Beriyal was lost forever, sealed behind the walls of the Qistool. None dared approach." The Blade gave Svorgin a look. "Until you, that is."

Svorgin was nearly to the top when the rope tying Aria to him gave way. She released an earsplitting shriek as she fell. Then her body stopped midair, and she stared up at Svorgin with desperation. The chain around their wrists had saved her.

"Stop moving," Svorgin ordered.

Aria squeezed her eyes closed. He saw the struggle on her face. She was terrified of heights. Svorgin gritted his teeth and tried to lift her with one arm, while his other desperately gripped the rope. The clawed end of the hook was sliding over the rock above. It would be a matter of seconds before they fell into oblivion. Svorgin gathered his strength. He spied the Blade above. The man was yelling something at him.

"Throw her up!"

The words registered. Svorgin knew he couldn't trust him, but he had little choice. He clenched his teeth and used all his strength to fling Aria upward. Her scream pierced the air. The Blade released his rope with one hand and grabbed Aria, using her momentum to propel her over the wall. Svorgin moved fast, covering the distance between their chains and feeling the pressure on his wrist. Aria grabbed the stone and hefted herself over. Pieces of the aged rock crumbled down. Svorgin moved in time to avoid being hit by one. He jumped over the wall a moment after her and saw Aria trembling like a loose leaf. Tears streamed from her eyes, and her fingers were shaking.

Svorgin gathered her in his arms. "You are safe."

She looked at him as though she could not believe she was still living. The Blade slid over the top of the wall, and Svorgin gave him a grateful nod. The Blade watched them without response, though Svorgin could see his mind whirring as he considered them.

Aria pulled herself together and stood. Svorgin glanced back over the wall and could see land for miles, the distant lights of far-off towns barely visible through the fog. They had made it over the Qistool. So far so good. Then Svorgin turned and instantly froze. Beneath them, in the crumbling ruins of the once grand kingdom, were hundreds of rotted corpses.

32

Honzio
Savoria

THE FREEZING WATER soaked into his skin and pulled him under, the waves gripping him as if they would never let him go. Honzio's head bobbed over the surface, and then he sank back down. He blinked, seeing nothing but endless blue. There were sparkling rocks beneath the surface, and if he wasn't so concerned with breathing, he might have pondered their beauty. His arms battled with the strong current, his right pulsing with agony the harder he slashed it to propel himself up. The surrounding blue grew blurry as a tightness gripped his neck and chest. How could Saga have jumped? How could *he* have followed her down into a waterfall? Who in their right mind did such a thing?

A hand grabbed him and yanked him through the water. Honzio broke through the surface and landed on a rock. A fist slammed into his chest, then rolled him onto his side. He coughed, desperate for air. Water poured out of his mouth and nostrils. He wheezed then, inhaling much-needed breaths. When he gathered himself in the knowledge that he was still very much alive, he propped himself up onto his elbow. Saga was kneeling beside him. Her hair and clothes were drenched in water. The formerly luxurious fur around her shoulders now resembled a wig he'd once seen a nobleman wear in Karalik Palace. The longer he stared at it, the more he remembered the way the nobleman's wig had shaken in fury when he glowered at Honzio during a council meeting. Honzio couldn't help the burst of amusement that coiled up his chest. He expelled a huff of a laugh, and Saga appeared concerned. She leaned over him, touching his head as though checking for fever. Honzio wheezed another laugh, his full body shaking. His chuckles sounded deranged when coming out of his shivering, freezing form.

"Are ye all right?" Saga said with hesitance.

Honzio slumped back on the ground. "Oh, I am perfectly wonderful. I just escaped a man who wanted to hand over my head to my enemies and ran more than I have in my entire life through a maze of trees and jumped off a waterfall that was the size of a watchtower and managed not to break any bones. I am perfectly wonderful."

Saga watched him with parted lips before she started laughing as well. It sounded just as strange as his did, as though she was not used to making the sound.

"Are you insane?" Honzio said, sitting up. "We could have died."

"It is not the first time I have jumped this waterfall," Saga said, finally sobering, but a smile still curved her lips.

The smile nearly froze all of Honzio's thoughts. She appeared years younger, and her eyes sparkled like jewels. But he forced himself to focus. Their voices echoed, and he glanced about. A continuous sheet of blue fell before them. They were behind the waterfall.

"I used to swim here in my childhood and go through this tunnel with my friends."

Honzio nodded. "I should have known. It sounds like exactly your kind of hobby. Saga the waterfall jumper."

Another laugh burst from her, and she shook her head. "It was only one time. My friend Britta—" She stopped for a moment, her humor fading before she continued. "She dared me to jump. And her brother, who annoyed me to no end, said I wouldn't be able to do it. So, of course, I had to."

Honzio sighed, running a hand through his sopping hair.

Saga glared at him. "I am not sure whether to despise ye or embrace ye, Honzio of the Empire."

Honzio frowned, tilting his head and at a loss for words.

"Ye made me break my promise to myself. I promised not to laugh until Savoria was free. Ye made me laugh for the first time in over ten years, and damn ye, it felt good."

An immense sadness swept through him. She had so

little joy in her life. Just a fiery need for vengeance that burned in her center like a lit candle. She didn't know she was only melting away parts of herself in her quest.

"If it means anything," Honzio started, "I am not sure whether to despise you or embrace you myself. I thought I had journeyed through all the stages of death until you yanked me out of there. But it is definitely a story to share when I get home. I jumped into a waterfall and lived."

Saga pushed herself to her feet. "Let us agree to either embrace or despise each other once we make it out of here."

Honzio grasped her extended hand, and she tugged him up. "Agreed."

Saga led the way into the tunnel. Honzio's stomach turned as they forged into the dark, the light of the waterfall dimming the farther they trekked. It reminded him of his days in the palace when he'd forced himself to take the hidden tunnels belowground. When he'd mem-orized the trails on the walls to find his way through. He grasped the wall now, but there were no comforting familiar marks. Only slimy, sticky weeds. He yanked his hand away and coughed, reaching for his neck. The beads he'd touched for strength were no longer there. The pieces had broken during the battle with the sea monster. Desperation filled him. He grew dazed. *No, this can't be happening now. Focus, Honzio, focus.*

"I know how to get through these tunnels," Saga called from ahead. "Leno will believe we swam on to the land. They will search for us at the end of the river. But we will be in the complete opposite direction."

Honzio tried to listen to her words, to stay rooted on her voice, but the darkness was calling him. It was pulling him back to the times in the oven when his father would trap him, alone and shaking. Honzio stumbled. His breathing was ragged, and sweat mixed with the wet hair clinging to his face. He grasped the wall for balance.

"Honzio?" Saga called from what sounded like a great distance.

Honzio tried to speak to her, but his words were incoherent mumbles. He sank to his knees and succumbed to the dark.

33

Saga
Savoria

S HE HEARD A thump and made out the outline of Honzio's form in the dark. Panic swept through her, and she rushed to him. She sank down and lifted him into her arms. Had he wounded himself in the fall? Hit his head? Endured some other injury? She loathed herself at that moment. This was her fault. She had once again put someone's life at risk because of her actions. She swallowed her self-directed anger and pulled him closer to her.

"Honzio? Answer if ye can hear me."

There was no reply. She leaned down, placing her ear over his face. It took a moment, and then came the puff of his breath against her skin. Relief bloomed through her.

"Did ye hit yer head?"

She probed his hair, ignoring how silky

the strands felt, and focused on searching for a bump. There was nothing.

"Wake up, Honzio. I cannot carry ye out of here. Ye must awaken."

He began thrashing and spouting words in Imperial. Most were phrases she didn't understand. She heard one word in particular that sounded familiar. *Mother*, she thought it meant. Her stony heart softened, and she placed her hands on his shoulders to keep him down.

"Ye will hurt yerself, Honzio. Stop."

But he continued shaking and mumbling, a pleading in his voice that she wished she could help. But she didn't know how. This wasn't some random injury causing his reaction. He bore a scar that ran too deep for her to understand. Something that haunted him. A wave of emotion surged over her, and she bit back the sudden wetness in her eyes.

"Honzio," she whispered. "Listen to my voice. I am here. I am with ye. Ye are not alone."

He trembled in her arms—and not from the cold water that plastered his tunic to his form. She ran her hand through his hair to comfort him.

"We will get out of here. We will vanquish the chains binding Savoria. We will do this together," Saga said in his ear. "I will make ye our famous dish that we serve to the greatest warriors. I promise ye. I will try not to insult yer emperor. Just fight whatever it is holding ye captive. Ye are stronger than yer chains. I will give ye a cot in the house. Ye won't have to sleep outside." She laughed against his hair.

Honzio had stopped shaking. She took it as a sign to keep going.

"We will find yer friends and save the villages. Ye will go back home safely once this is all over. Ye cannot give in so early. Please, Honzio," she said, her voice dropping to a pleading tone. "I need ye."

He stiffened in her arms, and she heard the scratch in his voice. "Saga?"

She could make out the shine of his irises in the dark. He'd broken out. She nodded and cupped his cheek. "I am here."

He coughed and sat up. Saga retracted her hand, burning with embarrassment. He was likely wondering why she was touching him. She cleared her throat.

"Good, ye are better now. We should get going."

She moved to stand when his hand shot out and caught hers. Saga stilled. Honzio's eyes found hers in the dark, and he uttered earnest words.

"Thank you, Saga."

The words were full of such gratitude. It was as if she had pulled him from a well.

"It was nothing."

"I sure hope it wasn't," Honzio said, rising. "I anticipate that famous dish."

Saga found herself smiling again. This Imperial was drawing too many from her. They continued forward, hand in hand. Neither bothering to let go. Warmth trailed up her arm, and she wondered at its meaning. She was startled by the knowledge that she had been truly worried about Honzio. It had been so long since she'd cared for someone this much. A stranger.

And a stranger was all he could be to her. He was an Imperial, after all. Just the thought of his land used to make her curse. They had taken advantage of her people and enslaved them as well. But Honzio . . . he was different. And he never looked down on her as the Tariqins did. Rather, he always watched her with an admiring glint in his eye. He treated her as an equal. And Saga didn't know what to do with this realization. Even as her heart pattered at his nearness and a part of her longed to surge forward and see what could come of this new beginning, she knew better than to hope for a future with him. She couldn't dare to imagine it. He would return home to the Empire, safe and alive, and she would continue living in her land. In a free Savoria. She would be content with that.

She loosened her grip on his hand, but he didn't release hers. In fact, he tightened his own, as though she were his guiding light. He was afraid of the dark or perhaps something else associated with the dark. *That is why he keeps me close*, she thought. There was no other explanation. As though sensing her thoughts, he spoke up, his warm voice echoing about them.

"Whenever I upset my father, he would lock me up in the large oven in the kitchen."

Saga froze in her step, horror making her swivel toward him. "What?"

"I would remain there for hours. Sometimes, almost a full day. My mother would come to retrieve me each time."

"Why would he do such a thing?"

Honzio shrugged. "He liked to experiment with different torture methods. That was one of his favorites, for me at least."

Disgust welled in Saga. "He was a nobleman?"

She had thought Honzio must be a man of status in the Empire or at least come from a wealthy family due to his demeanor, as well to be sent on a ship sent by the emperor.

Honzio hesitated. "He was. I grew up in the palace."

"Ye are close to the new emperor, then?"

Honzio seemed uncertain, a bit uneasy. "I am. Perhaps too close."

She raised her brow. "What does that mean?"

"Nothing. Just that I know his plans and approve of them."

"I see."

She wondered what he'd thought of her barrage of insults toward his emperor, especially since he saw him in such a favorable light.

"I was always alone in those prisons of my father's making, with no one to help pull me out of the dark until too late. You stayed with me in it. You helped me fight my fear."

"It was nothing. The least I could do," she said.

His eyes were burning with something when he stepped closer. "It was not nothing. Not to me."

A long moment connected them, and the space between them seemed to shrink. Saga moved into action before they did something foolish—like embrace each other like they'd spoken about. Honzio followed her after a second. Relief bloomed in Saga when she spotted a circle of light ahead.

"We are nearly there."

They quickened their pace. Saga stepped out of the tunnel, looking up and allowing the sun's rays to sink into her face. She basked in the warm glow and the scent of the surrounding trees.

"Took ye long enough."

She stiffened at the shout, and her eyes fastened on Leno. Savorians stood all around him, weapons at the ready. How was this possible? None knew of this tunnel. None except . . .

"Britta was kind enough to guide me here rather than letting me waste my time searching."

Britta stepped out from behind him. Her features were apologetic. Saga glanced about. There had to be another way. Somewhere she could go. Honzio's shoulders slumped. He looked utterly spent. He could not journey any longer. Saga finally looked back at Leno.

"It's over, Saga."

34

ARIA
REALM OF TARIQI
THE QISTOOL

Aria accepted Svorgin's hand, and he assisted her over the stone steps leading down from the wall. As soon as they reached ground level, the rancid scent that had assailed them before grew to an unbearable level. Aria covered her mouth and coughed into her palm, her eyes watering. Though her gaze was blurry, she could still see the corpses, who appeared even graver up close. Holes gaped in their faces, and their skin was receding. Parts of the bodies were so rotted that the bone beneath was in full view. Svorgin halted beside her, wheezing as he strained to breathe.

Aria tried to distract herself from the stomach-turning sight and focused on the buildings. Most had crumbled into themselves, but up ahead, the castle remained, high and proud among the destruction of the city. Though battered, it had survived. Carvings so beautiful they stole her breath etched the gates and towers.

Aria tried not to look at the corpses as they walked past, but she couldn't help but stare. The skin on the bodies was pale, stretched, and oozing with pus. "Shouldn't they have decomposed by now?" she wondered aloud. "It's been so long."

"It may be the effects of the poison," the Blade said, striding past them to take the lead. "Do not touch the bodies."

Aria had no trouble nodding at that. She had no wish to do so. Fox produced cloth that they tied around their mouths and gloves to protect their hands.

"You couldn't have given us these *before* the climb?" Svorgin grumbled, staring down at his shredded palms.

They continued onward without speaking, yet Aria could hear the silence shattering with each of their movements. The thud of their boots echoed in the dead city. There was a disturbance in the air, a sense of foreboding that made every muscle in Aria scream to escape. But she couldn't. Not yet.

By the time they reached the castle, Aria was dragging herself forward from exhaustion. The Blade called for a break, and they spent the night in one of the large chambers in the castle. The Blade took his time examining his map while the rest of them ate from the rations. Aria brushed spiderwebs off a wooden chair and sat upon it. Svorgin joined her and handed her a share of the rations. As soon as his weight settled onto the chair, it snapped, and they descended into a pile of broken wood.

Aria's jaw dropped open, and she and Svorgin stared at each other before bursting into laughter.

"Well, I suppose we expected too much of it," Svorgin said good-naturedly.

They remained sitting on the floor in the corner away from the others and ate in silence. Svorgin grasped one of the broken wood pieces and started using a familiar curved blade to carve into it. Aria reached into her sleeve. Her karambit was gone. She glared at him.

"How?"

"When we tried to escape. After you fell, I saw it on the ground and took it before Blade could see it."

Aria leaned closer, curious as she watched him work. "What will we do now?"

"We wait for them to sleep, and then we go back the way we came. I will gather what we need."

Aria knew he was referring to food and the rope they would need to get back over the wall.

"Again? That plan didn't work the first time. I doubt it will work a second."

"They won't be expecting it, not so soon and not the same method."

She couldn't wait to be out of this eerie kingdom and back in the land of the living. "All right," she told him.

He handed her the karambit, and while she tucked it away, he extended the carving.

"What is this?"

"You were longing for the sun."

Her heart thrummed, and warmth settled over her as she examined the carving: a depiction of the sky and a bold sun emerging from between the clouds. She glanced at Svorgin to find him watching her with a gentle smile. "This is beautiful," she said.

His smile widened in reply, and then he leaned back, lifting his arms behind his head. "Get some rest. I will wake you when it's time."

Aria watched him a moment longer, wondering at the feelings blooming within her before she curled down on her side and tucked the carving against her chest. It took a while until her eyelids grew heavy, and then sleep took her under.

She was beneath the bed. The roars of battle were dimmed here in the chamber. She pressed her hands over her little brother's ears. His luminous green eyes were too big for his face because of a lack of proper meals. How many days had it been? Ten? Twenty? Aria was giving up hope her father would come to save them. Then she slashed away the hopeless thought. Her father would come. Her hero never abandoned them.

She swallowed when she heard the jangle of the doorknob. She glanced at Alaric to ensure he was all right. He watched the door with a steady gaze, and she realized that, though she was trying to be strong for her brother, she was shaking more than he was. The door flew open, and Aria unsheathed the blade her mother had given her. The hem of a dirt-and-bloodstained dress appeared. Footsteps rushed to the bed, and Aria's heart pounded faster. Then a face ducked down.

"Come out, little ones."

It was their mother. Aria sagged with relief. She slipped out from under the bed and placed the knife in her pocket.

"Hold your brother's hand," her mother said.

"Is Father here?" Aria asked, her voice sounding so small and afraid.

"He will be here, my love." She placed a hand on Aria's cheek.

Aria stared into her mother's warm brown eyes, and a wave of comfort drifted through her. Her mother never lied. Her father would come. She reached back with newfound confidence and grasped Alaric's small hand. Her mother took hers, and they moved out of the chamber.

Aria coughed when she inhaled the smoke of the lit fire. Soldiers and servants stumbled against them. Screams and roars of the battle pressed against her ears now. Her mother never ceased her pace. Aria felt her brother's hand slip through hers. She gasped, looking back. She spotted a glimpse of round green eyes before a swarm of people surged in the way, concealing him from view.

"Mother!" Aria screamed. "Mother, Alaric!"

But her mother didn't hear her over the noise. Aria grabbed her mother's sleeve, and finally, she stopped. She pressed something on the wall, and a secret door slid open.

"Get inside," her mother ordered. Then she looked past Aria. "Where is your brother?"

The demand propelled Aria into tears. This was her fault. She had lost him. "I am sorry. I could not hold his hand."

Her mother kneeled before her. "Listen to me,

darling. You will hide here. Do not come out for any reason. I will get your brother."

Aria shook her head, her lips trembling. "Will you come back?"

Her mother kissed her brow. "Of course I will return. You can hold on to this until I do."

She unhooked her necklace from around her neck. A sole button hung from it—a gift her father had given her mother. The warmth lingering in the metal from her mother's skin sank into Aria's palm. Her mother ushered her inside, then pressed the lever. The door sealed, leaving Aria in the dark. She gripped the necklace within her palm, counting the seconds and then the hours that elapsed. But there was no sign of her mother or brother. She shook, rocking back and forth, repeating beneath her breath her hero's betrayal.

"He didn't come. He didn't come."

"Aria!"

Aria's eyes snapped open. She glanced around wildly before she found Svorgin standing above her with a finger pressed to his lips. It took her a moment to regain clarity. She was no longer huddled in that secret room awaiting her mother and brother's return. They were gone. All of them. She clutched the grimy wall and pulled herself up. She tucked the carving Svorgin had made her into her belt and then brushed her fingers over the front of her dress, feeling the shape of the metal pendant hidden within. A calming strength seeped over her. Svorgin bade her to follow him. They crept through the ruins of the chamber, past the sleeping forms of the rest of the company. Blade leaned by the door, his face angled toward them. Aria's breath caught, and she reached out to grab the back of Svorgin's shirt as they came close enough to see Blade's face. The dim light ensnared his features and open blue eyes that were staring directly at them. They waited for him to rise and shout for the others to awaken and grasp them. But the Blade remained on the ground with his eyes eerily open. He trembled and muttered, his fingers lashing over the ground.

"He is asleep," Svorgin said.

He was having nightmares. Not for the first time, Aria sympathized with the Blade. He may have been loyal to the queen of Devorin, but it was through her machinations that he had become such a vicious servant. Who knew what he'd suffered at her hands?

Svorgin continued on, and Aria cast one last look at the Blade's trembling form before following him through the crumbling archway. They had made it a good distance through the hall. Blade had put Fox on watch, but the man was nowhere in sight. She exchanged a confused glance with Svorgin. He shrugged. When they reached the end of the hall, Aria heard a noise. It sounded like wet slobber and gnashing teeth. Svorgin peeked around the corner and stumbled back. The blood had drained from his face.

"What is it?" Aria asked, fear clamping her in place.

"I think I found Fox."

Aria leaned past him to see what had disturbed him so. Her heart plummeted to the bottom of her stomach, and her mouth went dry. Fox was splayed across the floor, eyes staring upward, wide and unseeing. Crawling above him was the most horrific human Aria had ever seen. If it could even be called human. Loose flesh hung from its face. One eye dangled by its nose. The hair was matted and missing in several spots of the scalp. But the worst part was the wide-open mouth and the blood streaming in thick drops from its teeth—teeth that clamped down around Fox's throat, feasting. A strangled scream built in Aria's mouth, and the creature stilled before slowly turning their way.

35

SVORGIN
REALM OF TARIQI
THE QISTOOL

S VORGIN YANKED ARIA away from the horrendous sight and pressed her against the wall. His body shielded hers. They were so close he could hear her breath quicken, see the panicked look in her eyes. The urge to run gripped him just as he knew it did her. But if they did, that creature, whatever it was, would come after them. And he didn't know how to fight it.

The sounds of the creature devouring Fox had ceased. Svorgin could only hear his breath and the pounding in his chest. Then he heard a thump and could picture the creature moving away from Fox and finding its way to them. A frightened gasp slipped from Aria's mouth. Svorgin's hands came up of their own accord. He cupped her cheeks, lifting her head so he could meet her gaze.

"Keep your eyes on me," he whispered. "Do not think of anything else."

Aria stilled in his hands. Her eyes locked with his, and the green in them shone with terrified unshed tears. She nodded and clamped her lips closed. There was another thump. Svorgin leaned closer to Aria, praying in his mind for whatever this thing was to turn back. The panic returned to Aria's face, and her body shook. Svorgin touched his forehead to hers, and their exhales merged. There was a scraping noise. Aria's fingers dug into his skin. Svorgin turned his head slowly. Clawed broken fingers curled around the edge of the wall. Then the torn hair emerged, followed by those demonic eyes that had latched onto them. Svorgin swallowed and grabbed Aria's hand.

"Run," he said.

They took off, turning back the way they had come. The air brushed against them as they raced against time. A shriek sounded behind them, so loud Svorgin wouldn't be surprised if it raised the dead from their graves. They reached the chamber they had been in. Svorgin pushed Aria in first, and then he stumbled after her. Svorgin moved to close the doors. The creature appeared at the end of the hall. Its body twisted at an unnatural angle, and its head dangled forward as though broken. Gnarled hands reached up, lifting its head back into place. Its eyes glittered oddly as it focused on Svorgin. Then appeared a sight that made him freeze in terror. A line of more creatures appeared behind the first. All with the same horrifying bodies and decomposed flesh. It was then that Svorgin realized what they were. The lead creature screeched, and they charged toward him at an unnatural speed. Svorgin slammed the door closed and shoved the flimsy lock in place.

"What is going on? What do you think you're doing?" Blade demanded, glancing from Aria to Svorgin.

"Unchain us!" Aria insisted.

Blade shook his head. "What was that noise?" Then his brows lowered. "Were you trying to escape?"

He slammed Svorgin to the wall with a strength that surprised him. The cold blue gaze and thin lips were all Svorgin could see for a moment.

"There is no time," Svorgin grunted. "They got Fox."

Blade's hold slackened, and he paled. "What? Where is he?"

A blow rocketed against the door. The snarls and growls of the creatures slipped past the wood. The Blade stepped back, and Svorgin saw terror etched across his features.

"What is that?" he asked.

"Help me," Svorgin told him instead, rushing toward a table.

The Blade broke out of his daze, and with Aria, they pushed the table before the door. The shrieks continued.

"It won't hold them long." Svorgin glanced about in desperation.

"Hold who?"

The rest of the company watched the exchange, glancing at the door as the anxiety rose with every passing moment. Svorgin paused in his search for a way out and settled his gaze on Blade.

"The story is real." The words shattered the tension.

"Those corpses we saw . . . They were the nojori." He swallowed. "This is no kingdom of the dead. The city is alive."

36

Honzio stilled when the metal edge of an axe grazed his neck. Though Saga had attempted to put up a fight, they were soaking wet from the waterfall, and Honzio suspected on the edge of feverish. They weren't able to last long against Leno and the group of Savorians he'd brought with him. The former barked orders, shoving them both through the forest. Honzio shivered; the Savorian air was not helping matters in the slightest. His wet clothes were plastered to his skin.

"Ye will regret this, Leno," Saga spat.

Honzio had to admire her spirit. She never relented and had twice as many Savorians watching her with eagle eyes than he did. And thrice the number of weapons pointed at her.

Leno chuckled. "Is there a single soul who doesn't regret? I may regret it at some point, but I will tell ye this." He paused, and the group was forced to come to a halt as well. He stepped closer to Saga, who writhed against the grips holding her. "It will be my happiest day, the day I hand ye over."

His words were soft with an eager malice. They were low and intentional. The Savorians glanced at each other, some frowning. Honzio knew they wanted Saga gone for peace in the village and to prevent more lives from being taken, but he could see they were hesitant about giving up one of their own. And to witness Leno's unhidden willingness unsettled them.

Leno seemed to sense the gazes on him and stiffened, pulling away. He waved his hand at the group, urging them on.

When they reached the square, the sun had risen, highlighting the crowd awaiting their arrival. The entire village was awake. Smiles of relief coated some faces, while others looked on in disapproval as Leno had the both of them tied back to the pole. The village gathered around them. Leno looked at his audience before motioning to Honzio and then Saga.

"Look how desperate she is to save her own skin. She cares nothing for ye folk. Remember that now. She values the life of a foreign man over her own people."

"I hope ye choke on yer lies one day, Leno," Saga said, lurching against her bindings.

Leno pressed closer to Saga. "I speak only truth."

"Ye wish to be the shavka, but ye haven't proven yerself of it. Ye haven't sacrificed like those before ye,"

Saga said, and Honzio was proud of how strong her voice was. "Allow the people to vote if ye are brave enough."

Leno's brows lowered, anger contorting his posture as he angled his face closer to Saga's. A surge of protectiveness came over Honzio.

"Get away from her," he called.

Leno didn't move. The people began whispering, nods erupting among the crowd as they seemed to consider Saga's words. Leno clearly didn't appreciate how much her speech had affected their people.

"Perhaps the Tariqins do not need the Imperial," Leno said, but his gaze remained on Saga.

Saga had held his eyes, unintimidated until those words.

"Or at least not all of him." Leno's stare slid to Honzio. He stepped away from Saga, and the crowd went silent as he unsheathed a blade. "We can do away with a finger or arm." His eyes carried a wildness in them.

"Leave him, Leno!" Saga called.

Honzio's concern built. He didn't doubt the man would carry through with his threat. He seemed mad enough to do so.

"What is so important about ye, foreigner?" Leno asked, edging nearer. "Perhaps if ye tell me, I will consider sparing ye."

Honzio remained silent, trying to gather some of Saga's courage and hold the Savorian's brutal gaze.

Leno lifted the blade. "Perhaps a cut to yer face will make ye find yer sense."

"At least cut the right side," Honzio said. "The left is my good one."

Leno's jaw opened, and a peal of laughter erupted from the crowd. Honzio wasn't sure how the brazen words had escaped his mouth, but he was glad they did. With the small jest, he had taken power from Leno. Leno growled at the change in the air. He angled the knife against Honzio's neck.

"Well then, since ye won't speak, it is time for ye to bleed."

He flexed his fingers over the blade and readied himself to slice. Saga's curses and a few protests from the crowd followed. *It will all be over in a moment*, Honzio thought. Then a voice called out. Louder than the rest.

"Stop!"

All eyes shifted to a man standing at the entrance of the village.

"Do not dare harm him, ye fool. He has come to save ye all."

Confusion gripped the onlookers. Honzio smiled. He had never been so happy to see familiar faces in his life. The speaker, Daghvin, stood at the forefront of the newcomers. Lore and Silopar and ten other Savorians spread out behind him.

"That is no common man ye have imprisoned."

Honzio's elation disappeared when he understood Daghvin's intention. He felt Saga's gaze on him.

"That is Honzio Hartinza, emperor of the four kingdoms and ruler of the Karalik Empire."

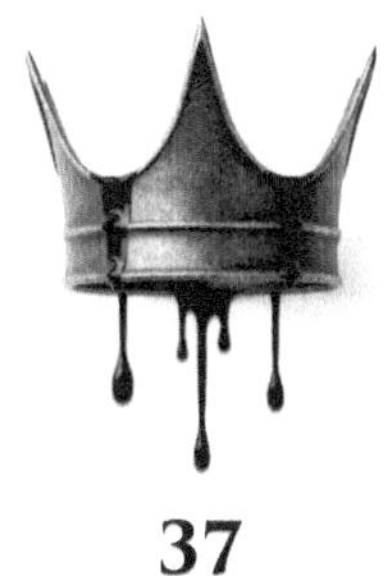

37

EMPEROR OF THE *four kingdoms and ruler of the Karalik Empire.*

The words turned around and around in Saga's mind. She tore her gaze from the man who'd shouted them and stared at Honzio. He was shaking his head at the speaker and then closed his eyes with a grimace.

Honzio. Honzio Hartinza. The emperor. Saga sagged against the pole. Embarrassment pooled through her as she recalled everything she'd said to him. The insults she had spat about him. Then a flicker of anger burst to life. Why hadn't he told her the truth?

Honzio opened his eyes at that moment, his gaze catching hers. Then his features shifted, turning apologetic. Saga's mouth tightened, and a muscle jumped in her cheek. She felt like an utter fool. The fact that she had begun to feel something for him—something more than an easy friendship—made her want to burst into flames and melt away.

"Daghvin!"

Saga turned to see Britta appear from the crowd and rush toward the newcomers. Saga's face went slack when Britta lunged into the arms of the man at the forefront. But this was impossible. Even as she shook her head in denial, Saga couldn't refute the truth. That young boy she'd grown up alongside resided in the hardened features of the man holding Britta tight to him. The familiar brown eyes and confident stance. He was so much stronger and wiser now. She could see it in the lines carved into his brow. The muscles decorating his exposed arms. His shirt was torn beneath a worn green vest. Brown trousers garbed his legs. He tucked Britta closer to his chest and looked up, those eyes finding Saga. He frowned, seeing her bound hands.

"Untie them!"

At his shout, Leno clamped his mouth shut and broke out of his mold. He glanced around, searching the crowd for someone to back him up, but everyone stared at him accusingly. Leno cleared his throat and brought his knife to the rope binding Honzio's wrists. He sliced through it in a fierce manner, the same way he probably wanted to slice into Honzio. He tossed the rope aside and stepped back. Honzio shook his wrists out and then raised his palm. There was a long second before Leno placed the knife in his hand. Honzio strode past him and stopped before Saga. His eyes were warm as he scanned her face. Saga didn't wish to read into his apologetic expression. He stepped closer, and her breath caught around his aromatic scent. The rope sliced away, and her hands were free. She wanted to scream at him and hug him all at once. How could this be happening? After all these years, the emperor himself had come to save her people? But the emperor seemed so distant, a faceless figure she had never imagined she would see. Not this kind, gentle man before her. Honzio's mouth parted to speak, but someone chuckled and called his name before he could.

Daghvin approached them. He slammed Honzio into a bear hug. Honzio choked on a laugh and the roughness of the embrace, patting the other man's shoulder. Daghvin pulled away from Honzio, revealing that easy smile Saga knew so well.

"Ye are a hard man to find, Honzio Hartinza," Daghvin said.

"I apologize," Honzio said. "I would have come looking for you if there hadn't been so many complications." He cast a meaningful glance toward a scowling Leno.

Daghvin waved his hand in the air, sending Honzio's regrets away. "It is no matter. I found as many of them as I could."

Saga followed his motion to the other Savorians joining the crowd. They looked like they had been through several battles, wearing torn clothes and gaping wounds. But despite their obvious injuries, their smiles were wide and infectious. They were happy to be home.

A younger lad approached Honzio and placed a

curled fist to his chest before bowing his upper body. "Your Majesty."

The formality and seriousness of the lad's tone reminded Saga, once again, of who Honzio truly was. He stared at the boy, a surge of emotions flashing through his eyes.

"None of that now," Honzio said and embraced the boy as if he were his own kin.

Saga's fury melted somewhat. How could she stay angry at him when he brought her defenses down so easily? Britta hung near Daghvin, who chuckled at Honzio and the boy's interaction. Tears hung on her lashes, and she stared at her brother as though he were merely a figment of her imagination. Daghvin turned toward Saga, and he grasped her wrist and tugged her toward him. He placed his forehead to hers, the greeting family members bestowed upon each other.

"Saga Barindaughter." His lowered tone still carried, and all eyes focused on them. "Ye haven't changed a bit."

38

Svorgin

Realm of Tariqi

The Qistool

"Alive?" Blade sputtered. "What are you talking about?"

The banging on the door increased. Chunks of wood broke free, and long bony fingers clawed through.

"The nojori," Svorgin told him. "Whatever that poison was that the Shadow Manos created to destroy the kingdom kept these people alive until now. They are sick and hunger for our deaths."

Realization sank into Blade's face before he glared at Svorgin. "This is a trap. You wish to kill us here."

"And myself as well?" Svorgin muttered with sarcasm. "Aye, that sounds about right. I told you already. It was all a lie."

"We do not have time to argue," Aria protested. "They are breaking in."

Svorgin glanced at the door to see more repulsive limbs slipping through the broken wood. Blade grasped his bow and nocked an arrow. He shouted orders at the Hounds and Mole, and they followed his lead. Arrow after arrow found its mark in the gaps in the wood, sending the creatures back with shrieks.

"Find a way out," the Blade barked at Svorgin. "We will hold them back."

Svorgin nodded, and he and Aria scoured the aged stone walls. Svorgin slammed his shoulder into a spot that looked weak. He caught Aria's grimace when his repeated movements yanked the chain against her blistered wrist.

"Hurry!" the Blade shouted.

The nojori were piling upon one another, eager to tear into them.

"Here!" Aria called, running her fingers along a wall.

Svorgin closed the distance and eyed the spot she pointed to. He wondered if anyone could have even spotted the hidden door when it was first built. It so seamlessly blended with the rest of the wall. Aria assisted him in moving aside a large chair, and then Svorgin slammed his body weight against the door. Screams rang behind him. Svorgin glanced back. The nojori had fallen into the chamber. One of the Hounds was yanked into them, his shouts disappearing in the cacophony of growls. His body was torn apart in mere seconds. Svorgin's revulsion and panic grew.

"Please," he whispered. He slammed against the hidden door one last time. It swung outward. "Come on!"

The Blade needed no further urging. He shouted at the two remaining Hounds to move. They broke out of their stupefied horror at the loss of their brother when Mole shoved them out of the chamber. Svorgin and Aria raced down the revealed corridor. Blade and his remaining company were seconds behind. The nojori's screams raised the hairs on their necks as they closed the distance.

"Svorgin!" Aria's pace slowed as she pointed ahead.

Standing before them was a solitary nojori. Svorgin didn't stop running. "Give me a weapon!"

He wasn't sure if Blade would listen, but the swish of a dagger swept the air. Svorgin reached up, catching the hilt and slicing it at the nojori. The dagger cut through the rotting tendons of the nojori's neck. The disfigured head met the stone floor. They had no time to rejoice; the pack behind them was gaining on them. Blade amped up his pace, appearing beside Svorgin.

"Head to the throne room."

Svorgin threw him a disbelieving glance as they continued tearing down the hall before barreling down another. "Why the throne room?"

Svorgin looked back, seeing another Hound devoured into the crowd of nojori. The remaining Hound and Mole were swept up seconds after. Their screams were short-lived. Their terrified faces would haunt Svorgin for the rest of his life. However many minutes he had left.

"There may be a way out through the throne room," Blade said. "Many such chambers have exits for the rulers in times of crisis."

This certainly was a time of crisis. Blade guided them, and before long, they entered the large domed chamber. Blade moved to close the heavy stone doors.

"Get the other side!"

Svorgin and Aria moved to assist him with aching muscles. The doors screeched across the stone. The nojori were so close. Their squeals filled Svorgin's mind. Aria screamed in frustration, sweat coating her face as she heaved the door with Svorgin. At last, it shuddered closed, but not fast enough. A nojori launched through, nails barely missing Svorgin's flesh. An arrow slammed into its skull, and it collapsed into a wriggling mess. The doors' heavy weight crushed two nojori between them, muffling the shrieks. Svorgin looked down at the creature that had been so close to killing him, his eyes riveted on the arrow. He slowly looked at Blade, whose chest was heaving, bow in hand.

"You saved my life," Svorgin said, grateful and surprised.

Blade shrugged as if he were uncertain why he had done it himself. He reached back into his quiver. His hand met air, and he winced. "My last arrow."

Svorgin glanced around the enormous throne room, checking for more of the nojori. There didn't seem to be any. The ones who'd followed them banged against the doors. They finally had a chance to breathe.

"We need to get these off," Aria told him, lifting their bound hands.

Svorgin nodded, and Blade tossed a key into the air. Svorgin caught it and made quick work of unlocking Aria's chain while Blade moved around the chamber, pausing to look at a dried-up fountain in the center and the engraving on the stone that led up to a crown. Blade tilted his head, staring at it with an imperceptible look. A smile creased his lips.

"What is it?" Svorgin called.

"The bastard," Blade uttered. It sounded like a compliment. "He truly did have it."

Svorgin frowned in confusion. A screech erupted, and then something pummeled into him. He crashed upon the stone, knocking his head hard. He saw stars and barely turned himself over. Aria leaped on the nojori, but it screeched and threw her off. She flew across the stone. Svorgin growled, and the nojori pounced back on him. Svorgin grasped the chain hanging from his wrist with his other hand and lifted it just as the nojori lunged for his neck. Jagged, rotted teeth gnawed around the metal. Wild eyes displayed its intent to end Svorgin. A roar poured from Svorgin's chest in his struggle to hold it back. His arms shook. A foul smell emerged from the nojori's torn flesh. Svorgin gagged, doing his best to keep it away from him. There was a sudden crunching noise. The nojori stilled above him and then collapsed. Svorgin pulled himself up. Aria's chest heaved, her hand shaking, and the end of her curved karambit stuck out of the nojori's skull.

"Are you all right?" he asked, scrambling to his feet.

She nodded, staring down at the nojori as a pool of grayish-black blood poured from its skull until an unbelieving chuckle tore their gazes from the corpse. Blade had climbed upon the fountain and torn the crown from the top of it. He stared at it like it was the greatest treasure in the world. The crown appeared aged and rusted, not worthy of the awe he was bestowing it.

"It was part of the tale, though most storytellers would leave it out. Morosta had gotten a gift for Lord Prolus. A gift he had searched for forever. And when Prolus declared him unworthy of being his heir, Morosta had sealed his gift in the kingdom of Beriyal. This is it." Blade lifted it toward them. "The Golden Crown."

Svorgin and Aria exchanged a glance. Worry built in Svorgin as the Blade slowly lifted it up.

"If this possesses the power the legends say, it will help me remember," Blade said. "I must know."

The slamming against the throne room doors had quickened. The doors would open soon under the weight of all the nojori.

"We should leave," Svorgin told the Blade.

But the man didn't hear him, lost in the past as he placed the crown upon his head.

39

The Blade
Realm of Tariqi
The Qistool

T HE WEIGHT OF the metal crown settled on his hair. Blade stumbled back a pace, gripping the edge of the fountain to catch himself. It was much heavier than he'd imagined. For a moment, nothing happened. Svorgin and Aria stared at him with their lips parted. Their eyes were rooted on the crown. Then a burning sensation overtook him.

"It's—it's glowing," Svorgin said, seeming partly astonished and partly apprehensive.

The weight increased, bringing Blade to his knees. He squeezed his eyes closed, bracing himself for the waves of agony radiating through his skull. It was far worse than the headaches he'd been suffering, but if this was what it took to find himself, he would face it. Images entered his mind, slowly at first before rapidly flowing past.

He saw himself in the academy. He'd been raised there, he realized. That was why he knew so much about healing and possessed knowledge of Tariqin history and land. It had been ingrained in him for years. He saw his uncle and his cousin Lilly. He saw Vykus, a mercenary that had torn him from his home in Devorin and sold him to the Tariqins because of the mark on his arm. *The mark.* Blade shuddered under the burden of memories. He had been a Shadow Manos once. All the judgment and bullying he'd faced for the mark slammed into him full force. He sank against the fountain, digging his nails into his palms and clenching his teeth.

They weren't just his memories though. Hundreds of other lives shifted into his mind. He saw Fox, just before he'd sent him off to take the first watch, just before he'd been devoured by the nojori.

"If something happens to me, Blade, I want you to find my daughter. Tell her that I fought for her. That I fought to return to her."

Blade's response was short. "You will do so yourself."

"Promise me," Fox insisted.

Blade nodded, and when the man turned to leave the chamber, he called after him. "Your name. Your true name. What is it?"

Fox smiled. "Teveris."

"Teveris," Blade repeated.

"I know you will find your own name soon enough. And it will be my pleasure to learn it."

The conversation faded, and Fox's face was replaced

by one that had haunted him for months. A pair of green eyes that stared at him with such care and compassion. A boy who'd grown up beside him. The boy had clasped his arm on so many occasions, giving him a nod.

"Brothers?"

"Brothers," Blade replied.

"Velamir," Blade whispered, the name breaking something within him.

"The Golden Crown grants its wearer unique abilities." The voice of his mentor at the academy echoed within his thoughts.

"Power."

"Knowledge."

"Eternal."

The Blade roared, his voice spilling from him and racked with so much pain.

"Oh, Jax, what did they do to you?"

Jax. *Jax.* The Blade smiled. That was his name. Jaxon Tana. *He* was Jaxon Tana. Through the onslaught of images in his mind, he made out a shape approaching him warily. It was her, Aria. She kneeled before him.

"Jax," he said aloud, so relieved to share his new-found truth. "I am Jax."

"Jax?" she repeated and then covered her mouth. Tears filled her eyes. "I have been looking for you."

Another surge of memories washed over him, and he groaned in pain. Velamir, the man Blade had been told had given him a mortal wound and left him for dead, stood before him. *When he tried to kill me,* the Blade thought. But then he saw himself stabbing Velamir's side. The utterly betrayed look on Velamir's face. It hadn't been Velamir at all, the Blade realized. It had been him. Jax. He was the one who'd done the killing.

"No," Jax whispered. "No!"

The shout poured from his lungs. His joy at recalling his past slipped away. Sobs clutched him instead. He shook as tears trembled down his cheeks.

"I couldn't have done this."

But the truth was there in his mind. He'd murdered his closest friend in cold blood. Jax looked down at his shaking palms.

"Look at me, Jax!" someone insisted.

Aria's demand pulled him from his horrible recollection.

"You should hate me," he mumbled. "It was me."

Her dark brows drew together. "What did you do?"

"It was me," Jax cried. "I . . ." He swallowed. "I killed him."

Her face went slack, and she slowly shook her head, unbelieving. The doors shook behind them. The nojori would be in at any moment.

Svorgin tossed his chain off his wrist and approached them. "We need to get out of here."

Aria hadn't moved an inch. Jax's head pounded as more memories poured forth still. Not just his own. He managed to grab Svorgin's arm.

"There is a tunnel behind the throne. Go through it. It will take you out of the Qistool."

Svorgin frowned. "How do you know this?" Then his keen eyes snagged on the crown that stabbed Jax's brain with every elapsing minute.

"Go," Jax said.

Svorgin nodded. "And you?"

Jax wanted nothing more than to drown in the sorrow of his newfound revelations. There was nothing more he could live for. Svorgin's features turned downcast as he seemed to read the resignation in Jax's face. He squeezed his arm, then stood.

"We must leave, Aria."

But Aria was frozen, her eyes far away as she continued to shake her head. Jax gasped. Agony gripped him as the memories continued. The barrier on the door cracked further. It would only be a matter of moments now.

"Get out of here!" he seethed.

Aria snapped out of her daze. "I am not leaving you. I am not going anywhere."

40

ARIA WATCHED THE conflict race across Blade's face. No, not Blade. Jax. The Jax she had been searching for. The Jax Velamir wanted to protect. The Jax that had killed him. Her brother. She buried her rising bitterness. He must have been under the queen's control. Otherwise, nothing could have made him kill his friend. Velamir had valued their friendship so deeply. Jax couldn't have betrayed him by his own will.

"I am not leaving you," Aria repeated, looking Jax in the eyes.

He blinked, leaning back as he struggled to speak. Sweat poured down his face, and his jaw flexed. The crown above his head flickered as whatever power it contained continued to affect him. She wanted to reach out and toss it away.

"Aria!" Svorgin called.

He'd gone to the throne and moved it aside with a rumble. He returned to them and grabbed her arm. She shoved him away.

"I am not leaving him, Svorgin. I promised."

She turned back to Jax, who was splayed against the fountain, seemingly devoid of any strength. "Velamir sent me a letter. He was trying to find you. He tasked me with the mission should anything happen to him."

Jax flinched. Another tear left his eyes as he drew in a rattled breath. "Let me do my last duty to him. I couldn't save him, but I will save his sister."

"We are all going to leave," Aria said. "Together."

Jax's gaze slid past her to Svorgin. "Get her out of here."

Svorgin nodded and moved toward her.

Aria shook her head. "No!"

But she couldn't fight Svorgin's strength. He grasped her around her waist and heaved her away from Jax.

"No!" The scream burned her throat.

Svorgin dragged her toward the throne. She fought against him. Her movements were too wild, her thoughts in such disarray that she couldn't break out of his hold. She couldn't think, couldn't breathe. Her throat was raw and aching as she continued screaming, her hands reaching out to Jax. Svorgin entered the tunnel and wrestled her hands behind her back.

"Stop fighting me!" She heard a break in his voice, saw the blood on his skin from her scratches, and a part of her knew he was in pain as well. "*Viila*, please." But it was only when he said her name full of sadness and urgency that she snapped out of it. "Aria."

She sank against him, tears streaming down her face. "But I promised."

Svorgin reached out, grabbing the back of the throne. Aria looked to where they had left Jax. He grasped the fountain and pulled himself up. He seemed to have gathered some strength and took slow steps toward the doors. He turned to them, his back facing the doors. Aria sobbed as a sorrowful smile crossed Jax's lips. A farewell smile. And then the throne room doors burst open at last, and a multitude of nojori spilled inside. The vile creatures swallowed her last image of his face. Then Svorgin heaved the throne back, sealing it with an ominous thud.

41

Honzio
Savoria
Vidrun Village

H ONZIO PULLED AWAY from Lore. The boy's face was sunken. He'd lost weight, and there was a haunted look to his features. Guilt rose within Honzio, and the regret of bringing him along plagued him. He should have stayed in Hearcross with Latimus. Safe and free to be the youth he was.

"Are you all right?" Honzio asked the boy.

Lore nodded, but the action was subdued, missing the intenseness the boy usually had. Honzio patted his arm, wondering what he could do to help him.

To his left, Daghvin pulled Saga close and enveloped her into his arms, his brow resting against hers. Something hot burned in Honzio's chest. He knew that feeling. He'd always gotten it when he watched Galvasirs jousting after his injury.

They'd been fully capable, wielding their weapons in either arm. Or whenever he saw a joyful family and was reminded of the lack of his own. Envy. Liquid fire that gripped his entire being. But this was another form of the emotion. One that made him want to tear Saga away from Daghvin when he had no right to. He was nothing to her, and she despised him after learning the truth of his identity. He was the emperor she'd cursed to no end. If she'd ever had any feelings for him, they were long evaporated now. Honzio swallowed the bitterness in his throat as he watched the couple. Daghvin withdrew, but his voice was loud and clear.

"Ye are just as beautiful as the last day I saw ye."

The inflection in his tone, the look in his eyes when he watched Saga, spoke of a history between them. Then Honzio remembered the Savorian's speech on the ship. He'd spoken of wanting to reunite with a lass. Honzio didn't want to believe it, but a part of him knew it was Saga.

"And ye still know how to make me furious, Daghvin," Saga said. "We thought we lost ye. What happened to ye?"

Daghvin touched her arm, and another spurt of jealousy enveloped Honzio. "It's a long tale. Perhaps we can wash off and then have a meal."

Saga hesitated and then said, "Ye are all welcome at my table."

Daghvin's mouth turned downward, and he glanced at Britta before throwing his arm around her. "It will be just like old times, the three of us."

Saga flinched, and Honzio saw Britta give her a pleading look.

"And we can check on yer mam. Last I saw, she was doing well."

Saga gave a curt nod and strode away. Daghvin followed her with his gaze until she disappeared between the forest trees. Lore patted Daghvin's arm, and the Savorian broke out of his daze to look down at the boy.

"That's her, isn't it?" Lore asked with a cheeky grin. "The girl you were speaking of."

Daghvin shook his head. "Look at the lad." He gave Honzio an exasperated sigh, and Honzio forced a smile in return. "Aye," Daghvin said with a grin he couldn't seem to hold back. "That's her."

"I will lead ye to the bathhouse." Leno appeared in front of them, and though Honzio detested the man for obvious reasons, he was grateful for the interruption.

Honzio followed them to the bathhouse, where he went to the private chamber rather than joining the men in the main room. He could hear their laughter and raised voices. They were quite comfortable with each other and didn't feel ashamed of their bodies. Honzio had accepted himself as he was months ago, but a part of him still twinged in discomfort when he felt the heavy stares on his arm. He shrugged his tunic off and looked down at the limb and the odd angle at which it had healed. He leaned his head back against the wall and shuttered his eyes. He wished he could transport himself back to that moment when Saga had stepped close to him and examined his arm. No judgment. No cruelty.

Her words had almost made him love his arm. Made

him see it in a different light. He remained still a moment longer, imagining it was her caress upon his arm instead of his. Then the door banged, and he startled.

"Ye almost done in there, Majesty?" Daghvin called. "We are heading to dinner."

Honzio moved toward the door, cracked it, and peered out at the Savorian. "You go on without me. You must have a lot to catch up on, after all."

Daghvin scoffed. "Nonsense. The lot of us are going. And ye are important to the group. Ye are coming."

Honzio opened his mouth.

"And I won't hear a word of protest." Daghvin pointed a finger at him before turning and heading away.

Honzio grimaced and closed the door. He wasn't exactly thrilled at the opportunity to watch more of Daghvin and Saga's interactions. But that was exactly where he found himself. He sat at the small table in Saga's home. All the bodies made Honzio feel cramped in the tiny space. The Savorians Honzio had met on the ship cheered and thumped tankards together. Honzio had been positioned at one end of the table and Saga at the other. Daghvin sat beside her and had been demanding her attention the entire time. Honzio made a point not to look in their direction. He focused on Lore instead. The boy was laughing again, a flush brought back to his cheeks now that he'd gotten cleaned up and food in his system.

The night never seemed to end. Honzio's hair had been wet when he arrived and was beginning to dry. His rumpled clothes that he'd taken care to clean no longer clung to him. He interacted whenever he was brought into the conversation—laugh on cue, smile and nod. It shouldn't have been hard. After all, that was what he'd been trained to do since he could speak. To act the exact way Emperor Malus and the Empire demanded of him.

"And how has Saga been treating ye, Majesty?" Daghvin called down to him.

Honzio blinked and forced himself to focus. "Kindly."

Saga's eyes caught on his, and his heart pattered a touch faster. She tilted her head, as though she wasn't sure what to make of him.

"Kindly?" Daghvin repeated. "Saga?"

Daghvin erupted into laughter that the rest of the table took on. Britta's laugh was forced, and she shifted, seeming just as uncomfortable as Saga appeared to be with the arrangements. When Honzio and Saga didn't join in on the laughter, Daghvin stopped.

"Well, I am glad our vicious little lass didn't tear ye apart." His voice was warm, and he leaned closer to Saga, pulling her against him affectionately and placing a kiss to her hair in a manner that Honzio and everyone else must have noticed was far more than friendly.

Honzio forced his gaze downward and caught on Saga's hand—particularly her fingers tightening around a table knife. Confusion and then uncertainty thrummed within Honzio. Did she not like Daghvin's approach? He looked up and saw she was already staring at him. He couldn't interpret the look on her face, but it seemed almost like she wanted him to interrupt Daghvin or do . . . something. But perhaps that was just his imagination. Daghvin continued jesting, entirely at ease as he touched Saga. Light brushes that might have gone unnoticed if Honzio hadn't been so attuned to them.

"You all right?" Lore asked, peering at him.

Honzio downed his water and shook his head. "I am feeling nauseous. I might retch upon the table if I do not get some air."

Lore's brows shot up. "That bad, huh?"

Honzio stumbled out of the chamber, feeling Saga's eyes on him, and entered the adjacent room where her mam was resting. Saga had been checking on her every so often. She didn't seem to be recovering, but she wasn't getting any worse either. Honzio settled in the chair beside her bed. He reached for the cold towel resting on the bedside table and replaced the one on the older woman's head. She shifted, her eyes opening and finding him.

"Thank ye, son."

Honzio froze while adjusting the towel. *Son.* His heart warmed at the term. She blinked, her eyes heavy as she focused on the door he'd left open, granting her a clear view of the merry table in the main room. Saga's mouth turned up in a smile. She was nodding at something Daghvin said. Daghvin reached out, wrapping his arm around the back of her chair and whispering in her ear.

Honzio whipped his head away and forced a smile at Saga's mam. She seemed to have difficulty staying awake. Her lids were closing. "I will leave you to rest." He had stayed here long enough.

He moved to stand when Yuva's arm shot out and

gripped his. Honzio froze, looking down at her aged, thin hand. Her eyes were wide.

"Take care of her, son."

Honzio frowned, then followed her gaze to Saga. Did she mean to tell him this? Was she mistaking him for someone else? But no, her eyes were clear, solely focused on him as she squeezed his arm.

"I entrust Saga to ye. I know ye will keep her safe." Her vise grip tightened.

Honzio cleared his throat. "I will." Then more firmly, he said, "I will take care of her. You have my word."

Yuva's face settled, and she released him, sinking back into her cot. Guilt wormed through Honzio. What had he just promised? He couldn't follow through with his oath. Saga would never be his to protect. He stood abruptly and walked past the merry party toward the door. He heard shouts calling to him from behind, urging him to join the fun, but he didn't have the energy to continue pretending. He opened the door, and a gust of cold air swept at him. Standing before him with his hand raised to knock was Leno.

"I heard everyone was gathered here."

There was silence until Britta stood and moved to the entrance, urging Leno and the Savorians accompanying him inside.

"Where are ye off to?" Leno inquired as he passed Honzio, giving him a bit of a shove with his shoulder as he did.

Honzio grimaced and turned. "I am off to . . . rest." Although he wasn't sure where that would be.

Perhaps he would be lucky enough to encounter Kalpara outside again.

"Well, we can't have that." Leno sat down and pulled Britta onto his lap. "Ye should stay. We will discuss our next steps."

"We should have a proper council meeting," Saga said, appearing frustrated.

Daghvin lifted his hand. "Wait now, Saga. Let's see what Leno has to say."

Saga rolled her eyes and sank back against her chair. Honzio remained. He leaned against the wall.

"Now, ye've come here saying ye've brought the emperor and that he will help us. How can we trust that? How can we believe he is truly the emperor? Why would the emperor risk himself?"

Daghvin huffed as he leaned forward.

Britta reached out, placing a hand to her brother's chest to stop him. "Leno, Daghvin is my brother. Whatever he says is the truth. I believe him."

Leno nodded. "Perhaps what Daghvin says is true, but how do we know this Imperial is who he says he is?"

Daghvin scoffed. "We saw the bloody man in the Empire surrounded by bodyguards and sitting upon the damned throne. Is our word not enough for ye?"

Leno paused and then his gaze flicked over Honzio. "I am surprised the Empire allowed a lame man to rule."

Shock coated the room, and then Honzio moved forward, anger guiding his steps. Daghvin shouted, rising so fast that his chair shot back and crashed upon the floor. But before either of them could act, Saga was there. She slid across the table, knocking over plates and cups, and angled the table knife to Leno's neck.

"How dare ye speak this way of the man who has come here to save ye? How dare ye speak of anyone in such a way?"

Leno gulped, the bob in his throat dangerously close to the glimmering blade. Saga's eyes shot down to Britta, who was frozen in Leno's arms.

"And ye . . . how could ye stay with a man who speaks so lowly of people? Especially after what happened to yer da. Ye should be ashamed of yerself, Britta."

Britta looked down, unable to hold Saga's stare. Daghvin panted angry breaths while staring daggers at Leno. All of Honzio's rage had dissolved seeing Saga's defense. He found his lips curving slightly. She was so beautiful, holding that dagger with vicious intent.

"Apologize to him."

Leno raised his hands. "Look, Saga, I did not intend any disrespect—"

"Apologize," Saga bit out.

Leno's mouth twisted before he finally spat, "I regret my choice of words, Your Majesty."

Saga scoffed. "That is nowhere near an apology."

Honzio moved closer to them. "That's all right, Saga. His words do not matter to me."

Saga held his gaze, and he could see she wanted to hurt Leno to make him pay, but Honzio shook his head, and she grumbled under her breath before relenting. She yanked the knife back and pulled away, then settled back in her seat. Leno touched his neck with a grimace, and Daghvin retook his seat beside Saga.

"There's the Saga I missed," Daghvin said, a grin overtaking his face again.

Saga didn't return his smile. Instead, she looked at Honzio. He nodded at her, hoping she saw his gratitude.

"I only want to know how we can trust this man." Leno waved at Honzio, daring to proceed in his speculation. "How do we know he will keep his word? He is not Savorian. His oath carries little weight to us. How can we trust him?"

Silence elapsed. Honzio glanced around. Several of the other Savorians seemed to be as distrustful as Leno, watching him with wary eyes. Honzio caught Leno's smirk. The man thought he had gotten the upper hand. Then Saga stood.

"Ye can trust him because ye can trust me. We will be bound as one."

Furrowed brows overtook the table as everyone glanced about.

"What do ye mean?" Daghvin finally asked.

Saga stared only at Honzio as she said, "Honzio and I will perform a binding ceremony."

42

FOR A MOMENT, all was silent. Eyes flicked to Honzio and back to her. Then the chamber exploded in a wave of noise. Daghvin stood. He demanded to know the reason, saying it was needless. Britta watched Saga with an open mouth. The smirk that had been fastened across Leno's face—the biggest motivation behind Saga's proclamation—faded away. Savorians stood all around the chamber, angry voices rising as everyone argued.

"It isn't done."

"Never has a binding ceremony been performed with a foreigner."

"Perhaps it is time for a change!"

"This is unreasonable."

The voices faded to a buzz as her gaze locked on Honzio's. He was leaning against the wall, as though using it for strength, a tiny frown on his brow. The line faded when he caught her gaze. She sensed all the questions he wanted to ask. The confusion, the uncertainty. Guilt plagued her. She had pulled him into this. He was the emperor. Entering a binding ceremony was no simple matter. The lives in a binding ceremony were forever linked. He would be forced to endure her, and likewise. Though the more she got to know him, the less it seemed like a heavy task. A part of her longed to know him better, his likes and dislikes, the view through which he saw the world and how different it was from hers. She wished to know what stories made him drift far away, what history had made its scars in him. And she wished for him to know hers in return. The realization scared her. But what was fear? It was an emotion she'd learned to conquer all these years of being under the Tariqins' thumbs. She wanted to choose for once what to do with her life. She just had to be certain Honzio wanted it as well. She couldn't force him.

"This is ridiculous." Daghvin snarled, his voice coming back into focus. "What say ye, Honzio?" He glared at Honzio, as though daring him to disagree.

Saga stood up, her chair screeching back. "This matter is between me and Honzio. Now, leave us to speak."

The others glanced at each other before slowly trudging out the door. As Leno walked to the door, Honzio moved past him, shoving his shoulder into him with an amount of force that wouldn't start anything but was purposeful. A retaliation for Leno's entrance earlier. Leno scowled and walked out. Daghvin's fists opened and closed before he left as well. Britta was the only one to remain with them. She turned to look at Saga.

"Are ye certain?"

Saga's gaze snapped to her. "What does it matter to ye? Were ye not the one who stayed silent as Leno considered handing me to the Tariqins?"

Britta tilted her head. "Please, I know it hasn't been easy lately. But I am still yer Britta, and ye are my Saga." She stepped closer and gripped Saga's hand.

Saga fought the urge to tear her arm away and inhaled to calm herself. "Those days are long over."

At her dismissal, hurt flared in Britta's face before she shuttered it away. She dropped Saga's hand but stayed a moment longer. "The binding ceremony will last a lifetime. Are ye sure ye want to do it with him? I want ye to be sure."

"I am the one making the choice for me. And I choose him."

Saga glimpsed Honzio's posture straighten at the conviction in her voice.

Britta finally nodded. "So be it."

The door closed behind her, and it was just Saga and Honzio. It dawned on Saga that it was the first time they'd been alone since the waterfall escapade, when she had known him simply as Honzio of the Empire.

"Emperor Honzio, huh?"

She heard the contempt in her voice before she managed to stop it. He flinched. His eyes tracked her as she moved around the table, suddenly in desperate need of water.

"I would have told you before," he started. "But then . . ."

Saga poured water from the pitcher into her glass. Ah yes, she had cursed him. She doubted anyone else would have made a different decision had they been in his place. She gripped her cup, keeping her back to him.

"I suggested the binding ceremony mostly to silence Leno and hopefully as a way to bridge the tension. I understand if ye disagree or do not wish to enter such a bond."

"Yes," he said, solidifying what she'd expected of him.

Saga downed the water. "Of course. I understand. After all, it would be strange for an emperor to enter a liaison with a Savorian, a race his people look down on. To form a bond with a Savorian that would last an entire lifetime."

"Saga—"

She wheeled around. "Ye do not need to explain. I assumed ye wouldn't agree. The binding ceremony is no simple thing."

He stepped closer, his eyes warming. "Yes. I meant yes, I will do it."

She stumbled over her words for a moment. "Ye will swear an oath to protect me and share a future where our paths align? It may not be romantically, of course. I am sure ye have plans to marry a noblewoman of yer own people if ye haven't done so already. But I would be forever linked to ye nonetheless."

He closed the distance between them, his deep-brown eyes delving into hers and ceasing the thoughts in her mind, settling the storm within her. "I am a man of my word, Saga," he said. "I will do it."

Saga couldn't find a reply. She was too frozen in place, her tongue tied with words she couldn't utter in order. The warmth of his stare traced her features, melting her harsh exterior. She almost longed for him to touch her skin to soothe the ache he left behind with his gaze.

"Shall we tell the others, then?" she managed to say.

Honzio nodded. He swept past her with a grace she wondered how she'd missed before. He had the bearing of nobility, the stance of a man who'd been raised to become something great. Even the intensity of his tone betrayed him. How had she missed all of it? Honzio paused by the door.

"And for the record, there is no noblewoman."

43

THE FOGGY AIR brushed her numb skin as they stumbled out of the Qistool through the tunnel. The screams from behind the large walls grew more distant the farther they traveled until they were silenced completely. Svorgin kept up a relentless pace, stopping only to grasp her arm and keep her moving. She didn't want to. She wanted to crumble upon the dead grass and shout into the sky until her lungs burned and throat ached. She wanted to release the dam and allow the tears she was gripping back to stream down her face. She wanted to mourn. But time would not allow it.

Svorgin's pace slowed, and the last torturous image of Jax lingering in her mind ebbed away for a moment as worry took over. She closed the distance between them.

"What's wrong?"

He shook his head, jaw tense. "Let's keep moving."

He tried to step again, but Aria pivoted before him. She glanced down to where his fingers splayed over his side in a protective motion. She reached down, ignoring his protests, and shifted his hand. Blood coated his tunic. She placed his hand back to the wound. Her throat was thick with concern as her eyes flitted back up to his. "How bad is it?"

"I do not know. I don't even know when it happened."

Aria spun around, glancing in the distance, and glimpsed flickering lights. "Can you make it to the town?"

Svorgin gritted his teeth and then nodded. Sweat trickled down his brow. Aria knew he was attempting to put on a brave face so she wouldn't worry. They continued moving, and soon Svorgin's feet began to drag. Aria placed herself under his arm to assist him. Though he tried not to, before long, he leaned much of his weight against her.

Aria glanced at the sky and sent up a prayer of thanks when they made it to the town entrance. A guard stood watch above the gate.

"Halt! What is your business here?"

Svorgin rose to his full height, attempting to look at ease, and waved up to him. "We are returning home."

His Tariqin accent was well done, better than Aria thought of her own. The guard frowned for a moment, and then another guard stepped up beside him.

"Let them through," the new guard said.

The former appeared conflicted. "We have strict orders to inspect every newcomer."

"They are not newcomers. They just said they are returning. Why are you so worried? They are just peasants. All the faces look the same. There is no need to do an inspection." The guard yawned, placing a hand over his mouth.

The first guard gave them another once-over and finally nodded. The gates swung open, and Aria and Svorgin strode inside. Their pace was slower than before, but they had to appear like a pair of ordinary civilians. She hoped the cover of darkness would conceal their torn clothes and the bloodstains, but as they continued through the town, she felt eyes tracing them.

"How are you holding up?" she asked Svorgin.

Svorgin grunted in response. She glanced at him, unsure what to make of that. His skin was paler than normal, and his perspiration had increased. The buildings they passed were dim—not a candle in a window, and curtains shuttered the interiors from view. Only one tall building in the distance appeared brimming with life. Torches and lanterns were lit all about it, calling to weary travelers. Aria wrapped Svorgin's arm around her shoulders and guided him toward it. They stepped inside and were swept into the bustling crowd. It was a struggle to navigate through the swarm of bodies while gripping Svorgin, but Aria did what she could.

"Pardon me," she called when she shoved past an older woman.

People watched them with odd looks, but only for a moment before falling back into their own world. Aria wondered why there was such a crowd. The gathering didn't seem to be a merry one. Frowns touched lips, and eyebrows were drawn down with worry. Arguments spilled out at the slightest insults. Aria reached the countertop at the back just as two men began pummeling each other with their fists near the entrance. A weary middle-aged woman was clearing off the countertop with a sopping rag.

"Jes!" she called behind her. "Get those men out of my establishment."

A burly, short fellow shot out from the kitchen area and maneuvered around the counter. The woman watched him go while shaking her head. Her gaze finally settled on Aria, and her brows shot up.

"Well, hello. Here for a room?"

Aria nodded. Svorgin began muttering something. She hoped he wasn't delirious from the loss of blood.

"I am sorry, young lady. We are all sold out. I wasn't expecting to be so busy this time of year, but I'm swamped."

Aria looked again at the crowd. "What is happening?"

The lady's eyes narrowed. "Well, I believe they are all here for much the same reason you are. You are from a town near the Borderlands, aren't you?"

Aria nodded, playing along. "I am. I didn't know so many others had left their homes."

The lady clicked her tongue, placing her towel aside. "They all had the same idea you two did, I guess. They are hoping to escape the wrath of Emperor Honzio's army."

"Have they set out, then?" Aria asked, a brush of hope stirring within her.

The lady shrugged. "I sure hope not. Our own battalions are not prepared. Our leaders are in disarray. We will be in ruins."

Aria nodded and then tilted her head. "We just need a room for the night. Please."

The lady considered her for a moment. "Like I said, I am full. And there are many others that were here before you. I have to serve in order."

"We would only be here for a night, and then we will be out of your hair." Aria became desperate. "We need nothing fancy."

The lady paused and then relented. "All right, come with me."

She led them through the kitchen and into a tiny empty room. There was a single cot in one corner and a lantern on the floor. "I will store my next shipment of grain in here when it arrives. But it should make do for you and your man for now."

Your man. Aria stiffened, a blush rising on her cheeks. "We are very grateful. Thank you."

The lady gave a stiff nod. "I will take your payment in the morn. I have too many to attend to for now." The lady turned to leave, then hesitated, glancing at Svorgin. "What happened to him?"

Aria stepped in front of him so the woman wouldn't catch sight of the blood along his tunic. "He's only wearied from the travel."

The woman waited a moment more. Something shifted in her eyes. Aria noted the suspicion in her stance before she finally nodded and stepped out of the room, closing the door with a soft thud. Aria spun around to Svorgin.

"Are you all right?"

He groaned and collapsed onto the cot, his blood-stained hand falling away from his tunic. He was still bleeding, and the fabric of his tunic was soaked in crimson. Aria could taste the metal tang rising in the air. She grasped her karambit and opened the lantern, then allowed the flames to dance over the blade. She waited for it to heat, meanwhile glancing at Svorgin, who watched her through half-lidded eyes.

"Remove your shirt."

His brows shot up. "Feisty. I see you took the inn-keeper's words to heart."

Aria glared, and he relented, slowly removing his tunic and wincing the entire time. She bunched the fabric and placed it against the slice on his side to stem the blood flow. Now that she could see it better, she noted that it wasn't too deep. She glanced at the blade, watching it coat over with an orange glow, and then retracted it from the flames.

"Are you prepared?"

Svorgin inhaled a deep breath before nodding. Aria moved forward before she could change her mind and placed the blade to his side. Svorgin's upper body tensed, and his head shot up. The veins in his neck bulged as he contained a scream. Aria's heart ached for the pain he was enduring, but it had to be done, or else the conse-quences would be far worse. Wetness coated his dark lashes. She couldn't watch any longer and moved back.

But his hand shot out, entrapping her wrist and keeping the blade plastered to his side. The burning scent brushed her nose as she continued to cauterize his wound. Svorgin's eyes opened, and a tear slid down his face. Aria tracked it down his cheek. Seeing his suffering brought tears to her own eyes. Despite the blurring of her vision, her hand didn't waver.

He finally allowed her to retract the blade, and it slipped from her hand, clattering to the floor. Svorgin sank back with an exhale of relief. Then he reached out, his warm palm cupping her face, and a finger dashed away the tears that had escaped her eyes.

"I have faced far worse, *viila*. Do not mourn for me."

At those words, something broke within her. He had endured too much at the hands of the unjust. Trapped and tortured, enslaved because of his race and because those with power believed he could give them more of it. He had endured far more than any person ought to. Just like Jax, Velamir, and Natassa, and so many others.

"They should be punished," she spat. "The cruel leaders who stand by and allow evil to reign. Who inflict the injustice themselves."

"That is why we need you," Svorgin said. "Your people. The Elders. The change they are said to bring. They are saving people one at a time. The Empire has already started. You said it yourself. Honzio is preparing to save my homeland."

"And his armies are coming to Tariqi as well."

"Patience, *viila*. It is just a matter of time. It will all be worth it in the end."

Aria was struck by the irony of Svorgin telling her

to have patience—the man who had faced some of the worst punishments. He reached up, touching his uneven hair. It was torn and sliced, in complete disarray from the events in the Qistool.

"My mother was so proud of my locks when I was a lad," he said, a smile touching his lips. "She said she could see me from the far distance because of the gold of my hair." His face saddened. "It was a custom of our people, to wear our hair long like a rumlok's mane. Mine darkened without the sun's heat once I was imprisoned, and now . . ." He brushed the torn ends. "It is a complete mess now."

At least Aria could do something about this matter. She moved toward him and sat beside him on the cot. She urged him to turn.

"What are you doing?"

"Trying to fix it."

Svorgin made a noise that sounded like disbelief. As soon as he turned, her breath caught at the sight of his back wrought with scars. She'd seen them before in Devorin but had forgotten how brutal they appeared. They extended so far that they even grazed his shoulders.

"They made a monster out of me."

Aria reached for her karambit and paused at his words. She shook her head. "They tried to break you, to use you for their gain, but you resisted." She smiled. "Instead, they made you a warrior."

There was silence, and then Svorgin glanced at her over his shoulder. His teeth shone as he grinned. "I like that term far better."

She got to work on his hair, slicing through the locks

that were longer than the rest, working on making them even. Svorgin leaned against the wall, placing his head to it. A peaceful silence elapsed. The lantern flickered, catching the lighter strands in his dark hair. The wisps fluttered onto Aria's lap as she worked. She noticed something on his neck. A symbol of some sort. She traced it lightly.

"What is this?"

He stiffened under her touch. "When Tariqi took over Savoria, they placed marks on all of us. On their *wares*." She heard the snarl in his tone. "So they could know which village we were from."

Aria's fingers closed into a fist as her hatred rose.

"Sometimes, I wonder if it was all worth it. I left them all, my mam and sisters." He paused. "And then Aylis came to search for me. My little sister and my mam were left all alone."

"You did it for them," Aria reminded him. "So they would leave them be."

"But how can I know if they kept their word? I hope they are safe. You should have seen her, my little sister. She was bright as the sun itself, barreling about the village." Aria could hear the smile in his voice. "She always wanted to be a part of the action and couldn't wait to become an apprentice to a trade. I hope she still has that fire and life in her. I hope this war didn't break her."

"If she's anything like you . . ." Aria gathered her words. She didn't want the strange feelings sprouting in her chest to be revealed. Finally, she settled for the truth. "If she's anything like you, I know she made it through the darkness. She is strong and brave and fierce. The Tariqins couldn't have destroyed her. She is still as bright as you remember her. She is still the sun."

"She is still the sun," Svorgin said softly.

Aria nodded, though he couldn't see her. She finished cutting his locks and ran her fingers through the thick mass. It looked presentable, and she couldn't help but admire her work. His hair fell just past his shoulders now, covering the tops of the scars.

"There! You look like a gentleman."

He didn't respond. Aria peeked around and saw his eyes were closed, and his chest rose and fell with a deep slumber. He'd succumbed to his exhaustion. She wanted to shift him so he could lie down properly but didn't want to wake him. She placed the knife down and settled on the edge of the bed. Aria stared at his back as her own eyes shuttered. She drifted to sleep with a warm feeling in her chest, and although she was in enemy territory, she felt safer than she ever had before.

44

THE COLD METAL of a blade touched his throat. Svorgin's eyes popped open and settled upon a man wearing deedan colors. He was large and brawny, with shifty eyes that marked him as unpredictable. Svorgin moved, prepared to fight, but the man shoved him against the wall, and the kilisham blade bit his skin.

Four more deedans stood in the cramped storage room. A woman by the door, who wore a captain's patch upon her chest, watched him with a narrowed gaze. Svorgin's eyes shot to Aria. She was curled into herself, an arm wrapped over her middle, her eyes still shut in a deep sleep.

"They looked off." The innkeeper who'd given them the room appeared beside the captain.

"And you were right," the captain said. "These are no Tariqins." She nodded at the deedan before Svorgin. "Inlo, check his neck."

The deedan shoved Svorgin from the wall. Pain burned in his side from his cauterized wound. He held in his grimace and fought the urge to touch it, lest he give himself an infection. Inlo grabbed Svorgin's hair, pushing it aside before looking up at his captain with a nod.

"He's Savorian, Captain Erda. Vidrun Village."

She sighed. "That's the one we were sent to inspect, isn't it?"

"Yes, Captain," Inlo said. "We haven't heard back from the deedans stationed there or the last group that was sent."

"What are ye doing so far from home?" Captain Erda asked in perfect Savorian, and Svorgin realized she didn't know he spoke their tongue. "Did ye escape yer slaver?"

"I was set free."

The woman's brow rose. She didn't believe him. "What is yer name?"

The question surprised Svorgin. Normally, his name wasn't the first thought on his captors' minds. They never saw him as human enough to ask.

"Svorgin Barinson."

"Well, Svorgin. I don't know if ye are a runaway or not, but we cannot leave ye here." She paused, contemplating before nodding. "I will return ye to yer village," the captain said before switching to Tariqin. "Wake the girl."

A deedan moved toward Aria. She shifted, awakening before he neared. Her eyes went wide when she saw the unfamiliar face, and she lunged for her karambit on the floor. Captain Erda clicked her tongue.

"Do not be foolish."

Aria's eyes darted to Svorgin, who was sitting upon his knees with Inlo's blade an inch from his throat. "And who are ye?"

Aria blinked, not understanding a single word of the Savorian the captain was speaking. Captain Erda switched to Tariqin, and recognition sank into Aria's face.

"I am traveling through the land."

Though she tried to mask her accent, it was easy to spot. The captain's surprise was apparent.

"An Imperial," Inlo growled, his grip on Svorgin tightening.

"She ran away with me," Svorgin said in his tongue. "We were enslaved in the Empire."

Captain Erda frowned. "She is not one of yer kind."

They would kill Aria, Svorgin realized. Now that they knew she was Imperial, they thirsted for her blood. He could see it in the eager eyes of the surrounding deedans, especially Inlo's.

Svorgin paused, thinking fast. "We married. She is my wife. Ye must allow her to come with me."

The captain tilted her head, regarding him. "And why should I do that?"

Svorgin reached toward Aria, placing his hand over her lower belly. He gave her an apologetic glance when her eyes widened. "She is carrying my child, who will belong to my village."

Captain Erda hesitated. She surely despised the Imperials, just like any Tariqin. But finally, she nodded. "Very well, then. Ye are both coming with us."

"Captain," Inlo protested. "We have enough prisoners on deck. Let's kill these two. Toss them in the sea."

The captain leveled him with a glare. "Load them onto the ship. Do not make me repeat myself."

Inlo glowered but did as ordered, although with far more force than necessary. Svorgin was hefted up and taken from the storage room. Aria was shoved along right behind him. Svorgin glanced back, seeing Captain Erda hand the innkeeper a heavy pouch no doubt filled with gold. The cold air stung his bare chest as they were shoved outside and then propelled through the town. The eyes of the civilians followed them until they left.

The captain provided a mount for them. Aria and Svorgin rode together, boxed in by the rest of the riders. They rode at a fast pace. Svorgin grimaced, the pain in his side increasing. He glanced down; it was bleeding slightly. Aria refrained from speaking to him in front of the others to conceal his knowledge of the Imperial tongue.

They didn't stop until they reached a harbor, where Svorgin and Aria were roughly pulled onto a ship.

"Captain!" a deedan called. "What is that?"

All gazes followed the deedan's pointing finger to the high towers of the Qistool in the far-off distance. Svorgin's stomach turned. The walls were falling. Crumbling to pieces. He exchanged a glance with Aria, who looked back at him with a horrified expression.

"We will wait until sunrise," Captain Erda said. "Let us see what is occurring, and then we will set off. We cannot wait longer than that. Ready the ship and take the prisoners belowdecks."

Svorgin and Aria were shoved down a set of stairs to the hold. More Savorians cowered below, crushed together. Svorgin nodded at them and tried to converse, but they were cold and untrusting. Svorgin settled down with Aria.

"What is going on?" she asked him.

"They think we are married and that you are with child."

She gave him a bewildered look, and Svorgin feigned a hurt one.

"Ah, come on, it can't be that dreadful to pretend to be my wife."

She continued staring at him without blinking until Svorgin said, "They are taking us to Savoria." He smiled and then whispered, "I am going home."

45

SAGA
SAVORIA
VIDRUN VILLAGE

EVEN WITH THE heavy frowns of disapproval from many of her people, the day buzzed with excitement. They could state their dislike, but they couldn't stop it. Once two people chose to become bound in the ceremony, it was done. Saga sat on the chair in the room she shared with her mam. Her mam brushed through her hair the same way she had done for years. Saga was eternally grateful she still had her. She may have lost everyone else, but her mam was the only one that mattered now. Her anchor.

She heard a growl and then a voice calling out. "Saga, call off yer guard."

It was Britta. Saga grimaced. She didn't want to see her. Especially not when she had once believed they would perform this ceremony together. She didn't want to think about the past and remember everything she'd lost. Kalpara's growls grew louder, likely spurred on by her thoughts through the mind link they shared. Britta yelped.

"Kalpara, let her pass!" Saga commanded.

A moment elapsed, and then she heard the door open and the sound of boots approach. Britta stepped into the chamber, holding a box in her arms.

"Welcome, Britta," Yuva greeted her.

Britta nodded, a strained smile on her face. "I came to speak to ye, Saga."

"I didn't know we had anything further to speak about."

"Please, for the sake of the years we spent together, at least listen to me."

At her desperate plea, Saga nodded. Her mam finished the intricate plait. Saga placed a kiss to her mam's brow and followed Britta into the main chamber.

"What do ye wish to speak about?"

Britta sat down, and Saga sighed inwardly. That meant she intended for the conversation to be a long one.

"Do ye remember when we were little girls, when we would dream about our binding ceremony? We would scavenge for scraps of leather and fur whenever we could to add to our dress for the special day? When we finally got to be grown and go on missions together for the village? When we became blood sisters, sisters in truth."

Saga stiffened. She placed her hand on the table, fingers splayed out so she wouldn't make a fist. "I remember. I also remember how that day never happened because ye bound yerself to a coward instead."

Britta flinched. "My choices are mine, and what's done is done. Ye may hate Leno, but ye do not see him the way I do."

"I do not know what ye see in him at all."

Britta stood up, flint in her face, a fire that surprised Saga. "After everything that happened, who was there for me? When my mam passed and my brother vanished. When my father was sick in bed from a fever and nearly died from the injuries he sustained at the hands of the Tariqins, who was there?"

Saga's mouth parted. "I stood by ye, Britta. I know what ye faced."

Britta nodded. "Ye offered me yer support in words, but ye had yer own things to worry about. Ye only cared for vengeance. Ye were blind to all else and did not care to heal the wounds we suffered from the attack. Ye wished for them to fester and allowed yerself to wallow in that hatred."

Saga flinched. No matter how much she wanted to deny it, Britta's words struck true.

"But I wanted to heal. And Leno was there for me. He was the one who kept the smithy running when my father was ill. He was the one who provided the coin for food so my da and I wouldn't starve. He was the one who wiped my tears and promised that there was a future for us."

Saga was startled by the passion and anger in Britta's voice. Tears rested on her lashes. "So, ye may see him as a coward, but he was my hero. He still is, despite what he's done. And I know he has done wrong. But I spoke to him. He is willing to change."

Saga was at a loss for words. Britta motioned to the box. "But I didn't come here to talk about Leno. Olava told me years ago that ye tossed yer binding dress away. She showed me where ye put it, and I took it from there. I finished it."

Saga swallowed the emotion rising in her throat. "Britta."

Britta opened the box. Flower petals caressed a folded garment beneath.

"Ye do not have to wear it," Britta said. "I know ye may never forgive me or understand me, but I want ye to know I am always here. Whenever ye need me, I will be waiting. And if ye do wear it, wear it for that little Saga who dreamed. Who loved and had hope. Do it for yerself."

Saga stood still, afraid if she spoke, she would crumble into a teary mess. Britta nodded a final time and moved to the door. But Saga couldn't let her leave yet.

"Wait," Saga said.

Britta froze and slowly turned, and when their eyes met, Saga's wall of anger came crumbling down. She wished they could turn back time, erase all hurts, and be the two little girls playing with their rumloks once again. Britta read the unspoken words in her eyes and started toward her. Saga crossed the remaining distance, and their arms wrapped around each other. They gripped each other tight, knowing through the embrace that all was forgiven.

Saga pulled back. "Stay with me."

Britta smiled. The time slipped by as the two friends spoke and laughed, falling into that warmth they used to share. Though so much was different, the connection had never severed. Britta helped her prepare, and soon, Saga was ready, garbed in the dress she had begun as a girl. She ran her fingers over the familiar patches of fabric. Britta had used gold and green thread to match the rest of the dress. She placed flowers into Saga's braid. There was a knock at the door, and Britta went to open it.

Honzio stood in the doorway. "I was sent to retrieve Saga for the ceremony."

Britta nodded. "She is ready."

Honzio stepped past her and entered the home. He stilled when he caught sight of Saga. It was the first time he'd seen her in a dress, Saga thought. Her concerns over her appearance faded when he cracked an admiring smile. His hair was wet and combed, the ends curling up as it dried. His beard was trimmed neatly, and he'd changed his clothes. Someone must have given him theirs. There were so many who stored the belongings of their loved ones, hoping they may one day return. Saga stepped closer to him, and his throat bobbed, his eyes flitting away.

"What do ye think?" she asked when he remained unresponsive.

He blinked, bringing his gaze back to her. "I didn't recognize you at first."

Britta burst into laughter, and Saga narrowed her eyes at him.

"Did ye not learn how to compliment in yer palace, L*srar*?" The old nickname spilled easily from her tongue.

Honzio laughed softly. "I did."

"Then, they did not teach ye well enough, it seems."

He stepped closer. Saga lifted her chin to hold his gaze. "They taught me how to compliment anything and everything. I could probably charm a rodent I encountered in the palace hall."

Saga's mouth dropped open. This was getting more insulting by the moment.

"But they were all false words of flattery. No honesty to them." He stepped even closer. "I want to tell you only the truest of words. And the truth is, you are beautiful in every form, Saga Barindaughter. Covered in blood and dirt, with hair wet from the waterfall. You are beautiful. You are *real*." The last word was a whisper as his eyes searched hers.

Saga's breath hitched, and her eyes stung with sudden emotion. "As are ye."

"Beautiful?" he murmured, his head tilting nearer and a lock of his hair sliding over his face.

"Real," she said.

She had never relied on anyone after her father and siblings had left. None but herself. And despite how much she'd fought for freedom and for her people, she'd been stuck in the dark. Then he'd come. He wanted nothing from her or her land except to help save it. He came with the hope she had so desperately needed.

A throat cleared, and Saga startled, looking away from Honzio and finding a smiling Britta watching them.

"They are awaiting ye both."

Honzio extended his right arm for her to hold, an internal debate waging across his face before he lowered it and raised the left. "Shall we?"

Saga ignored his extended arm and moved around

him, wrapping her fingers around his right one. "We shall."

He gave her a tender smile that melted the brown in his eyes. They stepped out of the house and walked through the trees into the village. The darkness shadowed the buildings. Flickering torches guided them forth. Kalpara bounded behind them, her tail flicking in excitement as she tasted the anticipation in the air. Saga gripped Honzio's arm tighter when she spotted the crowd ahead. The hums began, the start of the binding song. Many disapproved of their union—a binding between a Savorian and an Imperial, an Imperial emperor in fact, was unheard of and had never been done before—but they respected their decision, and so they honored it. Saga and Honzio sat down before the roaring fire. Her neighbors and elders closed the surrounding gaps, their voices growing louder. The hums became words and soaked into Saga's skin with passion that warmed her more than the raging fire.

> *Sons and daughters of Rasdor,*
>
> *children of the first warrior,*
>
> *bind at heart,*
>
> *bind at fist,*
>
> *bind as one,*
>
> *sons and daughters of Rasdor.*

The voices rumbled around her. Using charcoal, Saga drew customary lines across Honzio's face. He replicated her movements when she finished, grazing the color over her skin. It was typical for a parent to hand off the binding blade and rope, but her mother could not rise from bed. Saga spotted Britta's father approaching. He gave her a fatherly smile and extended a knife. But before Saga could take it, the crowd parted ways, and Britta appeared with Leno, carrying Saga's mother between them. Saga's eyes welled, and she smiled so widely her cheeks hurt.

"Thank ye," she told them.

Leno gave her a nod, and Daghvin appeared, placing a chair down before her and Honzio. They set Yuva in it, and Uncle Bodvar gave Yuva the knife. Yuva's eyes shone with affection as she handed Saga the blade. Saga gazed into Honzio's eyes as she sliced the knife across her palm. Her skin parted, a thin river of blood appearing.

Sons and daughters of Rasdor,

children of the first warrior . . .

She handed the blade to Honzio, and he followed her motion, though not as stoically.

"Bind at heart," she whispered along with the voices and lifted her palm.

Honzio followed her movements, and their palms melded together.

"Bind at fist."

Her mother reached out and wrapped their hands with rope, further connecting them.

Bind as one.

Cheers erupted, and Saga lifted their bound hands

in victory. A few people glanced and pointed overhead. Saga looked up to see a flock of sparrows flying past.

Honzio helped Saga return her mam to their home. They placed her on her cot. Saga smoothed her mother's gray hair and kissed her head.

"Rest now."

Her mam's face was weary and sunken. "Saga, listen to me."

Worry rose within Saga. She nodded and sat beside her mam's cot.

"Time has flown too fast. Ye have grown and become a beautiful woman. I was proud to see yer binding ceremony. As was yer da."

Saga squeezed her mam's hand. She had somehow conjured Saga's father at the ceremony in her mind.

"I know ye will be safe with yer brother and sister's protection. And the lad, he promised too."

Saga followed her mother's gaze to Honzio standing by the door. His features were downcast as he watched them.

"But even without them, I know ye are strong enough to take care of yerself," her mam whispered.

Warmth from her mother's belief in her tugged at her chest.

"Ye are a brave woman, and ye can overcome anything. And I can go in peace knowing this."

Saga's insides froze, and she grabbed her mother's hand tighter. "Ye aren't going, Mam. Ye will stay here with me. Like we've always been. Ye and I facing the storms together. Ye and I."

Her mam's lips trembled in a gentle smile. Those warrior eyes regarded Saga with pride. "It was always ye, Saga, that made us survive. Ye lived for us all, and ye will continue to do so. To conquer whatever fate throws yer way."

Saga's eyes teared at her mam's words, which sounded dreadfully like a farewell.

"Know that I have never been more proud in my life," her mam said.

Those icy eyes just like hers slowly thawed until they stared off into a world Saga couldn't reach. Saga shook her.

"Mam!" she cried out. "Ye cannot leave me. Mam, please. I can't lose ye too."

Her chest shook with cries, and she continued rocking her mam. A strong arm wrapped around her. She fought against his hold, and Honzio groaned when her fist smacked his chin. Despite the connecting blows, he didn't let go. They sank to the floor when the fight in Saga died out. The door opened, and Kalpara entered. The rumlok wrapped her warm body around them, joining them in sorrow. Honzio held her against him, whispering in her hair. Saga broke through her numbness, and his words became clear.

"She stayed for you, Saga, and once she knew you were strong enough to take on the world, she could go in peace. She will always be with you. In heart."

Saga knew he spoke the truth, but a part of her didn't

accept it. Didn't want to. But she had no choice. She broke out of his hold and strode past him and Kalpara.

"Saga!" Honzio called.

She retrieved the supplies she needed. Then she lifted the needle to her ear and breathed out. For the first time, she pierced the needle through the flesh of her lobe herself, marking a new era. She didn't even flinch at the pain and inserted the hoop. She closed it, her fingers dripping with blood. She turned to Honzio, and he watched her with a knowing expression.

"She will always be with me," Saga repeated.

46

ARIA
TARIQI

THE SOUND OF footsteps awakened Aria. She lifted her head from Svorgin's shoulder and glanced at the stairs. Captain Erda emerged into view, along with her second-in-command, Inlo, a large burly man who wore a constant scowl. He tossed flasks at the other imprisoned Savorians. The flasks smacked the ground, several opening and spilling precious water. The prisoners lingered back until Inlo moved away from them. Fear was evident in their tense postures. As soon as he approached Svorgin and Aria, the others lunged for the flasks, many of them covering their faces as they took greedy gulps. Aria frowned. Something was off about these prisoners.

Inlo leaned over as he handed a flask to Svorgin. Then he snarled, addressing Aria in Imperial. "The captain pitied you, but do not think I share the same concern. I will not hesitate to murder you, scum."

Aria glared at him until he moved. Captain Erda stopped before them and spoke to Svorgin in Savorian. She extended a bag to him, and Svorgin motioned to the other Savorians. She replied and then turned away. Inlo cut in front of her, and they spoke in heated whispers.

"What did she say?" Aria asked Svorgin.

His brow was furrowed. "She told me to eat and that the jerky was for you. For the wee one."

Aria scoffed but reached into the bag anyway.

"I asked about the other prisoners, why they weren't giving them food. She said because of her second's mistake, they are now in this state and cannot eat proper food, so they have been giving them broth."

"He unsettles me," Aria said. "He would've killed us if it weren't for the captain. I wonder what he did to the others."

Svorgin frowned, a muscle in his jaw jumping as the captain and Inlo's conversation grew louder. They were speaking in Tariqin, so Aria was able to make out most of the words.

"We must give them the same treatment," Inlo was saying, one hand on his dagger.

"You will not touch them," Captain Erda replied in a warning tone, her gaze flicking toward Aria and Svorgin. "I forbade your interference with the handling of the prisoners after your last horrendous display."

The man sneered. "You protect them because she is with child. You are too soft."

The captain stepped closer to him. "Speak again,

and I will show you how soft I am by feeding you to the monsters that rule the sea."

Inlo flinched and lowered his head after a defying second of holding her enraged stare. His face still spelled disobedience even as he retreated up onto the deck. Aria glanced at Svorgin, wondering what to make of that conversation. What had the man done to the other prisoners? And why was Captain Erda defending them so much? The captain gave them a lingering glance before walking up the stairs and disappearing from view.

Aria opened the bag of jerky, and her stomach growled, reminding her how famished she was. She took a bite and closed her eyes at the delicious smoky flavor. She didn't even mind that it was much harder to tear than jerky typically was. Svorgin's eyes creased in humor, and he reached to sample it as well. Aria tugged the bag out of his reach and shook her finger at him.

"You heard the captain. It's for the child."

Svorgin burst into laughter, and Aria joined him. After teasing him one more time, she handed him the bag, and they shared it. The other prisoners kept their distance, but Aria felt their eyes on them, watching. Svorgin moved toward a Savorian man, offering him a piece of the jerky. The man flinched back, his features contorting. Svorgin sank down beside Aria.

"It's almost like I tried to stab him or something."

Aria watched the prisoners with sorrow. They heard shouts above, and Svorgin stood.

"I will see what's happening. Stay here."

Aria stayed for a moment, but her curiosity won out. She followed him up, and they stood in the center of chaos as deedans raced about the deck. Most were leaning over one side, pointing into the distance. Aria squinted her eyes. Horror clutched her when she made out the swiftly moving shapes.

She gasped. "Svorgin . . ."

He was frozen beside her until he yelled at the captain. "We need to go. Move the ship!"

Captain Erda frowned, but something in Svorgin's tone must have convinced her because she shouted orders at once. The anchor was lifted, and the ship drifted into the sea. The shapes grew clearer, some nearing the ship. The nojori from the Qistool. The deedans shouted in terror, releasing arrows at the nojori to stop their approach. All aboard let out a relieved breath when the ship floated too far for the creatures to reach. They scattered on the edge of the waterline but didn't dare lunge into the cold depths.

Aria's relief was doused when she realized the creatures had been freed and could now spread the illness. There was no need for war when the land was already doomed.

47

HONZIO
SAVORIA
VIDRUN VILLAGE

A FORTNIGHT HAD ELAPSED since Saga's mam's passing. The funeral had been short and full of emotion, and Honzio noted tears on many Savorians' faces. Yuva had been loved and dear to all. The Savorians seemed to be convinced of Honzio's earnest intention to aid them, no longer questioning his presence or his words when he spoke. They had had several council meetings, but a shavka for the village had yet to be decided. They were more focused on how to defend the village when the Tariqins arrived.

"It will be anytime now," Leno said, coming to stand beside Honzio. "The weather has cleared. This is the perfect time for them to travel. And it has been too long since they heard from our village."

Honzio nodded. The man had barely spoken to him but had witnessed his dedication to helping the village over the past days. Though he didn't say it, Honzio knew he had won his grudging respect.

The clang of metal resounded in the open village square. Lore stood before a group of young girls. He lifted his blade. "You will have a firm stance, with feet shoulder width apart. Raise your blade like so."

The girls followed his lead. Honzio couldn't help but feel proud of the young boy, who'd been following orders and learning at every moment he could, soaking in as much knowledge as anyone gave him and now spreading it forth.

"Very good!" Lore called. He glanced up to the hill, seeing Honzio watching him.

Lore waved, and Honzio lifted his hand in reply. The boy grinned, and the lesson continued with more fervor.

"Not bad," a woman said.

Honzio glanced at Saga as she strode toward the group.

Lore beamed, nodding his head at her. "Lady Saga, please join us."

"Just Saga," she said and then motioned for him to lift his blade.

A flicker of tension swept over Lore's features at the sight of the ferocious woman standing ready before him. "You want to battle me?" Lore asked.

"We are demonstrating for the lasses, aren't we?" Saga quirked a brow. "Do not fear me, lad."

"It is not you I fear," Lore stated. "If I hurt you, Emperor Honzio will have my hide."

Saga's lips tugged into a merciless grin. "If ye manage to hurt me, I give ye my word that he will not say a thing."

Lore shrugged, her promise apparently putting him at ease. The audience looked on with bated breath as Saga and Lore circled each other. Then Lore struck out, his sword alight in the sun. Saga parried it with ease, the weight of her axe thrusting it aside. Lore retaliated with another swing. Saga ducked and thrust her leg out, catching Lore behind the knees. The boy fell backward onto the ground. Saga angled her axe beneath his chin, and Lore raised his hands in surrender. A furious blush stained his cheeks.

"That is why, even if ye have a proper stance and hold yer weapon just right, it will not matter if ye do not plant yer feet in the ground as if ye are one with the land," Saga explained to the girls.

They all nodded, *ayes* drifting about.

Saga leaned over and extended her open palm to Lore. "Ye are one brave lad. Not many have the courage to face me so boldly."

Lore's mouth curved up, and he accepted her hand. She hefted him up.

"Get back to training!" Saga called.

The clang of weapons started again. Honzio caught sight of a young girl in the back. For a moment, she appeared the spitting image of Natassa, with waves of brown hair and a determined hazel gaze. She looked young, couldn't be over six years of age.

"That is Clara," Leno said. "She lost most of her family long ago. Her father was one of the men left in the village. He and her mam were one of the happy ones, the couple the entire village envied. They remained whole despite losing everything. And when Clara was born, it was seen as a gift. Then Clara's father was killed by a Chishman inspector, and her mother passed shortly after."

Honzio glanced at him. "How?"

"She was found hanging in her home, a chair beneath her." Leno swallowed, looking away.

Honzio's empathy burst to life. "And Clara?"

"She was in the home, shaking in the corner and staring at her mam. We do not know how long she'd been like that."

Listening to the horrible tale gave Honzio another taste of what these people had faced. He looked at Clara, still brimming with life despite the horror she'd witnessed. She was so focused on righting her stance that she smacked herself with the blunt edge of her weapon. Tears spurted down her face. Honzio moved forward and kneeled before her, grasping her hands.

"Look up at the sky."

She watched him uncertainly, tears still streaming over her cheeks, until finally following his motion upward.

"Do you see that? Up there."

Clara shook her head, her lips trembling.

"That cluster of clouds gathered there. If you look close enough, you will see it is but a girl just like you. She is watching you, watching you fight."

Clara frowned, examining the sky overhead.

"If you cry, she will too. You must be brave so all

the little girls will follow you. You are their leader. You understand?"

The girl nodded. She wiped her tears, and Honzio gave her a soft smile, tucking back a strand of hair behind her ear.

"Up you go," he said.

Clara got to her feet and rushed back into the group of practicing girls. Honzio stood, brushing the dirt from his trousers. He turned and halted at the sight of Saga standing before him. She wore a beguiling smile that drew a grin from Honzio.

He stepped nearer. "Tell me the reason for your joy so I know how to summon it all the time."

Saga laughed, and Honzio's heart lightened at the sound. She shook her head.

"I was coming to help the lass, but ye reached her first. Ye have been helping us all, Honzio, just like ye promised. And that makes me happy. Ye truly are a man of your word."

Honzio wondered if she noticed his chest swell at the praise.

Saga stepped closer and then said, "But be careful, *Lsrar*. If ye continue being so kind, I may fall in love with ye."

She said the words in jest. Honzio could hear the smile in her tone and see it upon her face. But as soon as she uttered them, something shifted. Her smile faded as his eyes locked with hers. The words' meaning instantly deepened. A part of Honzio hoped she meant them.

"Emperor Honzio!"

At the call, Honzio tore his eyes from Saga and

turned. Lore bounded toward them. He slapped a half heart to his chest and bowed his head.

"Everything is proceeding as you wished. The girls are improving each day. Their archery is markedly better, and with Lady Saga's guidance, we have built a defense at the entrance of the village."

Honzio nodded. "Yes, Lore, I know."

He'd been a part of the construction of the barricade they had built. Lore's face became crestfallen. Honzio placed his hand on the boy's shoulder.

"I see what you are doing, and I couldn't be more pleased."

Lore looked up, his eyes lighting.

"I am proud to have you as my personal aide. I couldn't ask for anyone better."

Lore seemed to grow a full head taller at the praise. He beamed, and after several words of gratitude, he took his place beside Honzio. Saga shook her head on Honzio's other side and gave him a telling look, as if to emphasize her earlier words. *If ye continue being so kind, I may fall in love with ye.*

Honzio brushed the memory aside and glanced at Lore, who placed a hand on the top of his head and then, keeping the hand level, moved it toward Honzio.

"What are you doing?"

Lore jumped, startled, and then gave him a sheepish grin. "I am measuring my height."

"What for?"

"Once I pass you, I will only need two more hand widths to reach General Mordon's height."

Honzio shook his head and sighed. "So, I am your checkpoint, am I?"

Lore gave him an innocent shrug and looked away. Honzio didn't have the heart to tell him that Mordon was a bear among average men. Based on his brother and forefather, Lore would end up with a common height. But a lad could dream, and Honzio wouldn't take that from him.

"Well, since we are learning from Imperials, let's have a real bout and see who does better." At the loud voice, Honzio glanced toward the village square and found Daghvin's gaze pinned on him.

"What is he doing?" Saga muttered.

"I want to see the strength of the Imperial emperor," Daghvin announced.

Honzio started toward him, and the training girls parted a path. He reached Daghvin, and a crowd formed around them.

"Ah, there ye are." Daghvin smiled, but it didn't reach his eyes. "Do ye accept my challenge?"

Saga came to stand between them. "This is pointless. We need to focus on defeating our enemies."

"I do," Honzio replied to Daghvin.

"Good," Daghvin said, fire shooting from his eyes.

Saga sighed but backed into the crowd. All eyes were upon them as they circled each other.

"Draw yer blade, Your Majesty." Unlike every time before, when the title had been said with a kind jest, it now was laced with poison.

Honzio unsheathed his sword, and Daghvin lifted his axe up from his shoulder. The Savorian held back for a few moments more before he lunged at Honzio. The axe whipped through the air, the anger in the movements propelling it with a dangerous speed. Honzio ducked and rolled, barely evading the blows.

"I understand your anger," Honzio managed when Daghvin paused for a breather.

"Ye understand nothing!" Daghvin shouted and launched at him again.

Honzio parried the blow, but then Daghvin hooked his axe over the sword and flung it from his hand. Daghvin continued swinging. His axe flew toward Honzio's neck before cutting upward with the intention of splitting his skull. Honzio moved at the last moment.

"Ye knew I cared for her. I told ye of my affections," Daghvin growled.

He punched next instead of using his axe, taking Honzio by surprise. Honzio blinked back the darkness, and warm blood rushed from his nose. Another blow hit his temple, taking him to the ground. Cries of protest erupted, and Saga's voice swam on the edge of his senses.

"Ye will kill him! Stop!"

Daghvin dropped down and placed the handle of his axe to Honzio's throat, pressing down until Honzio choked. His airway felt tight and blocked. His vision grew dark. Honzio reached for Daghvin's waist, his fingers brushing against the end of the knife there. At the last moment, he managed to get a good grip around it. He unsheathed it and then placed it against Daghvin's side. The Savorian froze, his grip relaxing at the feel of the knife. Honzio thrust the axe aside and dove from under Daghvin. The Savorian fell onto his face at the sudden loss of balance. Honzio leaned over him.

"She was never yours, Daghvin."

Fury burned in Daghvin's eyes, and Honzio continued, "Or mine. She is not a thing for us to have, but her own person. And if I know her just the slightest bit, the only one who could truly have her heart is her homeland. She belongs to Savoria and no one else."

Honzio tossed the knife, and it bit the ground beside Daghvin's temple. The Savorian didn't flinch, but his features shifted to remorse as Honzio's words sank in. Honzio turned, seeing Saga amongst the crowd. She nodded at him, tears in her eyes. Before Honzio could decide to approach her, shouts of alarm rang out, and then Britta raced toward them.

"A ship has been spotted! The Tariqins. They've come."

48

Svorgin

Lagrima Sea

Aria stumbled against him when the ship shuddered to a stop. The anchor had been dropped. Svorgin grasped her arm to steady her. Aria blinked, placing her head against her knees.

"My head is killing me. I still haven't gotten used to the movement of the ship."

"We have arrived," Svorgin said. "You will be on land soon."

He didn't know what would await them. All he knew was that he was back on Savorian land and that they would return him to his village. He could hardly wait to see his mam and Saga and so many faces he'd grown up with. He prayed they were safe and well. Once he saw them, he could give them the good news that Emperor Honzio was amassing an army to free them.

Captain Erda descended the stairs, Inlo just behind her. He moved toward Svorgin and Aria, his gaze intent.

"Inlo," the captain hissed.

Inlo paused, and the captain swept past him, crouching before them.

"We have arrived to Savoria and are close to yer village. I plan on delivering each of the prisoners to their designated home."

Svorgin nodded, and just as he began to speak, he noticed Inlo approaching from behind the captain. In a flash, Inlo slammed the bottom of his weapon into the captain's skull. Captain Erda's eyes rolled, and she collapsed before Svorgin. Gasps echoed, and fear enveloped the hold as the prisoners scurried back. Svorgin stood, and though his hands were bound, they didn't stop him from stepping in front of Aria and challenging Inlo.

"Why are you doing this? I know you despise us, so let us go home. You will never see us again."

Inlo shook his head, his scowl widening. "It isn't that simple, Savorian. My family was slaughtered by your kind. Many years ago, a village rebelled against Prolus and killed all of the deedans stationed there. My father and uncle, my aunts. All of them dead in a poof." His face turned menacing. "I swore I would become a deedan just to avenge them."

"Our villages have been oppressed for years. If we fight, it is because we are battling injustice. We are battling for our freedom."

"Shut your mouth," Inlo snarled. "You are all meant to die. And today is your lucky day. I learned several weeks ago, from a friend stationed in your village, that your people there have gathered their courage, that they have risen, and so I plotted. And now, they will pay for their foolishness. And when I am done with them, I will bring you out to see their corpses."

Svorgin growled. He moved toward Inlo, but Aria held him back. "He is goading you. Do not listen to him."

Inlo clicked his tongue, then tied up the captain and tossed her beside Aria. He called for more deedans to assist him.

"Bring the prisoners up," he ordered.

Several of the deedans paused, staring at their unconscious captain with wide eyes.

Inlo growled. "Erda is no longer captain of this ship. I am your new captain. Now get a move on before I make you walk the plank."

The deedans sprang into action, dragging the prisoners up the stairs and out of sight until only Svorgin and Aria remained with a motionless Captain Erda. Svorgin worried for the prisoners. What did Inlo plan to do with them? Clearly nothing good. They were terrified of him already. Every time Svorgin had tried to communicate with the prisoners over the course of the journey, they'd remained aloof and silent. So frightened of Inlo that they wouldn't even converse with him.

Inlo smiled, an ominous intention lurking in his features. "I will return soon."

He gave Svorgin another menacing glare before he bounded up the stairs and disappeared. Svorgin breathed out, the erratic pace of his heart steadying once the man had left. That wild look in his eyes reminded Svorgin of the nojori they'd encountered in the Qistool. The nojori that were tearing around Tariqi wreaking havoc, perhaps at this very moment.

"We need to leave," Svorgin said, working on the ropes binding his wrists.

Aria nodded. "Turn toward me."

Svorgin did as instructed so she could pull at the knots around his hands. The captain stirred as they hastened, staring at them with bleary eyes before shooting up.

"Wha—what happened?"

"Your second struck your head," Aria told her. "He took the prisoners and headed for the village."

"No. No, no, no," Captain Erda whispered repeatedly. "I must stop him."

The rope around his wrists loosened enough for Svorgin to pull his hands free. He moved to the captain. "Ye must get ahold of yer deedans before Inlo causes damage we cannot take back."

She nodded. Svorgin untied her and then got to work on Aria's bindings.

"Why were you protecting us?" Aria asked the captain. "Inlo attempted to do us harm several times over the trip. Why did you aid us?"

Erda hesitated. "My sister was killed at the hands of mercenaries. It happened before my very eyes. That is why I became a soldier. To aid those who couldn't help themselves."

Svorgin nodded, understanding. But she had joined a cause that fought not for peace but dominion. Perhaps she hadn't known that. Just like Velamir hadn't, and who knew how many others?

"She was with child." The captain paused, taking a moment to gather herself before she motioned to Aria. "Take care of her. And stay here. I will get the troops in order and return when it is time to deliver ye to yer village."

Her footsteps receded, leaving Svorgin and Aria alone in the dim light of the hold. They remained for a while, but after some time had passed, Svorgin rose.

"We must go. Inlo is unpredictable."

Aria nodded and stood as well. They headed to the stairs. The ship was oddly still—no noise or rocking from the movement of the people above. Svorgin placed a finger to his lips and motioned upward. Aria nodded, and he moved past her, sneaking up the stairs. The door to the hold opened, and Inlo appeared. He was covered in blood and gore and vibrating with anger. He lifted a large, booted foot and landed a blow into Svorgin's chest. Aria screamed, and Svorgin rolled down the stairs, the impact of the blow sending pain ricocheting through his ribs. He grasped an arm around his midsection, groaning.

"You thought you would get off of this ship unscathed, did you? I slaughtered many of your people. They lay dying at this moment. I came to take you to them."

Inlo descended the stairs, each step an ominous thud. Svorgin breathed through his nose, attempting to rise. Aria was beside him, touching his face, asking him questions. But her voice was a buzz to his ears. Then the shadow fell over her. Svorgin gasped, reaching up as Inlo lifted Aria to shove her away. Aria spun under his arm before grabbing his wrist, twisting it until Inlo screamed. But then the screams turned into a laughter that sent terror through Svorgin.

"I so enjoy pain," Inlo hissed. "Even more so when it's the pain of the people I despise."

Svorgin hefted himself up, gathering his strength. Inlo broke Aria's hold and shoved her into the wall, his meaty hand grasping her neck. Aria gasped, hands clawing over his, her face turning purple. A roar burst from Svorgin as he charged the man. Inlo dropped Aria and swiveled to face him. Svorgin landed a hook that didn't budge Inlo in the slightest. Inlo spat a wad of blood and then swung back. Svorgin ducked in time. His movements were slower than normal, but his worry for Aria kept him in action. One of Inlo's strikes landed, hammering into Svorgin's jaw and sending him staggering against the wall of the ship, chest heaving and dazed. When he cleared his vision, Inlo was marching back to Aria, cruel intent in his gaze.

"Wait," Svorgin managed.

The man turned to him.

"Leave her. Kill me if you want, but leave her."

Aria shook her head, pulling herself up. Her nails were broken, and blood poured from her nostrils.

"I will kill you both," the man snarled. "But I will honor your last wish and start with you."

He charged at Svorgin, and then there was a crack. The sound of impaled flesh. The big man froze, utterly still before Svorgin, an unbelieving look in his eyes. Blood poured out from his mouth, trickling in swift drops that stained the wood below them. Then he sank to his knees before crumpling to the floor. Svorgin blinked, staring at Inlo's spasming body until it stilled. Aria breathed out, wiping her nose and then leaning over to yank wood from the back of Inlo's neck. Blood seeped out, forming a large puddle. Sharp and red-coated metal nails stuck out from the wood. Svorgin lifted his head. Aria dropped the piece of wood and placed a trembling hand over her lips. Svorgin moved toward her. She'd killed someone. Something that went against everything she stood for as an Elder. And she'd done it for him. To save him. Svorgin pulled her into his arms, holding her as she continued looking on with shock.

"Thank you," Svorgin repeated. "You saved me. Thank you."

"I murdered him, Svorgin. I killed him," she whispered.

He captured her chin between his thumb and forefinger, lifted her head so she saw only him. "No, you *saved* me, Aria."

He waited until his words soaked in before he said, "Let's go to the village." His voice lowered to a longing whisper. "Let's go home."

49

Saga
Savoria
Vidrun Village

S AGA PEERED OVER the fortified wall built to defend the village. All was still in the distance, not a trace of an attack. Honzio stepped up beside her. Saga glanced at the people gathered along the wall. Each one, whether young or elderly, held a bow in hand. Fingers reached for arrows tucked into quivers.

"Was it a false alarm?" Daghvin called.

"No," Britta said. "They spotted the ship. The Tariqins will be here at any moment."

Then there was a trembling in the earth. Saga inhaled the cold forest air and focused on the distant land. Her eyes squinted. There. A line emerged into view. Deedans charged forth, clothed in the signature black-and-red Tariqin colors. Gasps slipped out from below her. The younger lasses trembled, their fingers shaking around their bows.

"Steady," Saga called down. "Do not panic. It will be just as we practiced."

Her voice calmed them somewhat, but the fear in their gazes remained. The deedans moved faster, nearing the range.

"Prepare yerselves!"

Arrows slid free and were nocked onto strings.

"Draw," Saga commanded.

The united sound of bowstrings stretched taut filled the silence. Bated breaths, perspired brows, and clouded air. The Tariqins closed in.

"One moment," Saga said.

She counted in a low tone. The Tariqins were nearly there.

"Fire!"

The arrows loosed. They cut through the air and pierced the coming force, sending them toppling against each other.

"Draw!"

Saga's shout propelled them into action.

"Fire!"

More arrows. More fallen deedans. Saga frowned, examining the Tariqins. They didn't move with the practiced ease of trained deedans. Rather, they hobbled as though injured. The ones pierced by arrows lay still, blood spreading out onto the snow beneath them. Then something even more odd reached her mind. They didn't have any weapons.

"Saga?" Leno asked her.

Saga didn't reply. There was something peculiar about this. Something she couldn't put her finger on yet.

"Draw!" Leno continued the command. "Fire!"

After the third volley, Saga raised her arm. "Stop."

The bows lowered.

Saga hopped down from the fortified entrance and waved her hand at Leno. "Let's go out."

"But—"

Saga's glare silenced him. The doors opened, and Saga strolled out, Honzio to her right and Leno to her left. More Savorians streamed out of the gate behind them, their fists punching the air in cheers of victory. Britta and Daghvin were near the forefront. Saga moved toward the fallen deedans.

"Bind the live ones."

Leno followed her order, moving toward the deedans with more Savorians. Saga stopped by one of the Tariqins. The man was gasping for breath, a ragged sound ripping from his chest as he clasped his hands around the arrow embedded there. Saga kneeled, and his eyes looked to hers, desperation blooming in them. A chill gripped her then. She lifted the man's head, tucking his hair away, and focused on the lines marking his neck. Saga swallowed and lowered his head down. He opened his mouth, trying to speak, but not a word emerged. Then Saga realized why. His tongue had been severed. A gasp slipped from her.

"Do not harm them!" she called, then turned her horrified gaze to Leno.

Honzio kneeled beside her. "What is it? What's wrong?"

A tear slipped from her eye. "These are no deedans. They are Savorian."

50

HONZIO
SAVORIA
VIDRUN VILLAGE

SAGA'S WORDS SANK in, and he looked down at the dying Savorians with shock. His eyes caught on the red-and-black clothes the Savorians wore. This was planned.

"We need to go back." He shook Saga until her dazed eyes met his. "This was a trap. We need to go back."

She nodded slowly, then stood. "Retreat!" She waved her arms at the people still streaming out from the village to celebrate what they thought to be their triumph. "Go back!"

They stilled, uncertainty crossing their features. Britta continued moving toward Honzio and Saga. "What happen—"

An arrow sliced into her leg. Britta stumbled back just as a heart-wrenching cry slipped from Saga. Leno shouted, rushing to Britta. More arrows struck true, hitting other villagers. Honzio's thoughts ran wild, but most centered on Saga. He had to get her behind the wall. He had to keep his promise to her mam. He would protect her. But there was another voice inside that told him his promise was just an excuse. That if something happened to her, his world would be a wasteland without meaning. She was his sun, his moon, the stars themselves. Every lantern guiding him. He couldn't see his way forward without her.

So he grabbed her hand, dragging her whenever she slowed. He shouted at Daghvin to hurry as they rushed to the gates. Arrows were flying rampant. They were almost there. An arrow struck the wood of the gate just above his head. Then they were through. They slammed the doors closed. Honzio crossed the ladder that led up to the wall. He stared over it, seeing cheering deedans in the distance. The man at their lead smiled broadly as he maneuvered over the field, cutting the throats of the injured they hadn't been able to carry back. Rage poured through Honzio. The leader gave instructions to his deedans before disappearing into the trees. Honzio moved back down the ladder and into the erupting chaos. So many tears, so many wounded.

Honzio stilled when he caught sight of little Clara. Many were crowded around her, placing cloth to her wounds. Honzio shifted through them until he kneeled beside her.

"It's ye," she murmured.

"You will be all right," Honzio said, but one look at

her wounds made him grimace. They were far too many, and one was too close to her heart. "Look at me."

Clara smiled, blood coating her lips. "Do ye think she will be proud of me? The girl in the sky?"

Honzio nodded, biting back the rising emotion. "She has never been more proud."

Clara's smile widened, and then she fell still. At the trickle of blood slipping from her mouth and down her chin, Honzio coughed back a sob. The people surrounding Clara wailed. Honzio stood, wiping a tear, and turned. They had no time to mourn. The true deedans were approaching. He searched for Saga and saw her pushing through the crowd, a crazed look on her face.

"Britta!" Saga called.

Honzio grabbed her, forcing her to stop. "Britta is with Leno. She is safe. He took her into the village. The elder women will aid her."

Saga's blue eyes were filled with tears. "She needs me."

Honzio shook his head. "She needs you to fight. They all need you to fight."

More arrows slammed into the wood, and menacing cheers from the opposition rent the air. Saga held his gaze. The tears in her eyes faded with her next blink, and then he saw only burning vengeance there. She nodded.

"Let's finish these bastards."

She turned to her people, who were crying and shouting with despair. Honzio knew if anyone could break them from their stupor, it would be her.

"Brothers and sisters, awaken! It is time to end this!"

Her firm tone carried, and Savorians lifted their

heads to her. She moved toward the mountain of axes in the center of the village. She crouched down, muttered a prayer, and caressed the blade of one axe. She wrapped her fingers around the hilt and stood.

"It is time to avenge our fallen! I will do so by carrying my da's axe."

Her people nodded with approval, many of them moving toward the axes and lifting those of their fallen loved ones. Saga began a song.

> *We are the eagle's screech,*
>
> *the rumloks roar,*
>
> *the children's hearts.*
>
> *We are the captives of no one.*
>
> *We are courage,*
>
> *resilience.*
>
> *We are*
>
> *Savorian.*

Saga's powerful voice was joined by the others as one by one they stood. They hefted their weapons and wiped their tears and then turned to face the doors. Fear faded with each bang against the gate. And when the wood split apart, adrenaline rushed through Honzio. He charged with the others, lifting his blade high with theirs. His voice spilled out of him, joining theirs in a unified roar that sent the deedans staggering away. The fury of the Savorians repelled their confident attack. Honzio crashed into the melee to battle with the closest deedan.

He heard a heart-stopping growl before seeing Kalpara join the mix. Saga rode astride her, slicing through the deedans from her seat. The rumlok tore through the Tariqins with a vengeance that rivaled her rider's.

The voices of the Savorians continued bursting into the air with ardor.

> *We are the eagle's screech,*
>
> *the rumlok's roar,*
>
> *the children's hearts.*
>
> *We are the captives of no one.*
>
> *We are courage,*
>
> *resilience.*
>
> *We are*
>
> *Savorian.*

Honzio's heart stilled when a deedan lunged up and dragged Saga from her rumlok. They crashed onto the ground, rolling in a flurry of punches and kicks. Honzio fought his way toward her. The deedan lifted his kilisham, poised to bring it down toward her head. Saga's eyes squeezed shut. Honzio's breath slowed. Then an axe plunged into the deedan's back.

51

ALTHOUGH IT HAD been many years, Svorgin knew the path to his village like he'd left the day before. Aria moved stealthily beside him, but his clomping boots in the snow drowned out every other noise in the surrounding forest. They would be spotted easily if someone came looking for them.

Svorgin stared at the tracks in the snow ahead. Inlo must have gone this way with the deedans and prisoners. The clanging of weapons and screams of battle reached his ear. Svorgin tensed. He had no weapon, and neither did Aria. She looked at him with wide eyes.

"Did the captain not come in time to stop them from attacking?" she said.

"They might not have listened."

And if they hadn't heeded their captain's

words and attacked the village, then the clanging swords meant the villagers were fighting back. A lightness thrummed to life in his chest. He didn't want the hope sprouting within him to die if he said it aloud. Instead, the thoughts ran rampant inside his mind. The Savorians were rebelling. They were taking back the village. He strode forward, gaze intent.

"Wait!" Aria called, forgoing stealth in her haste to catch up with him. "Shouldn't we come up with a plan? We don't know what's awaiting us."

"There's no time, *viila*."

If it truly was as he thought, he didn't want to miss a moment of it. He wanted to be a part of saving his home.

"Svorgin!"

Aria's shout died off when she stumbled into the clearing beside him. A wooden-structured gate rose in the distance, and his people fiercely defended the village before it, battling the Tariqins with everything they had. Men and women, lasses and lads. Their angry screams filled the air. Emotion welled within him as Svorgin stared ahead, mesmerized. He'd never seen a more beautiful sight than watching Savorians fight for their freedom.

"Stay here," he told Aria.

Then he tore down into the clearing, the familiar drift of cold brushing his skin, the exhilaration of a coming fight boosting his speed. He jumped in front of a wounded lass, grasping the wrist of a Tariqin raising his weapon with a finishing blow. He knocked his knee into the deedan's ribs and then followed it with his head to the man's face. The deedan stumbled back with a broken nose and promptly collapsed to the ground.

"Ye all right, lass?" Svorgin asked the trembling girl.

The lass stared numbly, her fingers stiff around the handle of an axe. Aria appeared. Of course she did. She kneeled beside the girl.

"Go," she told Svorgin. "Fight. I will stay with her."

Svorgin nodded, squeezing her arm and knowing she could hold her own. He stood and flung into the fray. Savorians glanced at him as he appeared, confusion flickering across their features.

"Come on, lads!" Svorgin roared, and they smiled, adding their own shouts.

Svorgin caught sight of a lass atop a large white rumlok. His heart quickened. The lass—or woman, he should say—fought with venom, stabbing down at the deedans who managed to get past her rumlok's fangs. She was so familiar. The gold of her hair, the fierce blue of her eyes. Svorgin paused, watching her for a long moment. Could it be . . . ? Then a deedan grabbed hold of her, taking her into the snow. Svorgin didn't think. He flung his axe through the air, and it buried into the deedan's back.

Deedans swarmed before him, blocking his view of the woman. He fought with his bare hands, the cold weather numbing his bloody fists with every blow he landed upon the enemy. It felt like hours elapsed as the deedans dropped around him. He spotted Captain Erda through the bodies. She was on her knees, her eyes squeezed tight as a familiar man with his back facing Svorgin lifted his blade.

"Wait!" Svorgin called.

The man paused and then turned to view him. Svorgin's mouth dropped open.

"Honzio?"

Though the emperor's beard had grown even longer than the last time Svorgin had seen him, and his face was coated in blood and scrapes, and his clothes were far different from his typical style, Svorgin knew it was him.

Honzio stared back at him. Then a smile cut through his face, and his teeth shone bright. He lowered his blade into the snow. Savorians surrounded the captain, keeping her under the threat of axe blades.

"Svorgin?"

Svorgin moved toward him with a nod and yanked him into a bear hug. He knocked his head to Honzio's in the familial gesture, clapping his hand against the man's back. Svorgin pulled back and saw Honzio staring at him in amazement.

"I cannot believe it. I searched for you for months. Sent hunting parties to all corners of the Empire. But we could never find you."

"It's a long story," Svorgin replied. "I heard you were preparing an army to come to Savoria, but I hadn't expected you to arrive yourself or so soon."

Honzio placed his hand on Svorgin's shoulder. "I gave a promise, *mosori*. And I aim to keep it."

Svorgin placed his brow again to Honzio's. "Thank you."

The emperor nodded. Captain Erda called to Svorgin.

"I tried to stop the deedans, but Inlo filled their minds with his bloodlust."

Honzio glanced between them, and Svorgin nodded.

"This is Captain Erda. She aided us and delivered us here. Her second betrayed her and led the attack."

Honzio nodded. "I believe I saw him. He ran off after his heinous trick."

"Trick?" Svorgin repeated.

"He sent Savorians toward the village dressed in deedan garb. We shot at them, not knowing they were our own," a broad man said as he approached.

"The bastard!" Svorgin swore. "He met the end he deserved when he returned to the ship."

"Good," Honzio said with a grim expression.

The other man nodded. Svorgin tried to recall him, but he couldn't place his features.

"Svorgin Barinson, is it really ye?" Then, seeing that Svorgin didn't recognize him, he said, "It's Leno."

"Leno!" He'd been such a gangly lad the last time he'd seen him. "Ye've grown so much."

"Svorgin was the talk of the village. The bravest lad and the most handsome." This voice belonged to a man Svorgin remembered at once. He'd spent years keeping wary eyes on Daghvin whenever he noticed him trailing his sister. "We lads were mighty jealous of him."

More faces appeared, and hugs and claps on the shoulder were doled out. And at the back of them was the woman he'd seen earlier. She stared at him like he was a ghost.

"Saga?" Svorgin said, hoping he wasn't mistaken.

Her brow furrowed, and then she shook her head. Svorgin moved toward her, the voices of the others becoming muffled. He stopped when he was directly before her. He was certain it was her. The tiny slice at the edge of her eyebrow gave her away. The injury had happened when he was playing with her.

"Saga," he said, reaching for her.

"No, no." She continued shaking her head. He thought it was only in disbelief, but then she stepped away and ran through the village before mounting her rumlok and tearing off.

"What just happened?" He turned, seeing a crowd of gazes upon him.

"She thought you were dead," Honzio said. "Give her time."

Svorgin wanted to go after her but contained himself. He gave Honzio a brisk nod.

"What should we do with them?" Leno motioned to the bound deedans.

Svorgin nodded his chin at Captain Erda, lowering his voice so only Honzio could hear. "I believe she may help us if she has enough motivation."

Honzio approached the captain, who was on her knees surrounded by Savorians. "If you tell us anything useful, I will free you."

Doubt clouded her face.

Honzio lowered himself to one knee to look her in the eyes. "I give you my word. I, Honzio Hartinza, pledge to free you and, if you so wish, grant you permission to live freely in the Empire."

The captain's eyes widened as his words sank in and she realized his identity.

Aria stepped up beside Svorgin. "I am amazed we found the emperor."

Svorgin nodded. "Can you believe he used to think he was not worthy of becoming the emperor?"

Aria's brows rose as she glanced at Svorgin and then back to Honzio. Honzio leaned closer to the captain, talking to her in a low yet commanding voice. His presence was powerful, and it took only a moment for the captain to talk.

Aria smiled, shaking her head. "No, I cannot believe it."

"I am honored to have met him," Svorgin said. "I have experienced much in this life, fought many battles, escaped many dungeons." He wrapped his arm around her shoulders. "And I have never seen a more worthy emperor."

Aria smiled. "I think we've found something we can agree on."

Svorgin looked down at her. "We have so much in common. What do you mean?"

She rammed her elbow into his ribs, and he groaned. "I am just teasing you." Her expression grew serious. "That girl, was that her? Your sister?"

Svorgin's smile slipped. "Yes."

"Don't fret. She was probably overwhelmed."

"I hope so," Svorgin said, glancing off to where Saga had disappeared.

Once the deedans were rounded up and taken to a building previously used for storage, Svorgin faced his old neighbors and friends. He spread his arms.

"Who's hungry? I am ready to taste my mam's cooking. It's been too long."

The smiles that had lit everyone's eyes dimmed, and Svorgin's gut turned. Daghvin was the first who spoke.

"Yer mam, Svor—"

"No." Svorgin raised his hand. He knew before Daghvin finished what he would say. His entire being protested, and yet he could not deny what had already passed his lips.

"Yer mam's gone."

52

SAGA DIDN'T FLINCH when the knock came, just as it had the day before and the day before. She stared at the boarded window. Kalpara curled around her feet, gazing at her with mournful eyes. Saga reached down and ran her hand over her thick white fur.

"Saga, please. I want to talk."

Saga still wasn't used to the sound of that deep voice. Or the sight of the older version of her brother that had become permanently engrained in her mind. She saw it over and over, as his eyes had locked on hers and he'd moved closer to her. It wasn't real. He wasn't real. And yet the banging upon the door spoke otherwise.

"Ye cannot have much food in there. It's been a week, Saga. Do not torture yerself on my account."

Saga scoffed, closing her eyes and leaning back on her mam's bed. She smelled the pillow, searching for her mam's comforting scent. Though a trace of it remained, it had faded. Saga screamed into the pillow, her anger coming to the forefront. The pounding continued and then she heard a thump.

"I am not going anywhere, Saga. I will stay here."

His footsteps receded, and Saga breathed in, steadying herself. Then the knocking started up again.

"Go away!" she shouted.

The sound stilled, and then another voice called to her. "It's me. Honzio."

Saga's anger died down, and she stood. He'd come before, with food and news of Britta's recovery. She hadn't opened the door then, but she'd sat down by it and placed her ear to the wood, listening to the warm timbre of his voice.

She moved toward the door greedily now, eager to hear him.

"Everything is well, Saga. Britta is up and recovering. We lost a few, but you know that already. The funeral was this morning." He paused. "Your neighbors miss you." His voice cracked. He seemed to gather his courage and then said, "I miss you."

Saga placed her hand and leaned her brow on the door. She closed her eyes, forcing herself not to do as her heart commanded and throw it open.

"The Tariqin captain told us everything she knew. The routines of the other villages and the coordinates.

The Chishmans that are in charge and their weaknesses. Everything. We plan to start out in the morning and go to the nearest village. We will free them one by one until all Savoria is unchained."

Saga nodded against the door. It sounded beautiful.

"But we can't."

She stiffened.

"Not without you." Then in a lower tone that permeated through the wood between them: "We need you, Saga."

Saga's heart lurched against her chest, demanding and insistent. She swallowed, reaching for the knob. Then she felt his weight shift from the door as he retreated.

"Take as long as you need, Saga. We will be here when you are ready."

She heard his steps leaving, and she stopped thinking. She grasped the doorknob and wrenched the door open. The sunlight blinded her. She had been sitting in the dim candlelight for days on end. Honzio paused on the low steps and swiveled, a breathtaking grin overtaking his face. He retraced his steps until he was before her. He cupped her face in his hand.

"Thank God. I thought I would have to break it down."

She raised her brow. "I thought ye said ye were waiting till I was ready."

He laughed. "I would've. But I would've waited inside with you."

Saga smiled as his fingers warmed her cheek. He leaned closer.

"We are bound, remember? Forever connected now."

She nodded. "Forever."

A throat cleared, and her eyes shot to the man leaning against the side of the house. Saga stepped back out of Honzio's grasp and reached to close the door.

Honzio's fingers clasped around her wrist. "Wait, Saga. Please just listen to him once. Then you can slam the door in his face a hundred times if you wish."

Saga hesitated. She looked at the man who resembled her dead brother. He tipped his chin down in agreement with Honzio.

"Fine," she growled and stormed into the house.

The man entered, and Honzio walked away, giving them privacy. Saga's breathing was quick from her rising anger. They stood facing each other.

"Saga." He raised his hand toward her.

She flinched, and he dropped it.

"I had hoped that ye would be cared for. That our neighbors and Aylis had taken care of ye and mam over the years. I didn't know Aylis left too, not until I saw her in the Empire." The imposter swallowed. "They told me. Britta told me everything. How ye fended for yerself. I am so proud of ye, Saga."

Saga didn't reply, staring at the wall behind him. His words reached her ears but didn't sink in.

"I know ye must be furious that we left. But I had to—to save ye and Mam. To keep ye safe. That is why I left. But I am here now and—"

Her enraged eyes snapped to his, and he stopped talking.

"Ye left, and ye died," she said, the words blunt as a knife. "Ye died."

He shook his head. "I am alive, Saga. I am here."

She pointed a finger at him. "Ye are dead. So are Da and Aylis. I cared for Mam alone all this time. And she is gone too." Tears sprouted in her eyes. "I buried ye all in my heart. Ye are dead." She turned her head so he could see the rings on her lobe. "Ye all died, and I buried ye."

His chin trembled, and he reached for her. "I am so sorry, Saga. That ye had to face this all alone."

"Get out," she rasped, tears slipping down the planes of her face.

He didn't move.

"Get out!" she screamed.

She sank down to the floor, shaking with sobs she had held in ever since she was a girl. Svorgin moved, but not toward the door like she'd hoped. He crouched down beside her and pulled her into his arms. She tried to push him away, but he held her until she sank against him. He caressed her hair like he had when she was little, playing with the end of her braid. Then he placed a kiss on the top of her head, murmuring apologies with tears of his own streaming free.

"I am here now, and I will never abandon ye again. I promise."

53

ARIA GLANCED AT the sky overhead. Orange and pink lined the horizon as the sun dipped away and cast the village in the beautiful glow of sunset. The Savorian women she had grown acquainted with over the past days while assisting with the injured shouted their gratitude as she exited the small house they'd been using as a healing area.

She spotted Emperor Honzio in the square conversing with Daghvin. She had tried to speak with him several times, but he'd always been busy with the captured deedans or planning the next route with the Savorians. She had barely seen Svorgin either. He'd been sitting outside his sister's home ever since he'd learned of his mam's passing. Other than bringing him food and attempting to keep him company, she hadn't been able to spend much time with him. He was gloomy and closed off. So, she had spent her free time assisting the Savorians, moving about the village and helping with whatever was needed.

She walked toward the emperor. Just as his conversation finished and he headed a different way, Aria called out.

"Your Majesty."

He turned and nodded at her. "Aria, isn't it?"

"It is. I wanted to speak to you about something important. Months ago, you sent a request to the Elders to look into Queen Guin."

His brows rose, and he inclined his head. "You are a part of the Elders?"

"I see Svorgin hasn't told you much."

He grimaced, scratching his head. "No, we've barely spoken since his arrival."

Aria filled him in on the details. His face grew stormy at the knowledge of the queen's treachery and Svorgin's imprisonment. She gave him everything she knew about Jax, the Qistool, and the nojori. He listened intently, his expression growing graver with every passing second.

"If the disease spreads, the Empire is at stake. I must warn Latimus."

Aria frowned, unsure who Latimus was. Honzio seemed adrift in his thoughts, and Aria was relieved she had done her duty. She turned to leave when he called out to her.

"Thank you, Aria. You have done well."

"I am only doing my duty, Your Majesty."

He nodded, and she did in return before heading

toward Britta's home. The woman had given her a spare room to remain in after helping in her recovery process. She was upbeat and full of enthusiasm, and Aria was grateful for her kindness. Though she'd learned a few Savorian words during the journey with Svorgin, she was still lacking much in regard to the language, which made it hard for her to converse with most of the Savorians beyond pleasantries. Thankfully, Britta knew quite a bit of Tariqin. When she entered the home, Britta was walking across the room with the help of Olava.

"Very good, lass." Olava nodded. "Ye look much better."

"And there's a lot more color to your cheeks," Aria added.

Britta beamed. "Thanks to yer help—and Olava's, of course."

They sat on a long seat, and Aria joined them. Britta grasped a bundle of cloth from the table beside her and placed it on Aria's lap.

"What is this?"

"Just a token of my appreciation."

Aria gave her a smile. "You didn't have to, really."

"I wanted to," Britta said. "Now, come on. Open it up."

Aria unwrapped the cloth and gasped at the beautiful layers of fabric concealed within. It was a long green dress with a matching headdress and a brown band to keep it in place.

"I thought ye might want to get rid of those raggedy things ye're wearing," Britta said with a pleased smile.

Aria tilted her head. "This is so generous. And yes, my clothes have endured the worst of conditions."

"Ye have to try it on!"

At their goading, Aria went to the adjacent room and returned in her new garments. She even twirled for them, laughing as she did.

Britta squealed. "And the best part is that it's green. Svorgin's favorite color."

Aria stopped spinning, and her smile faded. Thoughts of Svorgin confused her. She didn't know where they stood at the end of this. He probably wished to settle down with one of his own.

"I don't know what you mean," she said.

"Lass, the lad's in love with ye," Olava said. "I could see it in his eyes from a mile away."

"You are mistaken," Aria told her, though a flutter of hope bloomed within her.

Britta shook her head. "She is right, Aria. Svorgin cares for ye. He never looked at anyone like he looks at ye. All the lasses would be jealous of ye. We used to wish he would even glance at us. Svorgin had many admirers in his youth."

Great, that meant there must've still been plenty of hungering eyes remaining. Still, they continued giving Aria hope when she tried to bury it.

"I don't think so." She moved toward the door and then paused, glancing back at them. "What does *viila* mean?" she asked before she lost her nerve.

Olava and Britta glanced at each other before exploding into giggles that made them appear years younger. Aria frowned, uncertain what to make of their reaction.

"The lad is a goner," Olava said.

Britta gave her a bright grin. "It means *fairy*."

SVORGIN

Svorgin left the home he'd grown up in, stepping outside to view the stars shining overhead. Saga had finally allowed him inside, and though she hadn't said she'd forgiven him, she had prepared food and slapped an extra plate on the table. It was a step, he supposed.

He sat at the foot of the stairs, wondering where Aria was. Guilt turned within him. He hadn't spoken to her properly since their arrival in the village. He knew she thought he was solely focused on Saga, but a part of him had been avoiding her, because he knew when he spoke to Aria, he would have to confess his feelings— the beginnings of the love he'd heard storytellers yap on about. He doubted she felt the same, and he didn't dare ask, afraid to hear her answer.

A shape appeared between the trees, coming nearer to him. Svorgin stiffened, squinting his eyes. "Who's there?"

"It's me." The soft voice reached him before Aria stepped into view.

Svorgin's breath caught. She was garbed in a green dress that only heightened her beauty. "What brings you here?" he managed to ask.

She frowned. "I can leave, if you wish."

"No, no, I didn't mean that." He scratched his head. "It's been a long day."

Aria settled down on the stairs beside him, and he

grew distractingly aware of the delicate summery scent that clung to her.

"How is she?" Aria nodded toward the house.

"She isn't shutting me out anymore, so I would say we are making progress."

Aria smiled. "That's good."

"What do you plan to do now?" he said and then regretted the words. He didn't want to hear her leaving preparations.

She paused. "I will be here until we free the villages and then . . . I suppose Emperor Honzio will prepare for a return journey. If there is nothing keeping me, I will return to the Elders."

If there is nothing keeping me. The words made Svorgin's head swivel toward her. Her green eyes were riveted upon him.

"And you?"

Svorgin cleared his throat. He shrugged. "After Savoria is saved, I will settle down. Start a home, a family."

She nodded, and her smile seemed strained. "A family," she repeated, frowning, her demeanor changing.

The envy in her tone was blatant and exactly what Svorgin had hoped for.

"Yes, perhaps with a beautiful lady in the village."

Her eyes widened, as though she couldn't believe him. Svorgin covered his mouth to hide his grin and continued.

"In fact, I have one in mind."

She shot up and stepped down the stairs. "Well, I wish you the best with your *family.*"

Svorgin grasped her arm to stop her, and a chuckle burst from him. Aria spun, her brows dangerously lowered.

"There is no one here for me," he said. "No one but you."

Her features softened, and she searched his gaze.

"You asked me once what I feared," he said. "I fear losing *you*."

She blinked, watching him intently.

"I care for you, Aria, more than I have ever felt for anyone. If you want to return to the Empire, I would go in a heartbeat. But I promised Saga I would stay. If we were to marry, I could travel to the Empire from time to time, but I would remain mostly in Savoria."

"I understand," Aria said. "And I wouldn't ask you to live in the Empire after all you've endured there."

Svorgin leaned closer to her. "But I was also blessed with many things there. I met Honzio and Velamir and so many others." His voice softened. "I met you there."

"Yes."

"We wouldn't have much in the beginning. I would have to build us a home here and earn from my trade."

"Yes," she repeated.

Svorgin's heart bloomed. "What did you say?"

"Yes, I will stay with you, you big oaf."

She pushed his shoulder. Svorgin laughed with joy, yanked her in for a hug, and then pulled back to ensure he hadn't hurt her with the fierceness of it.

"We can stay here as long as we need and go to the Empire when we can."

"Agreed," he said. "Agreed, *viila*."

She didn't glare like he'd expected at the nickname. Instead, her smile brightened. She pulled away from him and moved down the road.

"I need to get to sleep, and so do you!" she warned. "It's a big day tomorrow. Emperor Honzio wants to set out for the closest village."

Svorgin waved. "Sweet dreams, *viila*."

He stretched the word for good measure and heard her beautiful laughter as she continued down the path.

"You can call me that whenever you wish!"

Svorgin shook his head. Damned Savorians, they'd told her what it meant. Even so, a smile remained on his lips as he watched her fade into the trees.

54

HONZIO

SAVORIA

HONZIO UNTUCKED THE leather cylinder hanging against his chest and pulled free the parchment. He had been waiting for Latimus's reply ever since he'd sent him the news Aria had given him. It had been a day since. He unrolled it, spreading it across the rock he crouched beside. Words appeared along the parchment, and Honzio sighed in relief.

> *Your Majesty,*
>
> *We set out weeks ago, and when we arrived, it was just as you said. These creatures, whatever they are, wreaked havoc across Tariqi. Apparently, they were destroying only the battalions and command centers. They didn't touch any of the towns or civilians. Almost like they were*

directed or controlled, as odd as that sounds. Then they suddenly stopped attacking and gathered together. They didn't appear mindless, it was almost as though they were waiting for us. After shooting them from afar, we burned the corpses to keep the disease from spreading. The Tariqins surrendered without a battle. They had too many losses and no army to face ours. Tariqi is once again Imperial land. We are aiding the poor and helping any who need it. And are awaiting your further instruction.

Forever your loyal servant,

Latimus Blayton

Honzio scanned the words, his brows knitting in confusion. The creatures attacking the army exclusively and then dying off seemed very strange, but the rest of the words sank in and took the forefront. Tariqi had surrendered. The never-ending war of ages was over. Honzio smiled, wide and happy.

He heard a gasp and looked up from the letter. He was a good distance from the village they had trekked to, waiting for the deedans' approach. Captain Erda stood beside Honzio, her wrists bound.

"Here they come," she said.

As she'd told them, the deedans inspecting the village were leaving and heading to their watchtower. Honzio glanced at Saga, and she nodded, signaling to Daghvin and Svorgin. They moved down the snowy hill, approaching the unaware deedans. Honzio tucked the letter away and stood, stepping beside the captain. Guilt swam in her features as she looked at the deedans.

"You are saving many innocents," Honzio told her.

"I know," she whispered. "But they are my people."

"You are aiding them too," Honzio said. "We will not kill unless we have to. We will offer them a chance to stop fighting. Tariqi has surrendered to our armies. The war is over."

Honzio unsheathed his dagger, and the captain flinched. She closed her eyes as he neared. He sliced the rope around her wrists, and her eyes popped open. She glanced up at him in disbelief.

"I release you," Honzio said. "You can leave now, if you wish. Return home, where you can live in peace under Imperial rule. Or you are welcome to come back to the capital with me."

She smiled for the first time. "You truly are a man of your word, Your Majesty. I will be honored to make my home in the capital."

Honzio nodded and sheathed his blade. The sounds of battle reached his ears. He looked down, seeing Saga and the others surrounding the deedans in mere seconds. The deedans were taken by surprise, and fear spread over their faces when they heard the Savorian battle cries. They surrendered with little urging. Honzio walked down, joining the others as they entered the village, where a deedan was whipping a Savorian lad in the center of the square. Saga didn't hesitate, flinging her axe in the air and pinning the man to a nearby wall by the cloth of his tunic.

Gasps rang about. All eyes turned to them. Svorgin

grasped the whip from the hanging deedan's hand and tossed it onto the ground with a curse. Leno and Daghvin hefted a small table over to the square, and Saga jumped upon it to address all those gathered.

"I am Saga Barindaughter, from Vidrun Village. I have come to tell ye that ye are no longer under the oppressive rule of the Tariqins."

Hope sprang into the eyes of the observers. Some clasped their hands over their chests and shook their heads, as though they didn't dare to believe it. Honzio stepped closer to Saga.

"The war is over!" he said, informing her as well as the others. "Tariqi has surrendered."

Saga's mouth parted, and then her lips curved into the most beautiful smile he'd ever seen.

"The captivity is over. Ye are free!" Saga called out, her voice radiating joy. "We are all free!"

Cheers erupted as the Savorians embraced one another. Then, once all had settled, Leno stole everyone's attention with his booming voice. "I also wanted to announce something. Vidrun Village has long been without a leader. And there is no one I know who deserves it more than the woman standing upon that table." He pointed his axe toward Saga.

Svorgin and Daghvin nodded, and so did the others who had accompanied them. Honzio was pleased to see all enmity had faded away, leaving only a satisfied group.

"To many happy years," Svorgin called. "And to the new shavka! Shavka Saga!"

"Shavka!"

"Shavka!"

The others took up his cry until the entire village was rumbling with the title. Saga glanced about, and Honzio saw the tears in her eyes as she smiled.

55

T HE WEEKS FLEW by in a blur, and then the ship arrived, and suddenly, time stopped. The day became the longest Saga had ever experienced, not only because her da and Aylis had come and her family was almost whole again, but because it was finally time for Honzio to leave. He was returning to his home. Saga watched from afar as he embraced the other Savorians he'd bonded with. Even Leno and Daghvin appeared distraught. And especially her brother. Svorgin spoke with Honzio at length. His wife, Aria, also conversed with them, asking Honzio to pass on a message to the Elders for her. Saga glanced toward the ship, seeing the awaiting Imperials looking out for their emperor. Honzio made his way through the adoring crowd of Savorians until he stopped before her. Saga told herself to stay strong. *Don't make this harder than it has to be.*

"Thank ye for everything," she said. "Ye saved us all."

He shook his head. "I only helped. You were the strength at the heart of it." He stepped closer. "I know you will lead your people well. And I promise you that Savoria will not be harmed by the Empire as long as I live."

She smiled, but her lips trembled. "I know. We are connected, after all."

"Bound," he said.

"Forever."

"Forever," he finished, and Saga saw a sheen coat his own eyes.

"Who knows?" she whispered. "Perhaps this tie between us will pull us back together someday."

"I hope for that to be true." His throat bobbed. There were so many unsaid words, so much she wanted to tell him, and she knew he felt the same.

But they couldn't be spoken now.

"*Mavaalin*, Honzio of the Empire."

He nodded, blinking, and his hand reached for her. He touched her cheek and stroked her skin. Saga soaked in the warmth of his gaze. "I will never forget you, Saga Barindaughter," he said in a hoarse voice.

Then Saga watched him move past her. He didn't look back, mounting the ramp onto the ship and greeting the Imperials awaiting him. Young Lore joined him at the prow. Her da appeared, tugging her into his side and filling her with strength. Aylis emerged on her other side, her gaze full of understanding as she reached for her hand and squeezed gently. And when the anchor lifted, Saga felt a part of her heart was torn up along with it. It was then that Honzio turned and waved. His eyes roved over the crowd of cheering Savorians before landing on her. His hand stilled in the air, and his smile faded. She held his gaze until she couldn't see him any longer. And she remained standing in the snow until the ship was long gone.

"Someday," she whispered.

56

J AX STOOD BEFORE the castle gates. The guards thrust the doors open at once when they caught sight of him. He moved through the castle without a word to any who greeted him. But they were used to his coldness and aloof nature. The sack in his grasp felt heavier with every step. He crossed the stairs he'd taken hundreds of times over the past months. When he reached the tower, he found her, Queen Guin, standing among three soldiers. She spun toward him at the sound of his boots, a wide smile spreading across her thin lips.

"I didn't believe them when they said you'd come."

Jax forced his emotions to remain in check and continued until he was before her. "I have brought what you desired, my queen."

Her eyes glimmered with greed, and she jerked her head at the soldiers. They slipped down the stairs, out of sight, leaving Jax alone with her. She pressed her fingers together.

"Show me," she whispered.

Jax reached into the sack and pulled the heavy metal out. The queen stared at the crown, her smile growing wider.

"You have done what no one has ever accomplished before," she said. "You have brought me the greatest treasure in the world."

Jax didn't reply, but that anger deep within him flared to life. Still, he forced himself to be calm. He couldn't reveal it. Not yet. She took it from him, shuddering at its feeling. A surge of possessiveness gripped Jax as her hands clamped around the crown. He fought the feeling. She lifted it to her head, and when it settled upon her white locks, her smile turned to a tremble, and a tear fell from her eyes.

"So much power," she said.

She grimaced, and Jax knew she was receiving all the information she'd ever wanted. All the knowledge and power she desired. He stepped closer to her, and her eyes snapped to him. Her smile faded entirely as the Golden Crown shimmered upon her head and Jax's intentions became apparent within her mind.

"You—you want to—"

She reached for the dagger on the table, but it was too late. Jax had unsheathed his knife and rammed it into her stomach. She gasped, slowly looking down at the crimson spreading across her pale dress.

"That's for Lilly," Jax hissed.

She had thought he was still her captive, that his mind was still bound. But he'd broken free of her will.

"I remember everything," he said. "How you tortured me and twisted me into a monster to do your bidding. How you made me murder my own friend." Tears burned his vision. "I have known many villains in my time. But you—you are the worst of them."

Queen Guin looked up, meeting his furious gaze. Jax yanked the blade free and then shoved it into her chest.

"That is for Velamir."

She coughed, and blood trickled out of her mouth. Jax couldn't help but be satisfied by the sight of the life leaving her. He reached up and tore the crown from her hair. She shook her head, her hands lifting weakly as she reached for it.

"Please," she begged.

Jax tore the blood-covered knife from her chest and then lifted it higher.

"And this is for me."

The queen fell to her knees, the handle of his knife sticking out of her throat. Then she collapsed into a crumpled mess. But even in death, her eyes remained focused on the crown, on the power she had been so close to wielding. Jax tucked the crown back into the sack. He left the castle. A weight had been lifted from his shoulders, but even still, pain lingered in him—a wound no one could see and one he doubted would ever heal.

Jax heard the shouts of alarm and the rush of soldiers as the queen was discovered. The city bells clanged as he strode past the crowds of gathering citizens. He didn't heed any of it. He didn't stop walking until he reached the solitary home far from the town. His eyes tracked the distance to the barn nearby. The barn he'd once mucked for hours was in shambles now, torn apart from the harsh Devorin winters and left untouched since. Jax moved into the house, walking through the wreckage and placing the sack he carried onto a table that still stood by some miracle. The sack thumped onto the wood, the heavy metal within thrumming. Jax swallowed, his hands trembling as he released it. His body longed to take the crown and place it upon his head again. But the consequences of the previous time were enough to keep the temptation at bay.

After Aria and Svorgin had left, Jax had accepted his imminent death. Welcomed it. But even the nojori in the Qistool wouldn't grant him the peace death would give him. They had surrounded him but hadn't come near. Instead, they'd lowered themselves in deference. Jax had found himself in control of the most powerful army in the world. He had given in to his hatred and the power muddling his mind through the Golden Crown. He'd ordered the nojori to destroy the Qistool. They had done so with ease, proving that they could have escaped the Qistool long ago had their minds been their own.

When the walls had crumbled, Jax directed them into Tariqi, but a part of him was still aware enough to avoid the civilians. Instead, he made them attack all the places that had tried to use him like a puppet. The Chishman Academy, the deedan outposts. The screams of the Tariqins had done nothing to quell his fury. But it was when the nojori went rampant and started toward the towns that Jax realized he had to put an end to it. He thought of Velamir, Natassa, Lissa, all those dear to him and knew they would never approve of all this destruction or the death of the innocents. Lissa's final words had resounded in his mind. *"No matter the evil around you, never stop being the hero, Jax."* And so he'd stopped the nojori, gathering them all together and watching from the distance as the Imperials burned them where he'd trapped them.

He'd left then, traveling without stopping, entirely focused on coming to Devorin and doing what he had to. He traced the wood grains on the table. If he concentrated a bit, he could almost picture the times he'd spent with Lilly around the table. Crafting and laughing. His lips curved, but then the smile faded. There were only ghosts here now. He took the sack and trudged back into the snow. He had one last thing to do. Jax worked without pause for hours until he'd dug a hole so big he doubted anyone would unearth it. He tossed the crown inside and did the painstaking work of covering it. His hands were raw and bloody and body soaked with cold sweat when he finished. He tossed away the shovel. When he kneeled and placed his hand upon the ground, he felt the faint thrumming beneath.

A nicker startled him. His heartbeat a touch faster as Vandal appeared, racing toward him. Jax stood. Vandal came to a crashing stop before him, his hooves sending up snow and dirt. Tears welled in Jax's eyes. He felt more understanding in Vandal's eyes in that moment than he ever had before with anyone else. The same pain festered in both of them. He bridled Vandal and then mounted him before clicking his tongue, urging him into motion. It wasn't until they'd traveled a good distance that he swiveled Vandal around so he could look one last time at his childhood home. Then he turned his back on it and left. For good.

57

Seven years later
Honzio
Hearcross

ONZIO STRODE DOWN the palace steps and spotted Jax perched upon the fountain in the center of the garden, a gaggle of city children surrounding him and watching him with eager eyes as he told them another of his tales. Honzio had offered him so many duties and places to live so he could remain close by, but the man had refused, preferring to live alone. Honzio still hadn't figured out how to help him, but it seemed the children were a better medicine to his wounds than any other Honzio could provide.

An arm snaked around his waist, and Honzio grinned. He would know that touch and the scent that accompanied it anywhere.

"Did you have a restful morning?"

Saga nodded, placing her chin on his shoulder and watching the children with him.

"I did. The trip wasn't as tiring as the previous ones. It went much faster."

"I will have to speak to Svorgin. He continues to take my wife away from me for much too long."

Saga's eyes crinkled. "Svorgin is nearly twice as glad as I am whenever we return to the Empire. It is his opportunity to shirk his duties in Savoria and spend as much time as he wants with Aria." Her smile deepened. "But are ye saying that ye missed me?"

"Your daughter missed you," he replied.

She glared, and then he relented, glancing over his shoulder to smile back at her. "And I did too." He turned, gathering her in his arm, uncaring of the civilians and guards passing by. "I missed you terribly."

Saga's eyes sparkled, and she placed her brow against his. Jax's tale finished at that moment, and he stood, leaving abruptly. The children sighed in disappointment before one of them sprang up and rushed toward Honzio and Saga. A girl with bright hazel eyes and wild golden hair that resembled her mother's. She joined in on their embrace, and Honzio patted her hair.

"Did you have a pleasant time?" Honzio asked.

She nodded and then peered up at him. "Father, you promised that you would take us to the museum today!"

"Us?" Honzio repeated, racking his mind for a memory of this promise he'd apparently made.

She nodded. "Me, Das, and Mari."

Honzio's mouth promptly dropped. "General Mordon and Queen Coralie have arrived?"

"They came this morning. Ye better greet yer guests, Your Majesty." Saga smirked.

He planted a kiss on her temple and pulled away. "Come on then, Tassa."

His daughter bounded toward him, her joy evident. She tucked her hand into his arm as they walked past the sprinkling fountains before the palace entrance. He found Mordon and Coralie conversing loudly in the sitting room, the twins, their two rambunctious children, standing before them. Honzio grasped Natassa's shoulder so she didn't rush into the room and interrupt whatever family matter was occurring.

"Dasterion Velamir Vaz, behave yourself," Coralie said in a firm tone.

"But Father gave Mari the new dagger!" Das was protesting.

Mari, the devious little girl, stuck her tongue out at her brother. Mordon caught the look and sighed.

"All right, all right," he said in a defeated tone, placing a pouch of coins in the boy's palm. "Go to the smithy and have them forge one for you as well."

Das cheered, and his sister crossed her arms, glaring at him. They proceeded to play fight with each other on their way out of the chamber. They rushed past Honzio, and his daughter joined them.

"Children!" Coralie shouted. "Greet His Majesty, the Emperor."

They glanced back, calling as they ran, "Good afternoon, Uncle Honzio!"

Honzio chuckled, lifting his hand to wave after them.

Coralie looked at Mordon with a grimace. "You've

spoiled them, especially Mari. The girl has you wrapped around her little finger."

Honzio joined them in the room, and Mordon enveloped his wife's shoulders, pulling her into his side. "What can I say? She takes after her mother."

Honzio chuckled, and Coralie laughed, shaking her head.

Mordon leaned down, pressing a kiss into her hair. "And I wouldn't have it any other way."

EPILOGUE

I F IT WASN'T for the promise he'd made, Jax wouldn't have stepped foot out of his tiny home on the outskirts of the capital. He made his way into Hearcross, feeling the pitiful looks of people when he passed by. Most had assumed him to be a vagrant whenever he appeared, but now they knew him as the children did.

"Look! It's Master Hand!" a young boy called.

It was a matter of seconds before eager eyes and innocent faces surrounded Jax. He sat upon the fountain before Karalik Palace, his usual spot, his knees groaning in protest. The children's parents lingered nearby. They had long given up trying to keep their little ones away from him. Jax couldn't blame them. If he had a child, he would have tried to keep them from himself as well. Over the years, his hair had grown long and frazzled. He never trimmed his beard. When he had first entered Hearcross, a few people offered him scraps of food. Jax found he was resembling his old mentor Frumgan more with every passing day. And he couldn't help but smile at the thought.

"Master Hand! Tell us a story! Tell us a story!"

The children shouted, a red-haired girl the most boisterous of them all. Jax had ensured to keep an eye on her, and when she grew a little older—old enough to bear the sadness—Jax would tell her about her father and keep his promise to Fox.

Some parents hushed the children as they shouted, but others looked on with the same curiosity the children did. Master Hand. The children had begun referring to him by that title when he never bothered to provide his name. It was no doubt spurred on by discussions of half of his missing finger.

Jax cleared his throat and pulled out his sketchbook full of notes and stories. "Would you like to choose?" His voice emerged hoarse from lack of use.

At the children's demands, Jax told tale after tale. Scaring them with vivid details of the Karakan and even the Qistool. He wove the details of his life so they seemed fictitious rather than the gruesome truth that they were.

"And just as the humongous rumlok growled and pounced down, an arrow sliced through the air and sent him stumbling back. Vel had saved the town."

The children exhaled a relieved breath, and Jax's chest warmed at their sincere happiness hearing his stories. One boy leaned closer to him.

"You said once that the stories are real. Is that true?"

Jax winced. That had been a slip of the tongue. But he didn't want to deny it.

"It's true."

"Then who is he? Vel. The hero in all your stories. Did you know him?"

"Yes." Emotion burned his throat, and Jax took a moment to gather himself before he said, "He was my brother."

If you enjoyed this book, please consider leaving a review. Reviews are so crucial in helping spread awareness about the book.

ACKNOWLEDGEMENTS

And just like that, the four books comprising the Heroes of the Empire series are published. I am baffled at how fast time has passed, but I am also overjoyed that I can now hold the quartet in my arms and scream at all who care to hear that the series is complete. But how saddening that word sounds. Don't worry, I've got plenty more stories in the Empire, and more specifically the Uluz, waiting to be shared. So, be prepared to fall in love with more characters and experience more heartbreak. Cue malicious laughter. Haha, just kidding. (Not entirely) But for now, I want to thank all those who I couldn't complete this journey without. As always, my family, my moral support and the ones pushing me to the finish line with every book. My parents for telling me how proud they are and for never letting me give up on this path I have chosen, my siblings for being there always, you all have my entire heart. Gratitude to my relatives and dear friends who support me and cheer me on, I appreciate every one of you. Everlasting love and appreciation for my editors, Tanya Oemig, for meticulous developmental edits. Chelsea and Lisa from Enchanted Ink, for jaw dropping and lifesaving line and copy edits. You two are so amazing. I will never stop recommending Enchanted Ink to authors searching for editors—they absolutely make your work shine all the brighter with their work. Special thanks to my proofreader, Samantha Pico, the Goth Editor, found at thegotheditor.com

And to the readers. You make me smile so much. You have no idea that you make my day so beautiful with your feedback and comments. Through online messages or in person, you absolutely motivate me to continue writing, so thank you for reading my books and leaving reviews and letting me know what you thought.

Goodbye for now—until the next book, which may be coming soon and is a standalone from a brand-new world. But before I say too much, I will stop here. Thank you, thank you, thank you for reading all the way to the end of the series. It means the world.

ABOUT THE AUTHOR

Israh Azizi resides in the land of ten thousand lakes with her family and five cats. Since she was a little girl, she has been a lover of words and fanciful tales. It was her dream to one day share a story of her own with the world. With sheer determination, lots of love, and a decent amount of caffeine, she managed to make that dream come true. Besides reading and writing, she has a dizzying number of hobbies, some of which include bossing around her younger siblings, experimenting with new baking recipes, and playing board games with her family and close friends. When life's plot twists don't cross her path and her fingers aren't dancing across the keyboard building a fantastical adventure, she can usually be found in a quiet corner with a good book and a steaming cup of coffee.